D0712665

The Prisoner's Apprentice

"*The Prisoner's Apprentice* grabbed me on page one and swept me up into a rich tapestried world of mystery and intrigue that kept me turning page after page well into the night. Cheyenne Richards writes with such clarity and beauty that this novel cartwheels along, raising questions, and opening up a world that is sure to delight book clubs."

—LOLLY WINSTON, *New York Times* best-selling author of
Good Grief, Happiness Sold Separately, and *Me for You*

"This novel marks the debut of a gifted new writer. In *The Prisoner's Apprentice*, Cheyenne Richards tells the astonishing story of a young boy who befriends a brilliant murderer in 1846. She writes with a fresh voice that is both energetic and engaging. The story is part thriller, part psychological study—and completely riveting storytelling."

—ELLEN SUSSMAN, *New York Times* best-selling author of
A Wedding in Provence, The Paradise Guest House,
French Lessons, and *On a Night Like This*

THE
PRISONER'S
APPRENTICE

THE
PRISONER'S
APPRENTICE

CHEYENNE RICHARDS

BETTEREST
BOOKS

Editing by Alan Rinzler and Leslie Tilly
Cover Design by Laura Duffy
Design and Page Composition by Karen Minster
Proofreading by Debra Nichols
Author photo by Brian Bayley

PRINTED IN THE UNITED STATES OF AMERICA

978-1-7373022-1-6 (hardcover)
978-1-7373022-2-3 (paperback)

BETTEREST BOOKS™
BetterestBooks.com

For my incredible family—inherited and chosen.

Your inspiration, encouragement, and practical support for this novel has been boundless over the two decades I've wrestled with its radioactive subject.

I love you like mad.

Also, I've repaid your generosity by spilling the beans on the freaky serial killer lurking in our family tree.

You're welcome.

A Note About Language

Many words and concepts that we consider highly offensive today were commonplace in the nineteenth century. Choosing how to treat such words in historical fiction is never easy.

In the case of this book, there are some words I've chosen to avoid, no matter how common they may have been. Others that I've included may surprise or even shock a modern reader. These words were not written to hurt but to heal—to help build a more inclusive future by first acknowledging the mistakes of our collective past.

To anyone offended by my choices, I offer my most profound apologies.

It is plain that in the person of Rulloff one of the most marvelous intellects that any age has produced is about to be sacrificed.

Here is a man who has never entered the doors of a college or university, and yet, by the sheer might of his innate gifts has made himself such a colossus in abstruse learning that the ablest of our scholars are but pigmies in his presence.

What miracles this murderer might have wrought, and what luster he might have shed upon his country if he had not put a forfeit on his life so foolishly.

—SAMUEL LANGHORNE CLEMENS
Letter to the *New-York Tribune*

FIAT JUSTITIA, PEREAT MUNDUS

———

1846

*Justice must prevail even if
the world must perish over it.*

1

THAT SWELTERING JUNE BEGAN LIKE ANY OTHER. A FEW fighters and a buggy thief flowed through our jail. A man from the plaster company married a girl from Dryden. Eph Schutt lost his wife and baby to childbed fever. Mostly I remember the endless funeral sermon and Eph's sister giving me a hard smack on the shoulder for kicking at the pews.

By the Fourth of July, everyone with a boat was out on Cayuga Lake, dragging chains and hooks and fishing nets, looking for bodies.

Each had a theory about where Rulloff might have dumped the remains of his missing wife and child—poor Eph's sister and niece—but their chaotic searches led nowhere. The Independence Day parade that year looked more like a funeral march, with both the Friends of the Ithaca Railroad and the Anti-Slavery Society cancelling their lectures out of respect for unprecedented circumstances.

I was only six then, but as far as I can decipher, Edward Rulloff had once held a reasonable reputation in Ithaca, though always that of an outsider. I must have heard his name in passing, but had never met the man. He'd been a teacher for a while, but school cost a fortune in those days, even if Pa had believed in scholarship, which he most fervently did not. Later, Rulloff practiced herbal medicine, but again, paying for a doctor was not in Pa's perspective of how the world should run.

With my help, Rulloff would soon build a far more impressive résumé: doctor, lawyer, professor, inventor, philologist fluent in twenty-seven languages, serial killer.

AS THE SUMMER DRAGGED ON, voices grew more hushed. Mothers held their children closer in the folds of their skirts, and vague dread pulled at the whole town like an undertow.

Each time a rope went down, I wondered if they would pull a water-logged baby from under the glassy surface. I was still a novice to death then, but learning fast. The boy down the street told me dead people's eyelids fall open forever, that's how you know they're dead. I wondered if somewhere in the lake the lady and her baby stared at each other with wide eyes, never blinking. I tried to imagine it by leaving my eyes open but couldn't do it. The air was too dry, the sun too bright.

In those days, Pa and I headed to Grant's every night for supper. The sign said "Grant's Coffee Shop" to appease the pastor, but they only served whiskey and women. And while that time is fuzzy in my memory compared to what happened later, I knew there were three things I could always count on when we walked through that sloped doorway.

First, someone would have saved Pa's table, the best one in the place—closest to the south window. In the summer, the breeze carried the cool freshness of the lake in through that opening. The table was easy to spot—blackened on one leg from being used as a fireplace poker. There weren't enough chairs, so I was always relegated to the warped floorboards and took care to position myself as far as I could from both the spittoon and the older boys who stole my bread and marmalade.

Second, the men would talk longer than I could stay awake. Pa was officially Ithaca's jail-keep, but unofficially more like the mayor of our little village, leading talk on whether the Peterson land was too shaded for apples and who'd been lost over the winter to the blizzard, the pox, or buggy accidents. Gradually, travelers would pull one chair after another in his direction until Pa sat in the center of a big circle, each stranger in turn buying a half-pint to pass around. A patent medicine man would tell of a brush with bandits on the road, a boat hand of an explosion that lit up the whole Hudson, a circuit lawyer of Indian attacks in the ter-ritories. Or else there'd be a trapper with stories of giant bears chasing him through the woods. Or a logger who showed off his scars. And as the oil lamp's shadows danced over the bare plank walls, I learned by installments that my home town was meager and insignificant, and that the world outside was impossibly vast and full of adventure.

By the fourth or fifth round, someone would nudge me awake to remind me that before I was born, my fearless father had rushed into a blazing house and saved a whole family from a fire all by himself— the parents, five kids, and someone's cousin. Then every soul in Grant's would toast Pa, down the rest of the whiskey and sing "There Is No Home Like Mine Own" good and loud and stumbly.

I'd once asked Pa how I could become brave like him.

"It's in your blood, Albert. Your grandpa died fighting the Creeks. His pa marched with Sullivan. You'll grow out of this namby-pamby phase and become a man worth his salt. I'll make sure of it."

I wanted to believe him, but I could never shake a nagging certainty that instead of a hero like Pa, I was destined to become the family coward. For all Pa's encouragement to face down the bullies, I only learned how to run. And the day Pa tried to teach me to swim, he tossed me in the lake and I choked and coughed and windmilled my arms till he had to plunge in with his boots on and pull me out himself.

After, I clung to Aunt Babe's leg.

"You can't terrify a child like that," she snapped.

"How the hell you think I ever learned?" Pa'd yelled right back.

All this, of course, was before the nightmares about dead babies began.

EPH, STILL IN MOURNING CLOTHES for his wife and baby, had trudged into the jail and told Pa he was worried because now his sister and niece were missing. Mostly I remember feeling secretly avenged, thinking about that smack she'd given me, until the catch in his voice drenched me in shame. He was a big man, but his back trembled as he told Pa there was no sign of Harriet, baby Priscilla, or Doc Rulloff. At the house, Eph said, he'd found dishes caked in food and laundry strewn across the floor.

Pa'd told Eph not to worry, Rulloff had probably taken them for an afternoon row on the lake. Surely, they'd be back by nightfall.

"Awful things grief can do to the mind," he said to me later. "No one needs tell me. Terrible thing to lose a wife in childbirth."

THREE WEEKS LATER, Eph's sister and niece were still missing. Pa had to call the sheriff in from Elmira, and that's when things started to happen quickly. They discovered Rulloff had fled and tracked his movements as far as Syracuse by stage, but lost his trail at the canal. The sheriff brought in hounds to scour the acres around Rulloff's house, but found no sign of hastily dug graves.

I heard speculations around the water pump, not meant for my ears but not whispered either. The brewer's wife told the Clinton House cook that they'd found disemboweled animals in Rulloff's cellar. The tanner said bodies don't stay underwater forever. Eventually, they rot and pop to the surface. He knew because he'd lived in New York City once, and bodies were always floating on the East River there.

For all the lake dragging, no one could find the bodies of Eph's sister or niece, but someone recalled that Eph's wife and daughter had been doctored by Rulloff just before they died. Suddenly, the question swept through Ithaca like a chill wind—had they actually been taken by fever, or had Rulloff killed all four of Eph's kin?

A week later, a different doc from Dryden was brought in to exhume the remains of Eph's wife and baby—the only two bodies they did have. With all the newfound bloodlust, I remember feeling disappointed that he couldn't say for sure whether they'd been killed on purpose, only that he found copper in their bellies. Copper wasn't part of any cure he knew of, but he only knew medicine from Gunn's book. As a test, he tried feeding copper to a rabbit. The rabbit died.

That was good enough for the locals, and soon every conversation— at the Saturday market, in the lanes, at church—became an urgent cry to find and hang the dreadful monster who'd committed such abominable acts against innocent women and children. In my imagination,

Rulloff grew into a half-man, half-growling beast, covered in blood, with stooped shoulders and wolflike hair.

Every night I endured nightmares of meeting Rulloff alone in the woods, but in the real world, there was no word of him for weeks. The jail sat empty, so Pa kept me busy planting carrots, digging turnips, and piling wood for the kitchen fire. Meanwhile, Pa got new shoes for the horses and greased the coach axles and cleaned his gun, but although he sent urgent telegrams to all corners of the state, the replies came back with no new information.

Until one oppressively hot afternoon in early August.

2

OUT ON THE LAKE, A SINGLE, LAZY CLOUD DRIFTED above. I nestled into the bow of the rowboat under the glaring sun and draped my leg over the gunwale, dragging my bare foot in the water. Then I remembered the possible bodies down there and pulled it back in.

"When will we find him, Pa?"

I don't believe I ever considered the possibility that Rulloff wouldn't be caught eventually. All of Aunt Babe's Bible stories ended with good triumphing over evil.

"Keep your voice down," Pa snapped, concentrating on his line.

"Will we bring him back in the coach or make him walk, you reckon?" I whispered. I imagined pulling the man-beast on a rope like a stubborn steer. People would cheer, and we'd be men together, Pa and me.

"Stop scaring the fish."

Pa'd always been quick to temper, but he was angry more often now that people were asking him questions he couldn't answer. He'd even taken to skipping Grant's Coffee Shop, a detail I remember vividly because it meant I got stuck with boiled roots for supper every night.

I, too, had questions, ones that roiled inside me, ones I wouldn't know how to ask even if Pa was in a talking mood. I cupped my hand to my forehead and tried to penetrate the glittering diamond glare of the surface. *Were the bodies of the lady and her baby below, staring up at me?* I was glad my mother was deep under the hill, where I couldn't see her eyes.

"Watch that line," Pa said in a terse whisper.

I glanced at the stern, but the fishing line stretched back into the water the same as it had for the past three hours, without the slightest quiver. The only movement on the dead calm lake came from the water bugs skating circles. I picked at the scab on my knee.

"Why would he do it, Pa?"

I meant kill his baby. The other murders were too big for me—I couldn't penetrate the world of adults. What I really wanted to know was why a father might kill his child.

Pa squinted at me, brow furrowed under the shadow of his hat. He cleared his throat and I waited for him to say something, but he stayed quiet, pursing his lips and chewing on the inside of his cheek.

I did the same.

"No accounting for it," Pa said, forgetting his rule about whispering.

From shore came a loud whistle, then the crack of a rifle shot in the air.

"The fuck's that for?" Pa shouted. He tossed the rod into the boat and picked up the oars in defeat. We wouldn't see another fish for hours.

I squinted at the trees. Two men sat astride horses on the bank, one of them waving both hands. "Thomas and Josiah!" I shouted, trembling with excitement that the Dryden deputies were looking for Pa. That could only mean one thing.

It only took Pa a few minutes to row to shore, but it felt like years. I'd finally get to see the world outside Ithaca and get to catch the monster at the same time. I tried not to be scared of his fangs.

But if he stabbed babies, what might he do to a little boy?

"Chicago," was the first thing Thomas said, as he helped Pa drag the boat onto shore. "Found the bastard trying to enroll in medical school, if you can believe it."

Pa thrust the fishing rod into my hands and jumped on the back of Thomas's horse. The two horses and three men took off at a gallop for the jail, leaving me alone on the deserted lake path.

I tried like mad to keep up, but my legs were short and the wicker creel kept bouncing against my knees. By the time I got home, I was winded. The horses were already harnessed to the coach and a crowd had gathered to watch the departure. Eph stood in the center of them all, holding his hat against his chest, crushing the edges in his fists. I'd barely made it in time.

Gasping, I tried to climb to the driver's seat, fishing gear and all, but Pa grabbed me under the arms and set me on the ground.

"I left you a pot of stew," he said, "And the better flint and my old jackknife. Long as the train from Geneva to Buffalo meets the Lake Erie ferry in time, we shouldn't be gone more than two weeks."

I didn't understand at first and waited for him to explain about the stew. Then it hit me all at once. I stepped back and stared up at the men with a lump the size of a duck's egg in my throat.

"But Pa—"

He tucked his musket under his arm and squinted at me like he had a headache.

"Have some syrup with your porridge, if you want."

"You can't leave me behind!"

I knew Pa would be mad I was talking back in front of everyone, but I couldn't help it. I didn't want to be left alone, and I didn't want to miss the manhunt. But the desperation that stopped my breath was Pa denying me my one chance to ever become a man worth his salt.

"You're old enough to feed yourself," Pa said loudly, speaking for the neighbors now. "See you get your chores done."

"Please don't leave me, Pa!"

Pa ground his teeth, then leaned down and spoke in my ear. "You get yourself in trouble, your Aunt Babe ain't far away."

Pa stepped up to the driver's box and glanced in Eph's direction. Then, instead of goodbye, he looked out at the crowd, shook his head.

"I hate to think on it, but women and babies don't just disappear. Someone's guilty of something."

Then the black coach slid in the rutted mud and the team rode off down the western road. I watched until they were a speck on the horizon, then until there was nothing but road. The crickets were chirping before I could find the courage to go inside alone, before I could get over Pa thinking so little of me that he never even once looked back.

I MANAGED FOR almost ten days by myself: Lit the fire and boiled supper, tested the word *fuck* out loud, spied on the ladies filing into St. John's and tried to imagine the structures that stretched their skirts into upside-down pipe bowls. On market day, Mrs. Snyder and the brewer's wife both brought baskets of food and told me to wash my ears.

I broke Pa's shaving mirror on purpose for leaving me behind, then tried to fit it back together. The lizard I trapped under a jar for company looked so sad that after a day I let it go. I knew Aunt Babe would hold me and feed me rhubarb pie. But if I ran to her, when Pa found out, he'd have that clench in his jaw that meant I wasn't fit to be called his son.

Instead, I yelled "The hell's wrong with you?" like Pa would have when I spilled the cornmeal. And I practiced opening and closing his knife, thinking he might be proud of me if I could do it one-handed. And I crawled into Pa's empty chair at night as the rain thundered down in torrents, and wondered where he was on the road and if he was being brave and if he'd forgotten about me.

On the tenth day, the August heat baked the air and drove down a stillness that silenced even the birds. I pushed open the stable door, grabbed a pitchfork, and tried to muck it the way Pa had shown me—putting my back in it—but each load seemed heavier than me, and rank with the urine of both horse and horseman. I wobbled under the weight, banged into a post and fell into the wet, ale-colored straw.

I struggled to stand up and punched at a knot in the stable wall so I wouldn't cry, and tried to believe that one day I'd save a whole town from a fire. Then I'd march to the Pacific like Lewis and Clark and cross the Delaware like Washington. I wasn't sure how that made him worth his salt, but I figured it must be a mighty big river.

Then Charles Curtis and his brothers appeared on the other side of the fence and began lobbing clods of muddy weeds at me through the stable door.

"Get that scrawny wild Indian!" Charles yelled. Then he started making cannon sounds as he lobbed mud balls. I ducked away from the projectiles but one hit my shoulder so hard it knocked me half to the ground. The pack of boys began making war whoops and circling in for the kill.

"Come on out, you nasty Indian," Charles yelled. "This is our town! You don't belong here."

Pa's advice to 'fight them once and for all' was etched in my brain, but all three of them were bigger than me, and I was furious at Pa for putting me in this position. I dropped the pitchfork and threw myself out the back door.

"Yeah, keep running, you stupid Indian!" Charles shouted behind me.

I did. I kept running all the way up the hill near Six Mile Creek.

Below, Ithaca stretched out like Aunt Babe's quilt squares, with the Presbyterian church spire as the big needle in the middle. Across town, mules on the towpath dragged empty grain barges down the lake, ready to be filled and sent back north to the Erie Canal. A few people and a donkey moved in front of the foundry, but most everyone was indoors, escaping the heat. Everyone else had somewhere to be. Everyone else belonged.

Thunderclouds rolled across the sky and plunged Ithaca into shadow. The heavy air said the coming storm would be a fierce one, but I didn't care. I sat under the green umbrella of ash trees, scraping at the mud between my toes with a stick. I knew Charles Curtis was too lazy to follow me up here, but I couldn't escape the echo of his laughter.

Dank humidity clung to my arms as I waited for the storm to lash at me, but instead, I heard a faint sound—a rhythmic beat that made my hair stand on end. I lay down the stick and pushed up to my feet. The sound grew louder, drumlike. Way out on the western road, I spotted the galloping horses.

The shiny black coach streaked through a gap in the trees, horses straining against the leads. Thomas and Josiah galloped alongside, one-handed with the reins, rifles draped across their laps. Up high on the driver's box of the jailor's coach, tallest of them all, sat Pa. One thing I knew for sure: They wouldn't be rushing home if that coach was empty.

I sprinted down the hill, tearing through brambles, sliding over leaves and tumbling straight into the graveyard fence. I tried to catch my breath in the blistering humidity and felt the first trickle of rain down the back of my neck.

A streak of lightning startled me and I lost the coach behind the tannery. I ran through curtains of rain, past the gun house and the yeasty stench of the brewery. If I was fast enough, I could get there in time to see people slap Pa on the back and watch them pull the monster out of the coach, growling and covered in wolf hair.

At the bridge, I heard a crack and felt a shudder. I thought it was thunder until I saw that the creek, still swollen from last week's storm, had crashed a tree into the stone base. The water swirled in angry eddies below. Rain roiled the surface. I was about to take off running again when, fifty yards upriver, I saw a bundle of muddy pink fabric caught in the roots of a fallen maple.

A swaddling blanket.

3

THE BLANKET LAY AT THE BOTTOM OF THE BANK, CAUGHT
in the rocks just above the rushing river. I was terrified to glimpse the
open-eyed face of the dead baby, with her rotting skin, but still—after
the whole town had searched for months, I could scarce believe I was
the one who found her. It was like I'd won the Christmas goose raffle,
only bigger. There had never been a contest this big in the whole history
of Ithaca. Maybe Pa would believe I was worth my salt after all.

I started running to tell Pa, then stopped short.

*What if the river swallowed the baby up again? What if I dragged Pa all
the way back, only to find she'd disappeared?*

No one would ever believe I'd found her, least of all Pa. And Charles
Curtis would never stop taunting me. I'd be an outcast forever.

Unless I brought home the missing baby girl.

Maybe I could be like Seba Hornbeck, who never got beat up
because everyone knew he had an extra toe. I peered into the gorge. The
slippery shale bank plunged more than twenty-five feet before it hit the
riverbed, steep enough that it had been undercut by the water. Climbing down seemed impossible. Below, the water swirled in angry white
eddies, pinning her to the rocks.

*How would I get down there? More important, how would I ever get
back up?*

I spun around, looking from river to bridge to bank and back again
for anyone I could flag down. But this was the far edge of town, shielded
by a thick, summer-green forest. Hot rain pelted my face. There was no
time to go for help.

Everyone had looked all summer, but I was the one who'd found her.
If I could prove it, they would cheer for me as much as Pa.

I trudged through the thick black loam of the bank to get a better look. At the edge, I could still only see a corner of the blanket. The powerful crush of the river sprayed wet mist two stories up. I tested my strength, dangled a foot over the vertical slope, tried to grip my toes around a protruding rock. A skitter of fractured shale dropped into the rushing current as I grabbed a birch root for balance.

"It's in your blood, Albert," I said aloud, but my voice sounded weak, my conviction hollow.

Thunder shook the trees as I looked for solid footing in the pockets of moss, breathing in the thick smell of mud and fungus. Rain stung my eyes as I inched down the bank, sliding on wet leaves. My foot found a crevice. I grabbed a fern with my hand. The water plunged down the gorge behind me, loud as a steam engine.

I tried to think about Pa rushing into a burning building. About his pa fighting the Creeks, and his pa's pa marching with Sullivan. I tried to think about how I belonged in the story line: The one who found the lost baby.

Then the shale under my foot gave way.

I snatched at the fern, but it pulled out by the roots. I fell backward. The slick bank flew past. I glimpsed charcoal sky as I tumbled. My stomach lurched in free fall.

The river leaped up and swallowed me in a frigid shock. A sharp rock bashed my chin. I felt a terrible shot of pain that shook my skull. Then I was pulled straight down to the freezing, airless bottom—my arms feeble and useless against the heavy, rushing water.

I was desperate to breathe, to escape the giant weight that seemed to be sitting on top of me, crushing my lungs. I flailed and kicked until I struck something sharp and hard—found just enough traction that I could get a fist around a twisted root and pull myself up to gasp a breath.

As I thrashed against the current, I heard church bells in the distance, ringing for the murderer's capture. I shouted for help once, twice, but knew everyone would be rushing the other way—to the jail to see the man-beast. The eddies grabbed at my ankles, pulling me under.

I kicked my feet trying to push up from the bottom, but the roaring brown water wanted to envelop me. I was going to die a slingshot's throw from home. Never having shot a rifle, never having gone to school, never having had a friend.

Two shadows leaped from horses, faces hidden under hats, blurred by rain. "Over there!"

"Hold the rope, damn it!"

"I got you, Josiah—just get the kid."

A shower of pebbles rained down and I had to look away. A freckled arm encircled my chest, squeezed the air out of me, hoisted me out of the water like a dripping sack of grain. The man grunted his way up the bank and dropped me on the grassy lip, choking and squirming. I twisted on my side, cheek in the mud, retched black water onto the bank and curled into a ball, raw inside with cold.

"Hey, ain't that Jarvis's boy?"

"Little guy. Big ears. Your pa Jarvis?" The man leaned down. Thomas, the deputy. Under the brim of his hat, I saw his eyes narrow. He bent over me, scratched at his gray-blond whiskers, then laughed low and deep, a sound that was probably relief but that I heard as mockery.

"It *is* Albert. I'll be damned."

"Lucky son of a bitch, what he is," Josiah said. "The hell you doin' in the river, kid?"

Confused and hazy, I tried to stop shaking in front of the deputies, to halt the chatter of my teeth and think. The blanket. I wasn't a stupid kid. I was worth my salt. Hacking, I found my voice.

"Baby's down there."

Thomas stopped laughing. His face flattened.

"Josiah, go see what's down there." He spoke evenly, urgently.

"Hold the rope this time, damn it."

Thomas grabbed a thick coil of knotted rope, wrapped it twice around a tree trunk, and dug his boot heels into the mud. I pushed myself up to sitting, watched him strain as Josiah jumped down the bank.

"Whose babe?" Thomas interrogated. His right arm shook as he tried to steady the rope against Josiah's weight. "Whose babe'd you drop in that river?"

I wiped my face with my sleeve, tried to wrap my mind around his mistake.

"Didn't. Drop anyone." I couldn't stop shaking. "Saw her. From the bridge."

"Saw who?"

I could barely make my mouth work, my teeth were chattering so hard.

"Rulloff's baby." My wet shirt bloomed with crimson. I touched my chin and felt the warm smear of sticky blood.

"Rulloff—" Thomas stood from his crouch and the rope slackened.

"Aw, hell," Josiah said.

"What've you got down there? Is it a baby?"

"Lord, Thomas. Gimme a minute. I got my boots soakin' wet. There's somethin' down here."

Josiah huffed up the side of the bank, slipping on the shale, black hat askew. He cradled the muddy bundle of cloth in the crease of his elbow, the calico roses soaked and stained. I edged back toward the woods on my hands and feet like a spider.

"We got ourselves a deputy in training, Thomas. This what you saw kid?"

I nodded.

Thomas breathed heavy out his nose and frowned at Josiah. I looked back and forth between their faces but couldn't understand what passed between them. I wrapped my arms tight around my chest, tried to control the shaking.

"Is it dead?"

"It ain't living. That's sure."

He stretched out a smile, showed me his wide, square teeth, one stained brown.

"Good work, little man. You solved the mystery of the missing apron."

He threw the empty cloth to the ground with a huff.

"Got me good and wet for it, too."

Hot shame rose into dry heaves.

"Isn't there more down there?"

"Kid, there ain't nothing but river 'tween here and comeuppance."

"Alright." Thomas curled the rope and hung it from his saddle horn. "Let's get moving. The ankle-biter's gonna need stitches, I expect."

Thomas smelled of wet leather as he lifted me off the ground and sat me on his horse's neck, then settled into the saddle behind me. He was exactly the kind of man Pa wanted me to be, I realized. Practical. Brave. Strong. Exactly the kind of man I could never be.

I grabbed the mare's blond mane and tried to fight a dizzy nausea as I thought about how Thomas would tell the story, about Pa learning just how stupid I was about an old apron. Getting whacked with the belt felt like nothing in comparison to how he would see me now.

How could the town hero have fathered the town fool?

The mare twisted her head and gently rolled a big brown eye at me, the only being alive who didn't care what a failure I was. If she were mine, I'd give her clean straw and wash the mud from her legs with pails of water and bristle brushes. I'd feed her apples every day, look up into her wide brown eyes and watch them blink.

I wiped my bloody chin and tried to think of something manly to say.

"What's your horse's name?"

Thomas gave her an easy kick.

"Horse," he said.

4

AS THOMAS RODE ME HOME FROM THE RIVER, I WISHED like mad that he was taking me back to my *real* home with Aunt Babe. It felt like lifetime ago I'd moved in with Pa, but it had barely been two years since I first heard of the jail.

Aunt Babe had pressed her cheek against mine, once, twice, as she cradled me in her lap. The rocker creaked on the porch in a steady rhythm that matched our swaying. We were one warm, lumpy body.

"You're getting so big so fast," she'd said, glancing out over Cayuga Lake. I couldn't tell if her voice sounded happy or sad. "Four years old already."

I couldn't help but think of the hill beyond the barn, the pile of stones, and somewhere underneath, the person they called my mother. We'd just marked her passing on my birthday.

Aunt Babe had stopped talking, but I heard a dread build up in the silence until I pulled my head away, opened my eyes and looked past the arches of her thin eyebrows into her deep green eyes.

"Am I too big?"

She'd allowed a surprised laugh to escape her mouth, then pursed her lips and looked away at the lake with the same face she made before tackling a big threshing job.

"It's time you moved home with your Pa," she'd said, her voice stiff. She might have been telling the rooster to stay out of the corn hutch.

Back then, I knew Pa as the man who came for supper on Sundays and sat in the high-backed chair, twisting his left boot under the table and answering Babe's questions with either "Soon," "Soon enough," or "Goddamnit, you know better than to ask me that!"

I hadn't understood what she meant about moving home. I was home. I could only stare at the soft fuzz on her chin.

"I told your Pa that woman was too scrawny for babies. Anyone could see. Those tiny hips." She pursed her lips again as if to keep quiet. A screech owl hooted from one of the trees along the bank. "You think he ever listened to me?"

I tried to follow her gaze but only saw the waving, black-tipped tail of a weasel against the snow. A chill wind started up from the north side of the house.

"They're building a courthouse downtown," she'd said. "And they need someone to keep the jail."

I had no idea what that meant, but could tell from her tone that it wasn't a good thing.

She'd wrinkled her chin, wrenched a hand free, and tucked a loose clump of hair into her bun.

Then she'd patted my head the way she did when it was time to get off her lap for chores.

"A boy should be with his father," she'd said. "They're adding an annex in the back for the two of you to live."

Then she nudged me to the ground as if she'd explained things.

WHEN THOMAS TURNED the corner from Buffalo onto Cayuga, I realized he was heading to the front of the courthouse. The fancy public side had whitewashed walls and a grand staircase that led to the high-ceilinged courtroom on the second floor, filled with light from four big windows brought all the way from Boston. I'd never actually stepped foot through that carved wood door.

The bare plank annex where Pa and I lived sat behind the jail, and had its own rickety door in the muddy garden by the stable. The knot-holes whistled in the wind when the newspaper wadding got damp and fell out. Under the sleeping loft, the other door led into the stone-walled jail of the main building, a cramped room with three iron cells, two small windows, and Pa's squat desk shoved underneath the staircase.

I knew Pa'd be sitting at that desk now, furious about the mess I'd left in the stable, sure I'd run off to Aunt Babe's like the namby-pamby he expected me to be. He was about to find out I was much, much worse.

The ruts in the street were still fresh from where they'd pulled the coach around the raspberry thicket. The distant sound of hammering stopped. Then the lumber mill saw went quiet. The news was traveling like wildfire. The whole town would soon be raising their glasses to Pa and singing songs again.

Maybe I should have let the river take me.

Horse slowed from canter to trot. Thomas jumped off and tied her to the long post in front of the pear tree. Then he slung me over his shoulder and carried me up the steps and through the door.

"Jake? You here?"

He set me down next to Pa's desk under the staircase, facing the cobwebs on the back of the risers. From the annex came the tinny clunk of Pa's cup hitting the water bucket. The hazy light dimmed further as Josiah closed the door, trapping me in the narrow room.

"We were on our way to the telegraph office," Thomas said, squatting down to speak through the open fireplace at Pa. "We found your boy."

"Was he held hostage by wild Indians?" Pa's voice reverberated against the stone. "Is that why my stable's too mucked up to put my goddamn horses in after near thirty miles?"

Too ashamed to look up, I watched bloody water run down my leg. Behind me, iron shackles scraped across the slate floor, and then a long, blurred shadow overtook my feet. The smell of sweating mortar hung dense in the humid air.

"The hell?" The annex door slammed against the stone wall. "Why's he sopping wet?"

I snuck just enough of a glance to see Pa loop his right thumb through his belt, the big vein in his neck throbbing. I waited for him to jerk that belt off his waist, to hear the crack, and feel the whip against my backside, scorching my flesh deep as a hot brand.

"He fell in the river." Thomas said.

Pa said nothing.

"We were headed to send that telegram in Owego when Josiah heard him holler."

I swiped at a trickle of water down my back and waited for Thomas to say I'd imagined a dead baby, that I'd caused all this grief over a stupid old apron. I looked up, wishing Pa would shout at me. Anything would be better than the silence.

"Boy ain't got the sense God gave a toad," Pa said finally. "Ten days on the road and I come back. Stable half mucked. Turnips not sowed. Supper fire cold. There's not a boy from here to Chicago more helpless than my son. Gonna get himself killed 'fore he gets the rest of his teeth."

"He's had a bit of a time of it, I'd say, Jake," Thomas said. "You'd best look at that chin. Gash looks pretty deep."

Maybe he meant to keep the apron part of the story to himself. I was too afraid to hope. I felt sick to my stomach and light-headed at the same time.

"What do you got to say for yourself, Albert?" Pa glared at me and I looked back at the floor. "Bleeding like a stuck pig. You gonna look at me?" Pa's fat fingers grabbed my chin, wrenched my head up. "It's a hard world out there. You hear me? Ain't gonna bend for you, that's sure. You gotta learn not to break so easy." The sting made warm tears run backward down my cheeks.

Stubble lined the pink creases in Pa's neck. He smelled of briny man sweat, but not liquor. Finally, he let go, slumped in his chair, head back.

"You know what it's gonna cost me to get you sewed up?"

Woozy, I tried to recall the words printed on Doc Bull's door. Hebrew plaster cost a dollar. Three for bloodletting. Barter rates available. *What was it for stitches?* I remembered the answer but stayed silent, unsure if Pa actually wanted me to speak. But the silence lasted such a long stretch, not answering felt like the wrong choice.

"Two dollars or two chickens, Pa."

Pa scowled.

"I don't need stitching, though," I added quickly. "I'll go and finish the stable now." I took a step toward the door, but slipped in the blood and fell hard on my hip. I heard a gentle cough and the monster's shadow blanketed my whole body in darkness.

"Perhaps I may be of assistance."

The voice was surprisingly gentle. I pushed up to my knees and the room wobbled. I had to plant my palm flat on the slate to keep from falling. Behind the bars stood a man so tall his black curls brushed the ceiling beams. He held his enormous round head slightly to one side, as if engaged in deep thought. From his face peered the brightest blue eyes I'd ever seen—eyes that seemed to pierce deep into my soul and recognize all of my darkest secrets.

I was terrified of him, but I couldn't have said why. He didn't look anything like a monster. He wasn't even especially hairy. Not only that, but he wore a silk waistcoat, cravat, and a pressed shirt without a single gravy stain—and kept his hands folded deferentially behind his back.

He smiled warmly at me before turning to Pa.

"From what I can see, the young man requires stitches rather urgently," he said, calm but also serious. "The rate of blood loss is alarming for such a small child."

Thomas banged the butt of his rifle against the crossbar.

"You got nothing to say, you hear me? Three days I've told you to keep that trap shut."

The prisoner took a step back with a slight, submissive bow.

"I don't intend any offense. I only offer my skills. Whatever rumors may be circulating, I am a doctor, and I'm willing to stitch the lad." He waved his arm around the enclosure and smiled. "Under present circumstances, I'll even waive the two chickens."

No one laughed.

Pa didn't flinch. I waited for him to give the prisoner a boot shining or at least tell him to go to hell in a bucket.

"I don't need stitches, Pa," I said. I wiped the blood away with my sleeve, but warm ooze still slid into the hollow of my neck. Lightning flashed through the high windows. When it was gone, the room seemed darker than before.

"You know, Aristotle called youth a state of permanent intoxication," the prisoner said. "Errors in judgment are really quite common at this—"

"Don't talk to me about my boy." Pa leaned back in his chair, set his scuffed boots on the desk, and rubbed his thumb against his jaw with a faraway look I didn't understand. Thomas stood by the cell, waiting for an indication from Pa. Josiah picked at the grime under his thumbnail with his knife. Thunder boomed. I squeezed behind the chair.

"As you wish," the prisoner continued. "I understand the situation is a bit unorthodox. I simply mean to offer an alternative." Rulloff shrugged, then smiled, his full set of white teeth glowing in the twilight shadows of the cell. "Also, I assume one is innocent until proven guilty," he looked Pa dead in the eye, "Even in Tompkins County."

A loud bang made me jump. The front door rattled on its hinges. A voice echoed into the growing darkness:

"You catch the bastard, Jake?" It was Eph Schutt. "We're here to give him what he got coming."

"Fuck," Pa said, letting his boots drop to the floor.

He looked at Thomas, then at Rulloff and back again, barely breathing. Finally, he shoved me into the corner and turned to the deputies. "You two still loaded?"

5

———

THOMAS AND PA SHARED A SERIOUS LOOK. I HAD NO IDEA
what was happening, but I could see enough in that look to be afraid.
Thomas took a wide stance in the middle of the room, pointed his rifle
toward the door, and cocked the hammer. A flickering yellow light
reflected off the ceiling beams.

"Hang him!" I heard someone shout. Then another.

Then shouting came from all around—anger like I'd never heard
before. Maybe fifty or a hundred people, all with savage, vicious voices.
I wanted to peek through the window above my head but was sure
something would come flying at me if I did.

"Too late for help from that telegram now," Pa said. He grabbed the
old flintlock from the mantle, its barrel almost as tall as he was. I smelled
smoke from outside, heard a stampede of objects hitting the earth.

Pa glanced at Rulloff, then looked hard at me before he strode up to
the window, wedging his body between me and the crowd, boot on the
sill. Torchlight glowed across the bridge of his nose.

"Three dozen," he said to Thomas, "Maybe more. Fired up enough to
wake snakes." He twisted the latch and pushed open the windowpane.
Angry jeers echoed off the stone walls. "Evening folks," Pa said, as if it
was any other day at Grant's.

The hollers quieted enough for Eph's wavering voice to be heard.

"You get him, Jarvis? He in there?"

I STOLE A LOOK at Rulloff. He stood stock still, but a flash of terror
crossed his blue eyes. He caught me looking at him, and I felt ashamed,
not for the staring, but for the secret knot of fear I'd glimpsed inside
him.

"We got him, Eph," Pa said, steady as a stone fence. "Locked and chained. No need for a fuss now. You all can take down that rope."

"Let us in, Jarvis! We'll get Eph his due."

Pa took his time in front of the crowd, pouring a load of buckshot in the barrel of his musket, in plain sight of the window, drawing the ramrod to shove it down. "Now you know I've a sworn job to do here," he yelled over the din. "You all gave it to me." He squeezed a cap in the nipple, cocked the gun, and held it firm at his side like a walking stick.

"You brought him all the way from Chicago, Jake," Eph said. "You did your job. All we're asking is for you to step away."

I shook in the corner, losing control of my body from both cold and terror. Pa looked at Thomas, as if he might provide an answer, but he only stared deep at Pa and then shrugged.

"Your call, Jake," he said.

Rulloff carefully donned his frock coat and grasped his top hat with a barely shaking left hand. I imagined he was deciding that if he were to die he wanted to do so like a gentleman.

Pa looked long and hard at me, a look I didn't understand. He took a deep breath and tapped his four fingers against the barrel band.

"I'm sorry for your family, Eph," he said. "You'll get your justice after the trial. He'll hang proper soon enough."

"Jake, you ain't standing up for a baby killer?"

"You know I ain't, Ephraim."

I squeezed back as far as I could into the jagged stone of the corner. The flickering light grew brighter. I felt a wave of heat. Rulloff caught my eye from behind the bars and motioned to keep pressure against my chin. His face was calm now, his hand steady.

"Back up. I mean it." Pa pulled the musket to his shoulder and pushed it through the window. "Those torches get any closer and I'm gonna have to pull this trigger."

I heard the clang of a pipe against the stone and clenched my eyes shut.

"You wouldn't shoot your friends to save the devil."

"Stop that now!" Pa shouted. "You hear me? Listen, I took an oath to uphold the law, and that's what I'm going to do, one way or another. That means you take one step closer and I give the order to fire. The deputies here got rifles, so two of you die easy. But I got my Pa's old musket with shot, so everyone else in thirty yards gets sprayed and loses an eye. Or a leg. Or gets one in the stomach and bleeds for a week and then dies. Up to you. But you gotta think on if it's worth hanging him now or a week from now when the trial's all done and legal."

A blue flash startled me. I opened my eyes expecting the room to be on fire, but it was lightning.

"NEVER TOOK YOU FOR a traitor, Jarvis," someone yelled.

"This ain't over," someone else shouted, but the voice was farther away.

The glow from the torches faded and Pa turned into a dark shadow against the window. He kept his gaze out on the street for a long time before he hung his head. Finally, I heard him speak to Thomas.

"I don't think they're coming back," he said. "But I can't be sure. Josiah can go telegram the governor for backup. I'd be obliged if you'd stay the night, Thomas, in case there's more trouble."

"Whatever you need, Jake." Another look passed between them in the dark shadows.

"You did your duty."

Thomas hung his head and turned slightly away from Pa, staring at the wall and biting on the inside of his lip. If it had been anyone but Thomas, I might have thought I saw a tear in his eye.

In a hint of moonlight I saw Pa lower the hammer and lean his musket against the doorframe. He sighed, bit on his left thumbnail and then turned back to me.

"Hell, he's bleeding all over the floor."

6

I TRIED TO SOP UP THE STICKY MESS WITH MY SHIRT-sleeves, but it spread over the stone like slick paint.

Thomas cleared his throat. "You know how to stitch a cut?"

"Babe does the sewing," Pa said with the frown he reserved for all things Babe.

I crawled under the desk in a desperate hope that if they didn't see me, they'd forget about stitches.

"You know medicine?" Pa asked the prisoner.

"I've trained extensively in homeopathic remedies."

Pa spit onto the prisoner's shiny, shackled boots.

"I asked do you know medicine?"

Rulloff waited a moment before answering, perhaps deciding whether to ignore the insult.

"Yes," he said. "You're fortunate I'm available. That imbecile Doc Bull still adheres to archaic bleeding and blistering. Modern science shows us the human body is designed to heal itself. The proper role of the physician is to choose the right herbs and compounds to support—"

"Christ, man. Can you stitch the boy's chin?"

Rulloff took a deep breath and stared down Pa.

"I can."

Rain pattered down the chimney into the fireplace, sending up miniature clouds of ash. I'd never seen anyone get stitches, but I'd seen the scars left after the fact—thick ropes of tortured pink skin.

"You sure you want to do this, Jake?" Thomas cupped his hand on Pa's shoulder, softly, almost affectionately. "We've known each other a long while, and I'll follow any direction you give, but you recall this man murdered women and babes."

"Allegedly," Rulloff said.

"I don't need stitches, Pa."

I'd already made this point, but I hoped that it sounded more logical after what Thomas said.

Pa's looked at me under the desk, eyes hanging heavy with fatigue. I felt too guilty to hold his gaze.

"There's only one other option," I heard him say, "and Doc Bull was out there with that mob cursing me along with the rest, so I ain't got much choice."

Pa paused, then spat a fingernail into the fireplace.

"'Sides, boy's gotta learn his lesson."

Thomas lit the lantern on the mantle. The yellow light cast long shadows, more frightening to me than the darkness. Josiah brought in a load of firewood, crouched by the andirons with a groan, and dumped the wood on the hearth.

"When you're done, Josiah," Pa said, "we'll need some water and one a those rags hanging from the board."

"And a small glass of warm milk," the prisoner added, "if you'd be so kind."

Josiah sneered. "Shall I bake a plum pudding too?"

Rulloff smoothed back his hair and turned back to Pa.

"You'll find stitching needles in my trunk."

Thomas set the chair by the window, pulled off his hat, and fell into the seat with the rifle across his lap. He leveled his eyes at Rulloff.

"With all them smarts, I 'spect you can guess what'll happen to you if that needle slips."

Pa dragged a black trunk from the far corner and pulled out three heavy books, a folded shirt, and a stack of papers covered in delicate writing. Then he extracted a tied leather case. When Pa unrolled the bundle, I saw a half dozen gleaming surgical knives.

"Pa—"

"May I ask for your powder horn as well?" the prisoner asked.

"Pa! I've learned my lesson." I grabbed his leg, but he refused to look at me. "Please give me the belt. I'll never go near the river again. And I'll do all my chores. I promise."

Josiah returned with water, a rag, and a pot of milk that he set next to the fireplace. He crouched at the hearth, struck the flint, and blew until a twist of flame curled over the kindling. The firelight glinted off the needle—a curved bow as big as my hand. Pa handed it through the bars.

The smoke from the torches lingered in the air but Rulloff crouched in front of me, focused as a catamount waiting to pounce on a hapless rabbit.

"Young man, your fear is understandable given the things they accuse me of, but you are perfectly safe in my care, I assure you."

Even in the grip of terror, I noticed he called me young *man*. Not kid. Not boy.

"Today, we have the opportunity to bear injustice with grace. *Accipere quam facere praestat injuriam.* Do you know your Latin?"

I shook my head. Pa said Latin was for rich people.

"And yet, you remembered Doc Bull's prices perfectly. Such an intelligent young man should be learning his Latin by now."

No one had ever called me intelligent. Even Aunt Babe usually said things like "Not like that, Albert. Where's your head?" But Aunt Babe would never stab me in the face with a giant needle.

Pa grabbed the ring of keys from the table. The clank, muffled scrape, and loud click of the lock reverberated through my chest. He swung open the door and pointed for me to enter, but there was no way I was going in that cell. Pa stood stone-faced but for the twitch in his jaw that told me he was grinding his teeth.

"Did I hear your name was Albert?"

The prisoner swept his arm back as if inviting me into his parlor, as if a mob of people hadn't just tried to hang him from a tree. My heart was thumping, but I didn't hear the slightest tremble in his voice.

"Albert is Old German. It means noble, bright, and famous. It's a pleasure to make your acquaintance."

Pa kicked the back of my legs to move forward. I refused.

Rulloff took the rag and bowl from Josiah, then carefully removed his frock coat, folded it lining-side out, and rolled his sleeves. The navy silk of his cravat shimmered around his neck, and I was surprised to see his thick sideburns neatly trimmed, even after days on the road. When he reached out to clasp my hand, I flinched but couldn't back up because Pa was standing right behind me.

"May I see your chin?" He pulled me close, and continued to speak casually, but now I could feel his heart beating through his shirt as fast as mine. In that intimate rhythm, I realized I'd been right all along. He had been afraid of the mob, just like me. This man with fancy clothes and delicate handwriting and Latin words was the only person I'd ever known who felt fear the same as I did.

He dipped the rag in the bowl and wrung it dry. When he held the cloth to my chin, the sting made me wince.

"Now, the stitches will stop the bleeding, but afterward it's most important to prevent the wound from festering. Doc Bull would cauterize it with a hot poker—"

I gasped and pushed back against Pa's leg, but he shoved me back into the cell.

"But you can avoid such unnecessary pain, Albert. Fortunately, I've done many scientific experiments and discovered a gunpowder poultice far more effective than scorching."

I wasn't sure gunpowder sounded less scary than a poker, but his voice was calming.

"Can you lift your head?" he asked. "Perhaps look out the front window. Any stars out yet?"

"No, Sir," I tried to keep my voice from breaking, thought about what a young man might say. "Cloud cover."

"Of course."

Rulloff pressed the cloth with a gentle hand, as Aunt Babe would have. "I can see the gash now. About three inches along the jawline. It appears you have a perfect opportunity to show your father just how brave you are."

Or what a coward.

Rulloff spun his top hat off the bench like he was doing a magic act, and placed it top-side down, in the far corner of the cell. "Now come over here and lie down for me please, Albert." He smiled with kind eyes, but still held the massive needle.

Pa handed the black thread to Rulloff.

"Understand me. You do anything wrong with the needle and I call that mob back to rip out your insides, hang you from that tree, and light you on fire."

I lay on the bench, hugging my arms and legs in, tight as a dead beetle.

Rulloff smiled.

Up close, his breath smelled like he'd been chewing mint leaves. I watched him thread the needle, thick as the one Aunt Babe used for embroidery.

"We're going to put twelve stitches in, and then it will be all over. Can you count to twelve?"

His fingers were right at my neck, so I nodded only very slightly, glad Aunt Babe had taught me that much. I closed my eyes, heard the clatter and sparks from another log set on the fire.

"Now, one thing at a time," he said very quietly. "Very gently, I'm going to press the two edges of skin together, all right?"

I squinted tight, felt the gentle pressure of his large fingers. Maybe I could be a little brave, at least. Ever so slightly, I nodded my head.

"Excellent. *Bon courage!* And now the first stitch."

I felt a sharp prick at my jaw and wrapped my hands around the edges of the bench to hold in the pain.

"There," Rulloff said. "You did very well, Albert. It's not going to get any worse than that."

I felt another stab. The tightness increased into a hard pinch. A tear escaped and rolled down my cheek.

"That's two. I'm taking care to penetrate the skin at the perpendicular, so you'll grow into a handsome man with a dashing scar, not a jagged one. How old are you now?"

"Six." I felt another jab and drew in a breath.

"And do you like cherry or buttermilk pies better?"

"Ahhk." The pinch increased, and I stamped my foot on the bench. "Cherry."

My whole jaw screamed in pain. I focused on the dark splotches on the back of my eyelids as I clenched them shut, and the tender heaviness of Rulloff's large hand steadying my forehead.

"Delicious. And green snakes or ribbon snakes?"

I winced but took a chance with the truth.

"Don't like snakes," I confessed.

"I agree. I've never been much of a reptile fan either."

I almost smiled.

"Do you know your arithmetic? We've done two plus four stitches. How many is that?"

I felt a flush of shame and opened my eyes.

"Relax now. You'll find it easier with your eyes shut."

"I ain't had school," I said, then blinked my eyes closed.

I considered all the fights between Pa and Aunt Babe on the subject, but since we were in Pa's jail, I thought it best to express only his opinion.

"It costs too much."

"It certainly does," he agreed. "Now the proper grammar is *I haven't been to school*, which is a terrible shame, but no reflection on you." He tugged on the thread. "Two and four is six. And I just completed another, so six plus one is seven. That leaves only five to go."

He tugged again, and I couldn't hold in the gasp.

"My family's finances were also limited, so I am entirely self-taught. Do you know that many of the most accomplished people of history were autodidacts, Albert, from Leonardo da Vinci to Alexander Hamilton? If you apply yourself, you could accomplish great things, even without a formal education."

I didn't know what autodidact meant or who da Vinci was, but I'd heard of Alexander Hamilton. In the Revolution, he was a hero.

An insidious idea took hold like a weed in my heart. I'd always disliked the thought of growing up to run the jail, but that's how things were. You did as your Pa did like the sun came up over Freeman's fallow, like tomatoes ripened in August, and horse poop smelled better than cattle poop.

"How?" I opened my eyes.

Rulloff glanced away from his needle with a hint of surprise, then smiled broad enough to crease all the skin around his eyes.

"Well, you have more pluck than I expected. Let me see. Latin is always the best foundation. Under the circumstances, we could begin with Seneca. Can you say *Errare humanum est?* It means, 'To err is human.'"

"Stick to your stitching," Pa snapped. "Stop talking to the boy."

"As you wish," Rulloff said pleasantly, but I could feel his grip on the needle tighten.

After he knotted the thread I opened my eyes, feeling grateful it was over, but also strangely unsatisfied, like I'd missed something important and wanted to go back and figure out what it was.

Pa stepped in with his stag handle Bowie knife. He moved so quickly that I drew back as he ran the knife right up next to my chin. Tiny squares of firelight glinted off the blade as he cut the thread clean.

I wanted Rulloff to explain how someone could become a hero with an education—maybe it didn't require being brave—but he remained silent as he mixed the poultice in the cook pot. It stung like a slap when he put it on my chin, but he gave me a knowing wink, then wrapped my chin and neck in so many strips of muslin I could barely twist my head.

"That's enough," Pa said. "Straight to bed, Albert. You'll have no supper, but we'll save the belt for tomorrow."

I grabbed the doorframe of the cell, then pivoted to Pa, swollen with pride, shame, and uncertain courage.

"*Errare humanum est,*" I said, before the solid whack of Pa's hand caught me across the back of my head.

7

AT THE COURTHOUSE, THE GOVERNOR'S MEN RODE IN carriages with gold door handles and spoke to each other in titles: "Thank you, Mister District Attorney."

But to Pa it was always "Jarvis go fetch that book." "Jarvis, go send this telegram."

Most surprising, I never heard Pa tell them to take a fat mule to hell.

They set a reward of three hundred dollars for whoever found the bodies, and the fortune-seekers appeared overnight. Flatboats and lumber rafts, rowboats, and freighters still heavy with iron rails skimmed Cayuga Lake for weeks, dragging cargo hooks along the shadowy bottom.

The week before Rulloff's trial passed in what felt like a twisted festival: men shouting instructions at each other, boats colliding, oars churning, women selling meat pies, kids chasing fireflies, and men taking turns with the fiddle.

But no one found the bodies, and no one collected the reward.

Throughout these days, there was one phrase I kept hearing: *Corpus delicti*. Whatever it was, it made the prosecutor so mad he banged his fist on the table and broke his pinkie finger. And it made me hopeful that soon Rulloff would be set free, and maybe then I could finally have a friend.

"YOU GOING TO BOIL that egg or turn it to stone?"

Pa scraped the dried mud from the bottom of his boots with his knife. The dirt fell on the floor under the table. I ignored his short temper and set two forks on the table, but it did me no good.

"Let me see that chin," he demanded.

I knew immediately what was coming and threw both my hands in front of my face.

"IT'S FINE, PA."

"Show me."

I took a tiny step forward, hoping he would just look, but he grabbed my chin between his thumb and forefinger, and I winced with pain. He sniffed at the bandage.

"Don't smell rotten," he said, and surprised me with a gentle shove back toward the fire. "You reckon you've learned your lesson then?"

Before I could answer, Aunt Babe opened the door without knocking, set a stack of pamphlets and a blackberry pie on the table, then dusted her hands on her blue-checked dress. I was so surprised I nearly spilled the pot of water.

Just outside the door, I caught a glimpse of Bailey, her white-whiskered donkey, struggling to pull his lead closer to the wild mint by the paddock.

I wanted to hug her tight, but that would make Pa even madder.

Aunt Babe and Pa stared at each other as if seeing who would blink first. Finally, Aunt Babe spoke.

"Did you hear? Johnston's grain freighter washed out again. Second time in two years that drunken skunk has lost a boat. You'll be glad to know I contracted with Burrows instead of taking your advice."

I tried to imagine how far the freighters ran. The north end of Cayuga Lake was as far as I could see from the hill, but I'd heard the Erie Canal led all the way to New York City.

Pa shifted his weight.

"You expect me to be grateful for your scraps?"

"Your share should get you a hog to last the winter now, at least."

In the ensuing silence, I risked speaking.

"How far does the freighter go?"

Aunt Babe set her hands on her hips as she continued to stare at Pa.

"The grain's milled at Oneida," she answered, misunderstanding my question. Finally, she turned to look at me and must have seen the muslin wrappings around my face because she rushed over and grabbed me, which she never would have done normally in front of Pa.

"Lord, Jake. How'd he get hurt?" I heard her say, from the folds of her skirt.

"He's fine," Pa said. "Stitched up and everything."

She looked straight down at me and I felt the need to nod vigorously, which hurt my chin and made me wince.

Aunt Babe frowned, and I saw her hand shake before she reached her fist into her basket and dumped a small pile of coins on the table. A sheen of sweat glistened across the bridge of her nose.

"You get him some shoes with that," she said.

"Put that right back," Pa said. "I ain't taking your charity."

"I'm not giving it to you. It's for Albert. Shoes only, mind. Don't let me hear you spent this at Grant's."

Pa's jaw twitched, and I knew he was grinding his teeth again. Maybe she didn't know he was no longer welcome at Grant's.

Aunt Babe looked at me again, then back at Pa.

"He get hurt working? He's not even seven. You can't work him like he's seventeen. He should be in school."

"He's my son," Pa said and held the door open. "You hear me? *My son,* and he belongs with his Pa. You did me a favor when he was just a baby, and I appreciate that. I do. But don't think it gives you any right to tell me how to raise him up now that he's grown some."

Aunt Babe ignored Pa's hint to leave, pulled a chair from the table and sat mopping her forehead with the handkerchief she kept tucked under the neck of her dress.

"Lot of talk going round here, Jake. Not many folk who understand what you did, after all Eph went through." She moved the coins into a straight line along the table's edge with her finger, then took another glance at me. "Some are pretty upset."

"You think I should have handed the man over to be lynched by a lawless mob in front of the courthouse?"

"I am not implying that. I'm your sister. Why can you never believe I am on your side? I know you've got a job to do, and that in your world laws are the same as morals."

"Now that's just like you. You think the world'd be better off if folks could follow only the laws they liked." Pa stood, grabbed the pamphlets off the table, and pressed them into her face.

The tense silence was broken suddenly by the sound of the piss bucket being filled in the jail.

Aunt Babe barely blinked at Pa's outburst. "That's not what the Anti-Slavery Society is about, and you know it, Jake. We advocate for humanity and Christian decency."

"What's my job then, if not keeping laws as men wrote them? Why am I here if you and your friends—or that mob with a rope—get to decide what's right and wrong based on your version of morals? I've sacrificed everything for this job and can only pray they figure that out eventually. But meantime here's my very own sister handing out seditious pamphlets. Don't look at me that way. I ain't the one who let a dozen states enter the Union with slavery guarantees. I don't love it either, but it's the damned law!"

Aunt Babe ignored the cursing, placed one of the pamphlets on the table and smoothed out the creases. She placed the rest in her basket.

"Don't be dramatic. If you read the literature, you'll understand our aim is to bring about basic reforms and work toward a gradual end to the practice. For goodness sake, we are not revolutionaries."

"I don't need your pamphlets to know we ain't got room for more free Negroes in this state. Ain't enough work for the native born as is. Negroes and immigrants pouring in. You know there's even an Irish jail-keep in Binghamton now? Imagine telling our pa he died for his country so some Irishman's son could make a living good as his own. You figure out how to ship all the Irish and Negroes home, and then I'll read your pamphlets."

Aunt Babe squinted hard at Pa.

"Is there a difference between can't read and don't read?"

Pa refused to take the bait. "Whatever you think of me, I know my job. So you take these papers and hand them out somewhere else. This is a murder trial, not a ladies' tea."

"You're stubborn as Bailey out there. Always have been. But somewhere deep in your heart you must know slavery is an abomination."

Suddenly, Pa threw his fork clear across the room so hard it stuck in the wood post holding up the sleeping loft. I dropped the egg on the floor in shock.

"You used that word on me once, and I told you I'd kill you before I let you say it to my face again!"

Babe leapt from the chair and took a step backward toward the door.

"I didn't say it of you, Jacob." Her tone was firm. "I said it of *slavery*."

"You implied it well enough, so I'd appreciate if you would kindly leave. Right. Fucking. Now. I don't want you in my house, and I don't want you giving money to my boy. You understand me?"

"I didn't mean—"

"Out!" Pa thundered.

Aunt Babe pursed her lips like she'd swallowed a lemon, but she tucked her basket under her arm, smoothed her skirts, and strode out the door, pulling it closed behind her.

8

PA STORMED UP THE STAIRCASE TO THE COURTHOUSE, where the governor's men would soon gather. He'd forgotten his breakfast, but I knew from those angry bootsteps he wouldn't be back for it.

He also hadn't pulled the belt out yet, so I still had that to dread. I peeled the boiled egg that had fallen on the floor and rubbed my chin under the muslin wrappings until the throb turned into a dull ache. Then my chin started to itch, and I wished for the throbbing instead. I also wished the people I loved most in the world didn't have to hate each other so much.

When I could procrastinate no longer, my first chore of the day was to empty the chamber pots. This wretched job was often worsened by belligerent prisoners who deliberately missed. Luckily, if any one of them was too foul, Pa would deliver one of his boot shinings, and then they'd learn to use the pot well enough.

Stepping into the jail, I found Rulloff sitting still as a tree. I would have thought him asleep, hands folded over the book in his lap, except that I caught sight of his startling blue eyes. His cheeks were painted with snail trails of tears.

It was the first time I'd seen a man cry. Or a woman for that matter. I'd never even considered that self-pity could happen to a grown-up. I was still pondering this revelation when Rulloff's eyes met mine. I could see the man was shattered down to his soul.

"Why am I still here?" he asked, voice breaking.

I thought of answering that the trial wasn't until Thursday, but couldn't tell if he was actually talking to me.

"What kind of person—?" His back heaved as he curled in on himself and continued weeping openly. "I never, never intended—" He held up his empty, shaking hand as if holding a priceless object. "Oh, that dreadful hour."

The annex was waiting, warm and safe and uncomplicated. Pa would have told Rulloff to go screw the devil, but I felt too awful to leave him, also too afraid to speak.

He kept staring at his palm as if it was a book with answers, then looked straight at me, almost through me.

"Albert!" he said.

Startled, I drew back. I hadn't expected him to remember my name. To my mind, it felt as respectful as if he had said, Thank you, Mister District Attorney.

"*You* must have access to the woods. Do you know what snakeroot looks like?" He brightened suddenly, as if he'd discovered a double rainbow behind my head. "It's a simple poison to distill. There's a patch that grows just behind the quarry."

I desperately wanted to know the answer and be the intelligent young man he thought I was, but I didn't have it in me to lie. I had to shake my head. It killed me to watch how he deflated.

"People think your neck breaks when they hang you, but it rarely happens that easily. It's one of the worst forms of death imaginable—the excruciating torture of slow suffocation, worse than drowning."

I knew what that felt like.

"Like in a river?"

"Yes, like in a river," he said, then managed a small smile toward me. "And you don't get rescued in the end."

I felt unsettled and vaguely guilty at the same time.

"It's no matter. I suppose it will be over soon enough. Perhaps for the best." The way he forced himself to sit up on the bench reminded me of the way he'd carefully folded his coat inside out the other day, as if he was tucking away the inside bits of himself. "How are your stitches healing?"

I drew back before he could grab at me.

"Don't worry. I don't need to touch the wound. I can tell from here you don't have an infection. That's something good, anyway. All the experiments. I was onto something. I knew I was. Has your jaw begun to itch yet?"

I nodded.

"Good. Then the stitches can come out soon. When you're ready, I want you to get a cloth hot enough to steam. Then wet the muslin through, like this." He placed both hands, one over the other against his jaw. "That will dissolve the dried fluids and keep the sutures from tearing as you unwind the bandage."

I didn't quite know how to thank him, so I repeated what I'd been secretly practicing for days.

"*Errare humanum est.*"

Rulloff gave me a blank look, then threw his head back and laughed.

"Well. You are a persistent one, aren't you?"

"What's Seneca? You said it was Latin, from Seneca."

A genuine smile played across his cheeks.

"Now you remind me of my brother, William. Same endless curiosity. All right then. Seneca was a great man. A Roman statesman from the ancient days of the emperors."

I tried to imagine a great statesman, and suddenly, it was if a door had opened to an entirely different world. The idea that began brewing in the back of my mind was so powerful, I had to whisper it.

"Was he a man worth his salt?"

Rulloff tilted his head, thought for a moment, then tapped his forehead as if he was a salesman demonstrating an elixir.

"Seneca was the greatest kind of man—a hero of the intellect. Some men may change the course of a battle or even a war, but Seneca is still inspiring people to this day, thousands of miles away from Rome, eighteen *centuries* after his death."

I couldn't fight my awed smile. "What else did he say?"

"Ah. Would that I'd met you when I was teaching school, before—" A crease flashed across Rulloff's wide brow. He blinked as if he had a headache, then shook it off. "Seneca was, among other things, a Stoic, a philosopher. Since you memorized the first half of his statement, perhaps you're ready for the full thing. *Errare humanum est, perseverare autem diabolicum.* The meaning will be challenging at your age, but translated literally, he said 'To err is human, to persist is of the devil.'"

I flicked the hair out of my eyes. Pastor Isiah sometimes used the word diabolical the same way he used wicked.

"It's okay to make a mistake, but only if you learn your lesson?"

Rulloff drew back. "There's no need to waste my time if this has already been explained you."

I didn't know how I'd made him angry, but perhaps he read the confusion on my face.

"Who told you what it means? Surely, not your father."

"You did. Just now. I don't know anyone who speaks Latin but you and the rich boys." I felt my chin begin to tremble. "And they don't tell me anything. They throw mud balls."

Rulloff continued to stare. The tilt of his head reminded me of the shoemaker's Labrador. "You are only six?"

I stood as tall as I could, so my chin topped the chair rails.

"Seven next March."

"Well, if you came to the meaning by yourself, my goodness. You are correct—and quite a bit more precocious than I realized."

Since I thought he was telling me something good, I nodded and tried to look like I knew what precocious meant.

"You must come by your intelligence through your mother."

I held my finger to my lips.

"We don't talk about her," I said.

I looked at Rulloff hard, not sure how to explain the rest. Everyone else in Ithaca already knew I was to blame for her death, and never spoke of it, so I'd never had to either. I wanted to leave things be, but Rulloff was patient in my silence, and I reminded myself the man had cried in my presence.

"She died," I whispered, trying to push the words out. They felt like knives in my throat. "Seven years ago next March."

Rulloff nodded soberly. Then he reached his arms through the bars and took my hand in both of his.

"Albert, you must know childbed fever is an extraordinarily difficult condition to treat. The blistering and purging advised in many medical texts leads to pain, exhaustion, and nearly always death. I have theories on better methods, but few opportunities to test them. The important thing is you can't let people blame you. People can be terribly cruel when they're jealous of your intelligence."

That last part made no sense at all. I took my hand back.

"It's true. You're already more clever than most adults in this town, and your father knows it. It can be very difficult to grow up smarter than those around you." He stared off at something I couldn't make out. "It can also be quite lonely."

I felt a pain in my chest as if Rulloff had pressed on it with his thumb.

"I grew up in a town similar to this one," he reflected. "All a man aspired to in New Brunswick was a snort of Old Orchard, a twelve-point buck, and a woman's company."

I leaned in closer to hear, hoping he'd explain what he meant about being lonely.

"Like you, I was a different kind of child," Rulloff said. "Quiet. Curious. Those traits inspire ridicule in such places." He trailed off. "People don't like visionaries, Albert. You must learn this. New ideas make people feel ignorant, and people abhor feeling ignorant. When you're young, they tease mercilessly, but as you age, I'm afraid it gets much worse. They find any reason they can to persecute you."

I felt a deep chill. When it passed, I knew the world was an even more dangerous place than I'd understood.

"Seneca was ultimately forced to slit his wrists. Socrates to drink poison. Galileo, tortured."

"They crucified Jesus."

"Yes." Rulloff drew back in surprise. "See? Didn't I say you were intelligent?"

I felt warm inside, then confused and uneasy, as if I was being dragged on a feather bed to a place I didn't want to go.

"There's only one place on this entire godforsaken continent for men of ambition, Albert. My biggest mistake was leaving it for this backwater. One error, and what's to be the legacy of Edward Rulloff? Not an esteemed lawyer or eminent physician. All they'll remember now is a vile murderer."

He looked stricken again, like a jay with a broken wing. His eyes shone with grief, and the same man who a moment ago seemed to know everything in the world, appeared bereft. I wondered if he might cry again.

I didn't want to bother him in such a state to ask for his chamber pot, so I slunk back to the annex door, figuring I'd return after digging up the onions and potatoes for supper.

I wondered if that's what the governor's men were doing—persecuting. Palm on the doorframe, I pivoted back to the cell and said the one other Latin phrase I'd overheard that morning. *"Corpus delicti,"* I ventured. "Is that Seneca too?"

RULLOFF BLINKED at least a dozen times before he looked at me, then gazed up the staircase. His eyes grew wide enough to look almost natural on his massive head.

"It's a reference to Lord Hale," he said. "From English jurisprudence." He glanced at the thick book in his lap, then back at me. He didn't smile, but he sat up straight as an arrow. "Did you hear it upstairs, Albert? Maybe there's still a way out of this nightmare. *Corpus delicti* says that to prove a murder's been committed, you must first be able to prove that someone has died."

9

IN THE MORNING, I LADLED WATER FROM THE PAIL INTO
the pot over the fire, then grabbed a hand of coffee beans from the sack
and sat down on my chair. I let them tinkle one by one into the mortar
in my lap.

Pa had his straight razor in one hand, the mirror shard in the other,
tilted to catch the glow of the fire. I felt bad for breaking his mirror and
kept waiting for him to holler about it, but he set it down without comment.

A sudden bang startled me and I dropped the pestle, clutched the
chair rail and waited to hear men shouting again.

"Lucky for you that pestle didn't break," Pa said.

He opened the door, face half shaved. On the stoop, Thomas pulled
off his wet hat, flicked it twice to the side of the door and then walked
in, muddy boots leading a trail to the table. Through the open doorway,
an orange glow broke through the clouds, even as the rain continued to
fall on the stoop. The outside air that swept in felt sweet and thick. It
would be a hot day if the rain let up.

"We got a problem," Thomas said.

"D.A. again?"

Thomas nodded.

"Sheriff too. They're angry as hornets up there that the bodies are
still missing."

I already knew this, of course, and tried not to let them see me smile.
While Pa called me a namby-pamby and everyone else called me a
gibfaced ratbag, Rulloff had called me intelligent. And now the other
things he'd said had been proved right.

"We all know the bodies are in the lake. They weren't under the
floorboards and weren't burned up in a fire. If the dogs couldn't find 'em

buried, he threw them in the lake. Simple as that." Pa clutched at his razor but didn't wait for Thomas to answer.

"You know their plan?"

"I was just at Clinton House taking breakfast." He failed to contain a laugh as he sat. "Josiah thinks he's going to get the cook to marry him one day. I'd tell him that day'll come the other side of Judgment, but long as he's buying the bacon, I see no point dashing a man's hopes."

Pa allowed himself a tender smile.

"You always were the generous one."

Thomas looked down at his boots, the levity gone.

"Thing is, Jake, the big bugs are saying if the bodies don't turn up by the trial tomorrow, they can't go in for murder, or he could get off entirely. They want to try him for abducting his wife instead." The chair creaked as Thomas slumped farther into it. "They say it's the only conviction they can be sure of."

My jaw ached, and I pressed against the muslin, wondering if it would hurt less once I removed the bandages.

"What's 'abducting' mean?" I asked.

Pa wiped his sleeve across his neck, closed the front door and sat opposite Thomas, in my chair.

"Eph won't be happy." He thought long and hard. "But long as we can hang him, I suppose it don't matter much what for."

"What's 'abducting'?" I said it louder the second time.

Thomas shook his head.

"I hate to say it, Jake, with what happened—" He kicked at a loose coffee bean on the floor. "They said reformers been after the legislature. Made them cut down the number of hanging crimes."

His eyes hung so low I wondered how many days it had been since he'd slept.

Pa scoffed, lifted his chin.

"'Reformers' my ass. Take away the noose and you get more prisoners, more five-penny men. You know all these mill owners are just itchin' for a way to compete with slave labor."

"Be that as it may, the hard truth is the most that bastard can get now is ten years in prison."

Pa made a sour face and leaned heavy against the chair back till it cracked.

"In Illinois we coulda hung him for looking at us funny, and you're telling me we dragged that evil bastard all the way back to civilization to save him from the noose?" He stared at Thomas for a long minute. "I promised Eph he'd hang."

"Wasn't just you," Thomas said.

"But it ain't your town, is it?" Pa's mouth twisted in anger. He pushed the chair away as he stood, marched back to the mirror and pulled the razor up his neck and over his jaw. The scraping sound echoed from clear across the room.

"Damn it, Thomas." Pa turned back, holding the broken mirror tight, drawing blood from his palm. "You of all people know how it is. Your pa and mine carved this county straight out of the wild. Chased out the Indians, pushed the Redcoats to Canada. They were men, Thomas. And we are *what*?" He flicked the razor around his neck, missing a section of stubble under his ear. "You saying I can't even protect women and children in my own damn town?"

I picked up the spilled coffee beans and finished grinding, head down, waiting out the silence as Thomas paced around the table. I figured out that abducting must be like kidnapping, but I couldn't see why a man would need to kidnap his own wife, or why all the effort looking for bodies if they weren't there to find.

"I got spat on yesterday morning." Pa shook his head.

"Best let it pass."

I dumped the grinds in the water and watched the surface quiver as it got ready to boil. Pa's ragged breathing sent shivers through me.

"It's going to get worse. Oh Lord, Tommy, it's going to get worse."

Thomas stood and palmed the top of Pa's empty chair, pushed it to its place against the table and straightened it—not once but twice. I stirred the pot, as startled by Pa calling him Tommy as I was by Thomas not showing offense.

Thomas pursed his lips, set his palms on the table, and leaned in with a sigh.

"Maybe Sheriff Andrews could speak to the D.A. You know well as I do, a jury here would convict that fraud of killing Father Christmas, you give them a chance—bodies or no bodies. But the D.A.'s from Albany. He doesn't know your people."

The water boiled, and I ladled it into two cups.

"Sheriff never listened to me before. Ain't gonna start now."

"But maybe nobody got killed—" I pushed a cup into Pa's calloused hands. He took the cup but didn't look at me.

"Sheriff Andrews is a muck snipe," Thomas said. "I tell you, Jake, you get yourself some land, qualify to run next term, and I'd help you win Elmira. That might be enough to carry the county."

"Land?" Pa stomped hard with his heel on a nail sticking out of the floorboards. "You seen the prices since the mills came in well as I have. How's a man supposed to buy himself a piece of land?"

I flinched at the whine in Pa's voice. He would have smacked me for that tone.

"What about your sister's farm?"

"Babe's land is Babe's." Pa left it at that, set the cup on the basin. I wished he'd explained more. The past before I was born was a deep, dark hole that blocked understanding but vented wild fury.

Thomas scratched at his beard, set his wet hat on his head, and stepped toward the door. He set a gentle hand on Pa's shoulder.

"You give it some thought," he said.

"What for? I couldn't even win Ithaca anymore." Pa threw the razor in the basin with a clatter. "They spat on me. In front of my own damn house, Thomas—they spat on me."

THAT NIGHT, Pa set the fry pan on the table late, took his seat, and dug in. I spooned a heap of corn mush on my plate, stained pink with chunks of half-cooked beet, disappointed there wasn't any vinegar for the cabbage.

If Pa noticed I'd carefully removed the bandage the way Rulloff taught me, he said nothing. The skin on my jaw was still swollen and puckered with stitches and the whole left side of my face ached, but in the shards of mirror even I could tell the wound was starting to heal.

To say anything of the trial would only make Pa sore, so I cast about for a subject he would have cared about a few weeks ago.

"Traders are come through." I flicked the hair from in front of my eyes and tried to sound casual, the way Thomas would have. "Frenchies."

Pa stared at the rain streaming down the window. It was dark enough that he'd normally have lit the lamp by now. His eyes were saggy, his movements slow. The whiskey jug sat close by his elbow.

I scratched my nose with four fingers.

"How many pelts it take to buy a rifle?"

I pushed my tongue against the backs of my teeth and found a bottom one I could wiggle.

"Pa?"

"'Bout twelve." Pa used his leave-me-alone voice.

"That trader had a boat heaped full. Maybe twenty rifles worth."

Pa hefted the jug with both hands and took a long drink, skipping the glass. He sighed heavily and blinked at the window.

"Sundown what, an hour ago? Whole town's heard by now." His left arm rolled off the table and hung limp at his side. He'd barely touched his supper.

"Whole town heard what?"

Pa stayed quiet. There wasn't any meat. He hadn't even checked his traps. I sat there trying to navigate this new upside-down world where Pa's rigorous standards had disappeared like green wood smoke.

"About abducting, Pa?"

He stood up quickly, and I thought maybe he'd decided to give me a whipping after all, but he took three steps across the room and pitched himself onto his bed.

My attempts to cheer him were failing, so I switched to more dangerous tactics.

"Pa," I said. "Is it fair to say he kidnapped her if it's not true?"

Pa's voice was muffled by the pillow.

"When the world gets fair, Albert, you let me know."

He stayed quiet long enough I thought he'd fallen asleep, but then he spit out one last instruction.

"You gotta feed the bastard tonight. I swear, I don't know what I'd do to him right now."

10

"ANYTHING YOU EVER WANTED TO KNOW ABOUT, ALBERT, you'll find in New York City." Standing in his cell, Rulloff's heavy lips opened into a full smile, teeth straight and white. At least *he* felt cheery.

"Daguerreotype pictures and Chinamen doing dragon dances. You can see butterflies from around the world pinned to cards, some bright blue and larger than a grown man's hand, others red as fire." He put his thumbs together as if hinged and waved his hands as a giant butterfly. "A lecture on zebras in Africa one day, the sound of a symphony the next."

His eyes practically glowed as he created wonder out of thin air, like the traveling magician who'd pulled eggs out of his hat in the middle of State Street.

The fire had burned down to embers and the grease candle's meager flame left the corners eerily dark, but I smiled to myself. Telling him about *corpus delicti* had dramatically improved his mood. Maybe eventually I'd figure out the right words to say to Pa. I held the fry pan in one hand, candleholder in the other, trying not to breathe the stench of tallow.

"Best of all, there are entire streets lined with bookshops, shelves bursting with Homer and Hesiod, Cicero and Ovid, Plato, Aeschylus, Petrarch. More books than you could read in a lifetime."

Raindrops hit the open window ledge and reflected the candlelight like fireworks high above. The whole of New York City became a confused, fairylike jumble in my head, while Ithaca grew fearfully dark in comparison.

"Why did you ever come *here*?"

Rulloff shook his hand by his ear as if swatting a fly.

"I was naive then. A man promised legal training and an assistant-ship, but disappeared with my money and left me destitute. I had to take a job on a canal boat, leading the mule team. It was a hard lesson, but I learned it well: Never trust anyone." He sat down on the bench, elbows on knees, knees pressed together.

"It's funny to look back, I suppose. I wasn't on a career path, but the days on that boat were the only satisfying ones I've known in my life yet. I walked the canals and rivers all over New York, Pennsylvania, and Maryland, and learned every inch of the waterways. Give me a piece of paper and I could still map out each lock, hill, and farmhouse."

I thought about asking if he knew of Aunt Babe's house on the lake, but something stopped me. I held on to Babe as a comfortable secret.

"I saved up for a set of used law books and candles enough to read through the night. If I could have finished my studies, I'd be a promi-nent lawyer in the city now. Instead, my mother passed away. I could scarce leave my brother in the care of our stepfather, so I took a teaching post here in Ithaca, rented a modest room, and wrote for William to join me."

Rulloff sighed, then sat silent while the frogs croaked away in the garden. "By the time my letter reached home, he'd already sailed for Lon-don." His cheeks sagged as his piercing blue eyes explored the cobweb-strewn corners of the cell. "Barely fifteen and he wagered he'd be better off alone than with his older brother. That's my mother's doing."

I was missing something from the world of adults. Had it been any-one else, even Aunt Babe, I would have kept my questions to myself. But Rulloff had been as kind to me about things I didn't understand as about those I did.

"But why did you stay?"

He smiled softly, confirming I was right to trust him with my ques-tion.

"I could have left," he said simply. "Loneliness is a powerful force, Albert. I should have left, instead of marrying a woman as self-seek-ing as my mother. A woman who claimed to support my ambitions but thwarted them at every turn. Wanted a husband like that pompous know-nothing Doc Bull—but after I'd shifted my studies to medicine, refused to believe my methods worked better than his, even when I was accepted into medical college. I thought if I could just show her the good my ideas could do—" He trailed off.

"Anyway, tomorrow I'll be found innocent and this terrible episode will become a mere footnote in my biography, Albert. Seneca said, 'Throw me to the wolves and I will return leading the pack.'"

I felt like I was on a sled that had started to go way too fast, but it was thrilling at the same time.

"Because of *corpus delicti*?"

"That's part of it. A trial is a debate, and I have facts on my side and precedents behind Lord Hale. But for all that men consider themselves rational, they make decisions on emotion, then use facts to rationalize whatever is already in their hearts. So I will play to their emotions. The one thing I did learn from that charlatan in the city is that people will believe anything you say as long as you are confident, articulate, and poised." He stood erect, indicated his regal bearing and fancy clothing. "Appearances are everything. Do I *look* like a murderer?"

I shook my head vigorously. He looked like a gentleman. As fancy as the governor's men.

"What about—" I searched for the word that meant kidnapping. "What does abducting look like?"

"What 'abducting'?"

"Thomas says they're going for abducting 'cause there's no bodies."

Rulloff froze, and I thought I saw a look of panic cross his face before he rearranged his features. "The D.A. is more formidable than I thought." His eyes darted around the cell, distracted. Then he picked up the law book. "Reasonable doubt?" He blinked at the ceiling for several moments, then pressed two fingers against the beard at his chin, before flipping to a list at the front of the book. "Hysteria brought on by childbirth."

"You're not afraid?"

What I really wanted to ask was *How can I be brave too?*

"A setback," he said and half smiled, as if to assure me, or perhaps himself. "I still have presentation on my side. Confident, articulate, and poised—remember that. I have ten hours before the trial to adjust my legal strategy." Rulloff sat quietly for several minutes, staring into the dark. "Albert, I have much reading to do tonight. Would you mind leaving the candle with me?"

I rubbed a ball of half-melted tallow between my fingers, not sure how I'd made things worse. I had a dozen questions but finally whispered the only one I could put words to.

"So everything will be okay?"

"Of course," he said, "we will rise above our circumstances and change the world yet."

I heard the *we* in his statement and held back a thrilled smile.

"And become men worth their salt?"

"Absolutely," he nodded. "The world is full of opportunities for intelligent men, Albert. You remember that. You could be the next Seneca yourself with the right teacher. Now, if I might borrow the candle—"

The annex door slammed against the stone wall.

"The blazes is going on?"

Pa staggered forward with giant, angry steps.

I jumped and dropped the candle. The tin holder clattered to the floor, spilling grease as the flame sputtered out. In the blackness I could just make out the charcoal shadow of Pa pressed against the doorframe, backlit by the lantern in the annex.

"I was doing what you asked, Pa."

I never knew what Pa might do when he was either drunk or angry. Right now he was both.

"I heard talk of Seneca. That ain't what I asked."

"I'm afraid I got a bit carried away," Rulloff stepped in. "There's no need to blame Albert."

"I'm no fucking fool," Pa spat into the corner.

"Certainly not," Rulloff said.

"I could slit you from top to tail. You think I can't? You think anyone around here's gonna care if I beat the living daylights out of you?"

"Albert," Rulloff said calmly. "I shouldn't have kept you. Why don't you go to bed now."

I thought about telling Pa that it wasn't Rulloff's fault. I'd asked about New York City, and he was teaching me about books and charlatans and how to be confident, articulate, and poised. I thought about tugging on Pa's leg, so he'd spend some of his fury on me, or even standing behind him because he might be less vicious to Rulloff. Instead, I raced through the door like I was on fire and ran up the ladder to the sleeping loft.

"You're not to talk to that boy," I heard Pa say.

The key slid in the lock.

"As you wish."

Buried under Aunt Babe's quilts, hands over my ears, spilling tears into my pillow, I couldn't escape the thud of Pa's fists, the sound of him panting from exertion—the crack of a broken nose, crunches of fractured ribs, possibly a jaw. Pa was like a caged beast let loose, and I couldn't count fast enough to keep track of how many punches he threw.

Please don't kill him, Pa!

I'd been the coward that let it all happen. The lesson hit me hard, as I learned it was far harder to hear Rulloff get beat up than to get beat myself.

Eventually, the fry pan thudded into the bars, reverberated like a bell, and then everything went silent. The bench didn't creak, irons didn't clank. I couldn't hear weeping or moaning or even breathing. Even the rats didn't move in my father's jail.

11

A KNOCK AT THE DOOR PULLED ME FROM A GRISLY dream. I opened my eyes to see charcoal-colored sky through the holes in the roof. Pa was already up, downing a steaming cup of black coffee, but he stopped short when he saw who'd come. I barely recognized the man with the shaved face, combed hair, and tucked shirt. He didn't even smell like the tannery.

"Eph," Pa said. He lowered his head, took a step back, pulled out a chair. I crept down the ladder and stood as close as I dared, on the far side of the table.

Eph didn't move from the doorway. He stood stiff in his starched clothes and shook his head when Pa offered coffee, pie, and finally whiskey. He said nothing at all, as if he wasn't sure why he'd come.

"Jarvis," Eph finally said.

I hadn't realized our name could sound like a curse.

Then he turned and walked away, leaving the door open. Outside, dark clouds pressed in on each other with the growing energy of a storm. Lightning cracked in the distance. Pa made a fist again and again with his right hand, while I tried to guess what he was thinking, but failed. Finally, he shoved his hat on his head, turned to me, and said the very last thing I expected.

"You're to go to Mr. Snyder's right now and pick up a hog on credit. Tell him I'm good for it when the grain sales come through."

My jaw dropped, which still hurt like hell. The Snyder farm was miles away. It would take me an hour to get there, and several more to come back with a pig.

"But the trial—"

The words were out of my mouth before I could think, and I ducked instinctively from Pa's fist.

"Don't you dare say no to me," he said, enunciating every word till they felt sharp as knife points. "Not today."

"But—" My mind spun. Pa'd held me back from the manhunt. Now the trial? He hated me even more than I'd ever realized.

People can do terrible things when they're jealous of your intelligence.

"But nothing." His nostrils flared as his eyes pierced deep inside me. "I don't want you involved in this rotten business anymore."

Pa marched through the door and slammed it behind him. The annex reverberated with emptiness.

I sat on the chair, pulled my knees into my chest, and slumped over them, but pulled myself back from tears. I was six, almost seven, and I was smarter than Pa.

An idea crept into my mind—first as tentative as Eph's knock, then as unstoppable as Pa's fists.

CAYUGA STREET was a sea of people—more folks than came to town for the Christmas, Easter, and harvest festival combined. They pressed in from both corners, trampled flower gardens, and irritated the Millers's terrier into a never-ending bark. On the front steps of the courthouse, Thomas held out his palms as if he could push the whole crowd back.

"I can't make space out of thin air," he shouted. "They're already packed in there like Irishmen."

"But we're from just over on Lewis," the mill hand with the black beard said. "Why should he get in first?"

A fat woman I'd never seen before with a marble-sized growth on her forehead shoved her way in front of Thomas, dragging her husband by the arm with a lace-gloved hand. "We traveled more than forty miles to see this."

The crowd pressed forward, swelling like Cayuga Lake when the spring thaw came too close to April rains. Josiah leaned against the post, using his knife to remove grime from his fingernails. He looked bored by a duty that didn't involve a chase or a gunfight.

Rain began to fall, thick and heavy, carried by the wind at a sharp angle. It bounced off the upstairs windows, flattening leaves against the trees. The people near the front door pushed in harder, but those at the edges broke off toward the taverns on State.

I caught sight of Aunt Babe's blue-checked dress behind the hobble-bush and pushed my way toward her through the thinning crowd. She was talking to a black man with fuzzy white hair, but spun around when I tugged on her skirts.

"Pardon me, Minister," she said, "We can discuss this later." When he left, Aunt Babe turned to me, ignoring the rain. "What happened to your face, Albert? The truth now."

"I got twelve stitches," I told her proudly, remembering how I'd been brave. "Rulloff did them and—"

"Rulloff?" Her tone swung from comforting straight to demanding. "Your Pa let that man do *what* to you?"

I was angry enough at Pa, but didn't see any point getting him in more trouble, especially when Aunt Babe was missing the point.

"Pa didn't have a choice. The mob had torches and Doc Bull was one of them, but Rulloff was kind and said I was intelligent."

Like everyone else, she leaned down and sniffed at my chin.

"I don't smell rot," she said. "That's something, but only just. I can't believe even Jake would let a baby killer sew up your face."

"But they're wrong about that," I said. "He's the smartest man in all of Ithaca. And the bravest." I thought of how he took the beating for me last night. I couldn't bear to tell her how much of a namby-pamby I'd been, cowering in the loft, so I told her a story I hoped to make true.

"He's going to be my teacher."

It was an exaggeration that bordered strongly on a lie, but saying it aloud made it feel genuine, and even I began to believe it a little.

"He already taught me *Errare humanum est, perseverare autem diabolicum*. That means it's okay to make a mistake as long as you learn your lesson. And *Accipere quam facere praestat injuriam* means I bear injustice with grace. Albert means noble, bright, and famous in Old German.

Also two and four is six and six and one is seven." I stopped because, though I'd never been able to surprise Aunt Babe with frogs or jumping out of cupboards, she stood with her mouth agape, even as rain streaked down her face, plastering a dark snake of hair to her cheek.

"Well," she finally said. "Isn't that wonderful."

Except her tone didn't sound wonderful, and I thought maybe I'd mixed up the arithmetic.

"Now, listen to me, Albert." She looked back at the courthouse with a frown, then wiped the rain from her eyes. Her manner shifted back to decisive. "Schooling is important, and I'll try to find a way to convince your Pa, but after today, Rulloff will be imprisoned up at Auburn, so you'll have to be patient about getting an education."

"But they're going to let him go 'cause he doesn't look like a murderer and because he's confident, articulate, and poised."

"I see," was all she said, though it seemed like she wanted to say more. The downpour grew heavier until the sound drowned out even the Millers's terrier. "I'll find a way to help you with school somehow. Let me think on it."

She grabbed for Bailey's lead, then disappeared into a rainy blur.

For the first time I could recall, I didn't ache to follow her back to the farm. Instead, my heart felt as light as a dandelion seed. It was time to discover just how smart I really was.

MY BET WAS they had to open a window somewhere so all those people in the courthouse could breathe. With the rain hitting the front, the square window in the back over the annex roof would be a good choice. And if Pa was guarding Rulloff, and Rulloff was in the defendant's chair, Pa wouldn't be able to see me sneak into the back of the room.

I shimmied up the trunk of the pear tree and crawled over the sagging branches, careful to shift my weight as I edged onto the slick shingles. When I let go of the tree branch, it snapped back and shook like an awful wind had hit it, flinging water and half-grown pears to the ground. I scurried across the roof to the tiny window next to the chimney.

Open.

I stuffed myself through the opening, hung from the sill, then dropped to the floor. On my hands and knees, I squeezed like a mole behind hundreds of people packed in so tight the men had no room to remove their hats. The air hung thick with humidity, wet wool, and damp leather. I tried to get a foot on a pew Pa'd borrowed from the Unitarians, but a lady in a blue dress slapped me down with her fan.

I found a small patch of empty floor and squatted low, able to see only a triangle of sky and the black soot on the ceiling above the chandelier, but I could hear well enough. My plan had worked!

A woman behind me sounded aghast.

"No, Jules. There. In the corner. Follow my finger. I told you he was a monster. Dripping with blood as if he killed her this very morning."

I'd planned to stay hidden, but her words stabbed me with a sudden, terrible fear—far worse than Pa finding out I'd disobeyed him. I peeked from behind a man's shoulder, searching for the defendant's chair. When I spotted the man slumped in the seat, I barely recognized him. Rulloff's left eye was swollen shut behind a bright purple bruise, and his delicate nose had grown into a potato overnight. His hair was combed, waistcoat buttoned, and cravat fastidiously tied, but his neck and shirt were stained with rust-colored blood and his wounded nose kept leaking scarlet streaks he had to mop up with his shirt sleeve.

My heart constricted into a tight knot when I saw the result of my cowardice. Rulloff struggled just to breathe. If there was an opposite of confident, articulate, and poised, Pa had brought it down on Rulloff with everything he had, and he'd done it all because of me.

The prosecutor blathered on with complicated legal definitions and praise for the devoted mother, Harriet.

"Among the many facts are three crucial ones: First, Rulloff was known to have a furious temper. Second, he'd frequently displayed jealousy of Harriet's affection for her family friend Doctor Bull. And third, Rulloff ran away after their disappearance and was found hiding all the way in Chicago."

I watched a daddy longlegs inch across a tiny patch of empty floorboard as I waited for Rulloff to explain everything, but when it was his turn, his mouth was so contorted from the beating that I couldn't understand him.

"I can't follow a word the defendant says," the D.A. said to the judge. "Sounds like a lunatic."

I'd thought the trial would be exciting, but people just shouted out about how they'd never liked Rulloff, how he was an outsider, how he always placed himself a cut above everyone else. The whole town had lined up to throw mud balls at him.

People can do terrible things when they're jealous of your intelligence.

Eph, when his turn came, was surprisingly diplomatic and composed, hands folded in his lap.

"Hattie weren't a perfect girl, hadn't learned her place yet, but she was just a schoolgirl. So young to be married—beguiled by a trusted teacher. Spilled stew on his papers, didn't grind his potions fine as he woulda liked. That part was on her maybe, but those two fought like badgers right from the start, and she took a harder knocking for it than need be. But—" He shrunk into the witness chair, his voice dropping to a bare whisper. "But no matter what she done, ain't nothing in this life or the kingdom to come as gives a man the right to destroy my beautiful, defenseless sister. Or his baby. Or my family—"

While Eph collected himself, Rulloff used a pencil to write out his words for the judge to read. "Mr. Schutt," the judge said, "as the defendant is acting as his own attorney and is unable to speak clearly, I'm obliged to read what he's written here. For that, I beg your pardon in advance." He rustled the paper. "The defendant asks if you were aware of Mrs. Rulloff's intentions to abandon her husband."

The crowd burst into angry jeers and the pews scraped against the floor. The judge hammered his gavel against the desk to very little effect. The blue-dress lady did a better job of shushing everyone nearby.

"Hattie would never a done that," Eph said, looking about wildly. "She was stubborn, but she knew her place."

There was a pause as Rulloff carefully scratched out words on the paper with three fingers holding the pencil. Even from the far side of the room I could see the other two were broken.

"The defendant writes that perhaps you didn't know her as you thought. For example, the secret that caused her to flee Ithaca in shame." The judge looked around as if he expected to be pelted with rocks. "That a traveling Indian was the true father of the child?"

Eph jumped from his chair and dove at Rulloff. The crowd surged over me like the river, pressing down as I struggled for air.

"Yes he did," a man shouted to his wife. "Accused her plain of miscegenation."

I tried to protect my chin, rolled under a pew but got a button boot in the ribs anyway. I dragged myself toward the window, crawling past a dark smear that had once been the daddy longlegs.

12

MR. SNYDER'S HOUSE SAT NEAR THE FARTHEST OF THE three creeks that started high on South Hill, transected Ithaca like a cat scratch, and ended in the lake. By the time I arrived, the rain had let up to make space for a fragile rainbow.

Mr. Snyder was using his dray to furrow a cleared section of land as the afternoon shadows cut long across the new rows. Two dozen chickens followed close behind, going after the upturned worms like sewing needles.

I told him what Pa wanted, and he wiped his brow with his sleeve.

"First you get a piece a cornbread from Mrs. Snyder. You look skinny as a rail. Then you can take the spotted hog in the pen. Your Aunt Babe's credit is good with me."

I ate a whole feast at Mrs. Snyder's table. Not just cornbread but sliced ham and apples and two squares of lemon tart, as if I hadn't eaten in days—which I probably hadn't. Mr. Snyder was taking the yoke off his horse by the time I headed to the barn.

The gilt had a white patch on her belly and two tar-like spots that spilled over her right shoulder. The rest of her body was a glorious, fuzzy pink. I slid through the horizontal rails of the pen and crossed to where she rested on a patch of flattened brown straw, teats dimpled, legs sprawled out like sticks.

"Hey Pig Pig," I squatted just inside the sty, butt resting on the backs of my heels. She sniffed at the air with a passing interest, but I saw a hint of playfulness in the way she lay her head down, wiggling to scratch her fat rump. Then she snuffled her nose, caught an intriguing scent, and rolled herself up onto her forelegs with a shudder. When she shook her head, the motion rolled along her belly in waves, but I was surprised how gracefully a two-hundred-pound animal could walk. When she pressed her face into my hip, after the gift Mrs. Snyder gave me to take home, she almost knocked me over.

"Here, girl." I unwrapped the cloth around the lump of cornbread, and she pressed her baby-soft snout into my fist, tickling my knuckles with the stiff hairs on the side of her nose. I opened my fingers one at a time, letting her root deep into my palm and suck up the morsels with her warm, wet tongue. When the bread was gone, I brushed my hands on my trousers, but she still tried to follow the scent to the crumbs in my pocket and shove her mug-sized nose in my teaspoon-sized pocket.

"Hey," I laughed. "You're already too big a Pig Pig."

I tried to pet her, but her hairs were bristly, so I ran an index finger over her much softer ear, and she nuzzled her big face against my waist.

If only people could be more like animals.

Pig Pig barely needed the switch on the way home, which made me happy because I didn't want to hit her. I wanted to teach her to sit and stay and wag her fat behind. Still, nothing could make her walk fast. The sky glowed orange before we'd even passed the mill, and when we turned onto State, the sliver of moon cast gray shadows over the treetops and the lacy, bug-eaten vines growing up their trunks.

Loud singing and fiddle music came from Grant's and the Millers's terrier traded a volley of barks with the bloodhound who lived on the corner, but my street sat deserted.

Pa was gone—the annex, jail, and courthouse empty.

I tied Pig Pig up in the stable, lay down next to her in the straw, and tried to figure out a reason—other than Aunt Babe's prediction—that explained why Pa and Rulloff and the horses were all gone. If she was right, I'd never see Rulloff again. Just like that. I'd have no teacher, no friend, and no prospect of ever becoming worth my salt. I wouldn't even see Pa again until at least tomorrow night. I pressed hard on my stitches, feeling glad at the hurt, the kind of pain I could understand.

———

I SPENT THAT NIGHT and most of the next day in the stable with Pig Pig, crossing the garden to the empty annex just long enough to boil myself a potato for supper and return. I lay beside her, comforted by her body heat, and told her what I'd learned of Seneca and what I still didn't fathom of education and heroism. I confessed my guilt for letting Pa beat Rulloff, and my suspicion that Rulloff was taken away to spite me, and then shared all of the other wrong-headed things that grown-ups did, until the sound of the crickets drowned out my voice.

It must have been hours later that a bridle jangled and the stable door creaked open. Pig Pig moved, but I lay in the dark and let my eyes adjust. I tried to think of what to say to Pa as he unbuckled the carriage yoke and led Thunder and Eli to their paddocks. When he lit the lantern, crooked shadows crawled up the walls. He reached for the brush before he saw me.

"Jesus. You startled me. What in blazes are you doing out here?"

"You didn't have to take him away."

"Easy, Albert."

He brushed the sweat from Thunder first, her black coat almost blue in the lantern light.

"He could have stayed here with us."

"Man was guilty. I took him to the state prison. That's the end of it."

Still holding the brush, Pa leaned his back against the post, pressed his fists against the meat of his behind and cracked his back.

"It's high time you forgot about that devil."

"But he was innocent."

I pressed my arms to my aching chest like broken birds' wings.

Pa grunted, untied the scarf at his neck, and swiped his eyes.

"Jury convicted him."

He twisted his shoulder and his back cracked loud again, three times.

"That means he's guilty. What's got into you, Albert?"

I pushed myself up to a wide-footed stance, sweeping a thin layer of straw from the dirt with my left foot. "Pa, please can we have him back?"

"Albert."

He wrenched his mouth into a knot and looked at me, long and focused. Grabbing the lantern, he walked out of the stable—then spun around and strode back, leaning down into my face.

"I don't want another word about that man, you hear? There was some kind of unholiness between you two. That man's a monster and I never shoulda let you near him."

I wanted to say that it wasn't true, but the words got stuck behind sobs in my throat. Everything seemed heavier with Rulloff gone, as if a furious winter had suddenly roared back after a false spring.

Pa kept talking.

"You gotta forget his nonsense. Fancy words won't keep you alive in this world as well as a good hand with an ax will. If something happens to me, you need to be able to fend for yourself, understand?"

I kicked at the ground.

"You're just jealous I'm smarter than you."

Pa grabbed my shoulders, his mouth twisted in fury. I was sure he was going to hit me, but he turned and smacked the post with his palm instead.

I hung my head, barely able to breathe.

What was I doing? I couldn't lose Pa too. Not now.

"I came straight from Mr. Snyder's. Like you asked, Pa. I kept Pig Pig on the road all by myself and didn't even have to use the switch."

Pa's whole body stiffened. "You brought home *what*?"

I remembered how much he hated to be my pa.

"Pig Pig."

"Pig Pig."

He drew his shaking hands into claws in front of his waist, like he wanted to wring my neck. I swallowed, tried not to look away or breathe too heavy or say anything at all. Finally, he pointed a vibrating finger straight at my chest.

"You named our winter meat like some fancy poodle? Do you know what it feels like to starve? To feel death scraping you away from the inside out? Your aunt and I been there, but you—you think you're the king of Siam. I swear by the fucking—" He bit his lip and went near cross-eyed. "Bring me my knife."

I tripped onto my back. Looking up at the scowl on his face, Pa seemed nine feet tall. I didn't know whether to follow his orders or not. I crawled to his saddlebag. The knife trembled in my hand as I gave it to him.

"You gotta learn what it takes to survive in Ithaca, not some fairy castle where animals drink tea and play hopscotch."

"Pa!"

I didn't want to cry.

"This is my fault and I mean to fix it." He spoke in monotone. "If the Lord takes me young as he took my Pa, you gotta be able to fend for yourself. Get work in a mill. Plow stumps. Argue the price of a barrel with men three times your age."

He grabbed the rope around Pig Pig's hind leg and dragged her backward to the center of the stable. She squealed up a storm and Thunder kicked at the stable wall. I tried to step back but bumped into the rear wall of the barn.

"You," Pa waved the knife at me. "Haven't a blowfly's belly of common sense. Not a single animal in nature is so helpless. Wolves, muskrats, hares, I don't care what, they fend for themselves. You're near seven years old, and I've done you no service by letting you skip the trapping and skinning for so long. It's time you learn what animals is for."

"Don't hurt her, Pa. Please. Don't hurt her."

"I'm not going to touch her," Pa said. He thrust the knife, handle first, toward me. "You are."

I dropped the knife in the dirt.

13

"PICK IT UP. CLEAN IT OFF." THE VEINS IN HIS NECK
bulged. Eli pounded the ground with his hoof. I peered around Pa at
the open stable door, but he took a stride closer, blocking the exits.

"Now," he bellowed.

*What would Rulloff say if he were here? He'd know how to change Pa's
mind. He'd be calm and say just the right thing, but I wasn't that smart yet.*

"You forget that Latin crap and learn this: The world you live in ain't
no fancy London town. This is the edge of the frontier, and here, you
gotta make it yourself. You dig your own ditches and grow your own
food and by God, you kill your own meat. That simple. Ain't no room for
those soft places you got inside you, Albert. You may think I'm the cruelest man alive, but one day you'll understand. Now pick up the knife."

I stooped and picked it up by the handle, wiped the dirt on my trousers and looked at Pig Pig. Her soft brown eyes were wide open and
darting around the stable. If I hadn't been so stupid as to say her name,
she'd be sleeping quietly in the hay.

"Here's how it's gotta go," Pa said. "There's an artery just here, under
the jawbone at the top of the neck. You feel that?"

Pa moved my fingers over Pig Pig's scratchy skin, next to her birth-
mark, and I felt her pulse, each beat trembling in her neck. Pig Pig
shook her head and backed away, but I'd felt her heart's quivering
thump, like a tiny miracle.

"That's where you need to bury the knife," Pa said.

I couldn't breathe. I thought about death and eyes that never close.

"I'll hold her for you but she's heavier than I am. If she wants to
make this hard, it's gonna be hard. But you do this right, and it's nice
and easy for her, just like she's gone to sleep. Put the water bucket down
there, out of the way 'cause she'll stagger. If you can catch any blood,

we get black pudding for breakfast. But you hesitate, it's bad for her and bad for you, understand? You've got one chance. Keep her calm, find your spot, and then bury the knife. Nice and easy."

I held the handle tight in my right fist, shaking. I'd told her I'd feed her carrots and lettuce every day and pears when they ripened.

"Will she go to heaven?"

Pa snorted. "A damned—"

He took a deep breath, looked into my face with saggy eyelids and hung his head.

"That hog will go to a real nice place in heaven, Albert. You don't worry about that. With green fields and plenty a slop to eat."

"And cornbread? She likes cornbread."

A tremor ran along Pa's jaw.

"Lotsa cornbread. God likes to feed cornbread to all the pigs in heaven, for Christ's sake. You just think about being steady and strong with that knife."

I ran the back of my hand over her velvet soft ears.

"You've been a good Pig Pig," I whispered.

"Albert, you take care of business now."

"We had fun, didn't we?" I nuzzled my face into her head. "We played in those puddles, and you let me tell you stories."

"She ain't your damn friend, Albert. She's a goddamned pig!"

Pig Pig twisted under the rope, alarmed again by the shouting.

"You make that slit right now. I ain't gonna wait another minute."

Pig Pig kicked out and knocked me over with her hind trotter.

"Get this over with, Albert, before you get yourself killed with that knife."

I stood up, angry with myself for being afraid, furious at Pa for making me do this and mad at Pig Pig for not trusting me. I raised the knife and struck at her. She pulled away and I missed the artery. The knife jabbed into the bone of her shoulder blade instead, and she squealed in shock, then kept squealing. Blood poured from the wound as she flailed in terror.

"Do it now!"

I made a bloody rip in her cheek, just under the eye, and she screamed. A sickening shriek. The skin peeled away in a big flap and I could see the bone beneath. She was no longer a soft pig, but a violent and terrified animal, jaws open, fighting desperately.

"Help me, Pa!"

"I will not. You are going to learn to butcher a damned hog, or I'm going to butcher you. There!" He pointed. "See that artery? Slice it right there."

I dug in the knife. Her head twisted savagely. Blood sprayed from her throat and showered my face and chest in hot stickiness.

"That's the messiest job I ever saw," Pa said. "Grab the bucket and save the blood," Pa said. Pig Pig kicked and shuddered and stared at me, then collapsed onto her belly. The bucket filled with thick, crimson blood. I watched her legs jerk softly for a full minute as I panted, my eyes full of tears, and then she stopped moving. Her eyes lay open, unblinking.

I staggered back from the dead pig, wiped my face with my sleeve and watched Pa, still squatting, clean the bloody knife on his trousers.

When he leaned over the mess, I sprinted past him, out of the stable and into the night, where no one could see me cry.

I crashed through the black forest, feeling the path by foot, tripping over roots and gopher holes, stubbing my toe and nearly wrenching my ankle. Over the desolate lake came the echo of a lone screech owl. The rusty smell of gore followed me past every clearing, every silent farmhouse cloaked in darkness.

I ran for seven miles straight.

WHEN THE GROUND sloped up beneath me, I knew the terrain on the other side of the hill would finally break into the wide, flat plain that flooded in spring, saturating the ground with silt. The wheat would be high, trees heavy with fruit, the donkey and cow snug in the barn.

Aunt Babe's house would stand in the center, quiet and secure, and she'd hold me and agree that Pa was the cruelest person who ever lived.

She'd clean away all the blood and wrap me in her arms and make the nightmare disappear.

But as I rounded the hill, the moon slid from behind the clouds and washed the valley in ghostly light. Five shadow figures moved in the darkness next to a mule and wagon—three towering men, two women.

Bandits? I sniffed back my tears and searched behind the mossy logs for some kind of weapon—a rock or heavy branch—but only found a uselessly thin stick. I grabbed it anyway.

I crept through the tall summer grass, quiet as a catamount. Despite my terror, I was driven forward by the worst kind of desperation: If I lost Aunt Babe, I'd have no one left in the world.

When I got closer, I saw a blue-checked dress. Babe stood in mud up to her hem, a shawl around her shoulders, hair in a thick braid down her back. She pointed into the house and three of the shadows climbed the steps. The lantern briefly illuminated their faces.

Negroes.

She was directing the other four figures in the night, but if they weren't bandits, who were they? I crept to the edge of the clearing, clutching my stick.

The mule driver handed her a small bundle and I recognized the fuzzy white hair of the Negro minister.

"Bless you, Ma'am."

"Nothing for it. Just pray we can get Wilmott past the Senate and at least put an end to slavery in the territories."

I crouched in the grass, not sure if I should hide. But where else did I have to go? What other friend did I have in the world? The emotions of the day overwhelmed me with desperation that quickly outweighed any fears of whatever was happening around me. When I finally spoke up, I meant for my voice to sound confident, but instead the sounds left my mouth in a wail.

"Aunt Babe!"

She spun around and thrust the lantern toward me.

"Albert!"

The shadow people around her stopped dead. Her lips pursed in the flickering light as she stared hard.

"It's my nephew," she said with the same steely determination as the night the wolf got in the stable. Without turning, she said, "The three of you go inside now. I'll follow shortly. A safe journey to you, Minister."

He looked long and hard at me, then spoke a soft *haw* to the mule and left.

Aunt Babe watched him go, then turned to me.

"What are you doing here?" she hissed.

I didn't answer.

She took three steps in my direction.

"What's happened? Lord, is that blood you're covered in?" She ran to me, set the lantern in the dirt and dropped to her knees, squeezing my arms, lifting my shirt. "Where are you hurt?"

I shook my head, my throat swelling closed. I had no words to explain what had happened.

"What is it?"

I collapsed into her shoulder, choking on sobs.

She put an arm around my back, but her pats felt stiff and wary.

"Who's hurt? Is it your Pa?"

I pressed my head against her chest.

"Pig Pig's dead. Pa made me stab her, and she screamed and bled everywhere. She's dead, Aunt Babe. I *killed* her!"

The scratchy wool of her shawl rubbed against my cheek.

"A pig," she said, and pushed me away until the lantern light was bright in my face. "That's pig's blood on you?"

I couldn't speak for the sobs in my throat. I nodded.

"This is important, Albert. Is your Pa with you? Did anyone else see what just happened here?"

Her brow furrowed, green eyes locked on mine.

Her face looked dark and distorted in the shadows of the lantern. I shook my head again, shattered that she didn't care at all about what had just happened to Pig Pig.

She pulled me back into her chest again.

"Shhh, then," she said, cradling my head. "It's okay. Your Pa will come looking for you, but not till afternoon at least. We'll be ready by then. You and I will be ready. There were no lanterns here and no carts and no people, Albert. Nothing at all happened here tonight."

14

IN THE MORNING, I PUSHED MY FORK IN ANGRY CIRCLES around the plate of griddlecakes. Aunt Babe thrust a paddle in the brick oven and pulled out two steaming loaves of bread. I waited for her to slice off an end piece for me, but she wrapped them in cloth and put them in a hamper with a wheel of cheese. Finally, she sat across from me at the kitchen table, eyes tired, shoulders hunched over her elbows, breaking all her own rules about posture. Her hair, never outside its tight bun, lay carelessly braided across her shoulders. She took my hands between both of hers, but I refused to look up. Her house had been my one sanctuary. Now a rifle leaned against the door jamb.

"You're growing up so fast, Albert," she said. She didn't ask about Pig Pig or Rulloff or any of it.

"They're runaways," I said, testing the theory I'd put together overnight.

"People in need."

I shook my head. I didn't want her to feel bad for them, I wanted her to feel bad for me.

"It's illegal to hide them." My voice came out spiteful, stormy as my heart. Everything I had was ruined. "Pa says only savages don't follow laws."

Instead of slapping me for talking back, she bit at her lip, squeezing my hands so tightly I wanted to pull them away.

"Your Pa's a good man, Albert. A soldier, following orders. But in this case, the laws are wrong, and sometimes people need to be brave enough to stand up for what they believe."

"Laws can't be wrong," I said as if she were the child. "Laws are laws."

She paced the floorboards in bare feet—stark white with long toes and clusters of blue veins.

When was the last time I'd seen her with her boots off?

"Sometimes there's a difference between what's legal and what's moral," she said. "What would God tell us to do for people in need? People desperate enough to risk their very lives to seek freedom. Would you have me send them back to be tortured?"

I heard what she said, but barely. I was too furious about what she didn't say. *You are the most important thing in the world to me, Albert. Your Pa is a tyrant, and you don't ever have to go back to the jail. You can stay with me, and I'll get you a new pig and everything will be alright.*

"I don't care," I said.

Aunt Babe spun toward me suddenly, grabbed my wrist, and yanked me away from the table. I tried to pull away, but she held me firm, dragged me to the pantry. I was afraid she was going to lock me in so I kicked, but instead she lugged a sack of flour away from the wall and felt along the underside of the beadboard molding until I heard a loud click. A panel sprung open two inches.

I stopped fighting, stunned into curiosity, but she was still mad. "You think you know what heroes are, Albert? You and Jake think my pa was a man worth his salt? He may have died in the war, but do you know how he lived before that?"

She didn't continue until I pulled my eyes away from the opening in the wall and looked up at her face.

"He wasn't a hero, that's sure. Until he ran off with the army, Nathaniel Jarvis was a drunken brute and a rum-runner who smuggled British liquor into Ithaca and sold it under the table at Grant's. He was a *criminal*, Albert."

I could tell she didn't want to have to reveal so much, and I wrestled with the idea that a hero could also be a criminal. But mostly I was fascinated by the secret panel.

"He built this room under the house to hide his contraband. I tell you, everyone—including your Pa—knows him as a soldier who died in battle, but I was your age when he marched off to war, old enough to know what kind of man he really was. Jake wasn't even born until our Pa was in his grave, so a fallen soldier is all my mama would tell him. She made me promise it's all he would know. So much as I hate to see old

Nate Jarvis revered, Albert, this room is our secret. You can never tell your Pa."

She stared at me hard, and I realized she was extracting a solemn promise in exchange. I felt dizzy with the realization that I knew something Pa didn't.

I nodded.

In the space between shelves of colorful preserves and squat sacks of beans, she pulled open the hidden door, revealing a ladder. The smell of earth and musty wool was overpowering.

She pushed me forward. "Grab the rail," she said. "Careful on the way down."

I found one rung after another and descended, trying not to be afraid of what was below me. I waited anxiously in the dark until Aunt Babe reached the ground, then clutched the back of her skirt as she crossed the secret cellar, planting my feet carefully in the cold dirt. From somewhere came a putrid stench, like a dead animal. Aunt Babe struck a lucifer match and lit a lantern hanging from a nail.

With the light, faces appeared out of the dark. Two men and a young girl, all of them black, all sitting on a heap of straw covered with a saddle blanket. The girl held the younger man's hand like they were a couple, or maybe sister and brother. The other man, the older one, had white hair, lighter skin, and freckles on his cheeks. The rotting smell was coming from bandages around the girl's feet.

"This is my doing, and I wish you didn't have to be part of it, Albert, but what's done is done, and you're going to have to make an adult decision now."

I looked at the people on the straw, but couldn't meet their eyes, so I focused instead on their knees. The younger man was taller than his trousers and his bare shins displayed several scars.

"These folks have endured terror and hardship you and I cannot imagine, pursued by hounds and men with guns, never knowing if they could trust the next stranger with their lives. The girl's feet are rotting away from a week in the Maryland swamps, and it's a wonder they don't all have cholera. You said I'm no hero, Albert, and you're utterly right on that score. But they *are* heroes. True ones, trusting their lives to strangers every day, to creep away from bondage a few miles here, a few more there. Can you see that, Albert? They've come hundreds of miles, and now they're two days from freedom. From safety. Two days. And *you* are the next stranger. Are you going to send these heroes back into slavery, to be whipped and tortured and worked as if they're beasts?"

I waited for the people to beg me, or to cry, but they sat stock still, questioning me with flat eyes rimmed in red and lips pulled tight.

Aunt Babe chewed on her thumbnail.

"Sometimes *justice* means going against the law. Can you understand that?"

I couldn't forget that Rulloff was gone and Pig Pig was dead and Aunt Babe loved the slaves in her cellar more than me. She handed me the hamper of food. "You give this to them," she said. "Tell them tonight we'll lead them to a boat on the lake. They'll need to row all night, but at the north end they'll see a white house with yellow shutters and two lanterns on the gate post, and then Mr. L. will ferry them across Lake Ontario into Canada. To freedom, Albert. That's how close they are."

I held the wicker hamper. It was heavier than I thought. I bit my lip and tried to think straight, but my head felt like a hive of bees that had been poked with a stick. I could still smell Pig Pig's blood on my clothes and the whole conversation made me dizzy.

"Pa made me kill my pig," I said. I was disappointed by how childish the words sounded.

Aunt Babe winced, and seemed to consider her words carefully. "That must have been very hard."

Water seeped through the earthen walls of the cellar. It was a wretched place to hide. When I looked at the old man, he ducked his head in a small nod that I imagined was intended as sympathy, but was probably terror.

"Rulloff got sent to Auburn." I said. "He said I was smart and that scholars are the best kind of heroes. He was going to teach me, but Pa took him away." I stopped talking because I heard the whine in my voice and knew tears were next. I wasn't a baby anymore, and I wasn't going to cry. Not in front of strangers.

"Albert, you're a smart boy. Whatever else Rulloff may have been, he was right about that." She put her hand on her hip, in her thinking way. "There are all sorts of heroes, you know." She caught my eye then nodded at the basket I held.

"You want me to lie to Pa."

Aunt Babe cleared her throat.

"Were you folks warm enough last night?"

Each nodded, warily.

"Many thanks, Ma'am," the girl said. Her voice was sugary.

"Perhaps you don't need to tell your pa an untruth. You can just keep what happened here between us. Sometimes guarding secrets can just be as courageous as doing great deeds."

I allowed myself to imagine the consequences of telling Pa, but I already knew I wouldn't do it. I didn't want these people to get sent back, certainly not the girl with the sugary voice, and I didn't want Aunt Babe to get in trouble.

"When you're older, you'll understand, but right now I know the principle isn't enough." Her fingers tapped at her waist, fast as a woodpecker. "What if Rulloff could still be your teacher? How would that be?"

"Good," I said.

"He's at Auburn Prison," she sighed. "If he's willing to teach you, I believe I know someone who could arrange letters."

"So I could be a scholar? Like Seneca?"

"If he's willing, mind. I don't have money to pay him."

"He will be. I know he will." He *had* to be.

"Of course," she said as if she'd just thought of it. "That would be another secret you'd have to keep from your pa."

I stepped forward, set the hamper on the straw, and pointed to the girl's bandages.

"A poultice is good for infections," I told her. "I'll fix one for your feet."

ERRARE
HUMANUM EST

1846–1856

15

Dear Mister Rulloff,

Im sory your trial went bad on account a me and Pa. I wish Id been
brave that nite. I got a pig but Pa made me kill it. Aunt Babe had to use
the donkey brush to get all the blood off me. She said the stitches all
heald up good. She says she can get letters to you. Would you rite me?
You know so much and I want to learn more about latin and senaca.
Your friend Albert. Noble, brite & famous

Dear Mister Rulloff,

Aunt Babe says theres no letter from you. Probly yer still mad at me.
It's been real quiet in our jail a long time now. Pa says folks is scared
strait and hes sore cause he dont get paid when the jail is empty. Hes
hunting alot now so we ken eat. Can you tell me more about senaca?
Your friend Albert.

Dear Mister Rulloff,

Its cold here. Is it cold there? People dont talk to me or Pa much
anymore. The baker's wife on Aurora gave me a piece a turkey pie but
said I had to take it home to eat it cause her husband be home soon.
Pa tells me to fite the boys but now they put rocks in the snowballs.
I hope you have a good Crismis. Aunt Babe says I cant write again less
I hear back cause it means you dont want my letters. So I guess Ill stop.
Albert.

Dearest Albert,

Please forgive the tardiness of my reply. Your letters reached me only recently—inmates at Auburn are forbidden the luxury of communication—but your aunt seems to have friends in powerful places.

This has been my first opportunity to respond to your thoughtful dispatches, as I've run somewhat afoul of the warden here, a Mr. Atwater, whose punishment has included forcing me into freezing baths of water for hours. This brought on a grave fever that very nearly killed me over the holidays, but it was in the midst of this dark time, while I shook with tremors and hallucinations, that a guard passed me your letters in secret. Your kind words, Albert, meant more to me than you can know, and I found myself looking back on our conversations in Ithaca quite fondly. You have not only inspired me to recover my health, but have helped steel my resolve to win over Mr. Atwater and use the next nine years, eight months, and three days to my best advantage.

Thus, acting as your teacher would be a very agreeable role for me.

As you know from our study of Seneca, the core of modern education rests on the mastery of languages—the prime separator of the educated classes from the rest. The simplest newspaper article begins with a Latin or Greek quotation, establishing the writer's credentials and testing the worthiness of the reader. To hear a speech, to see a club motto, to argue a case in court, to regale a table full of dinner guests, to gain the trust of the upper echelon—the secret to all is linguistic fluency.

Therefore, we will focus all our efforts at the beginning on languages. Once you master a half-dozen or so, we will extend your education to other areas.

When I taught school in Ithaca, I was forced to follow traditional techniques that required years for a student to achieve even the most woeful Latin. For you, I'm hopeful that more rapid progress can be made by using the method I used to teach myself as a boy. Instead of rote memorization, we'll focus on the root sounds that form the foundations of all languages. Once these are mastered, I believe you'll find you possess the skeleton key that unlocks every language on the globe, both modern and archaic.

The most important root sounds are the vowels—think of the sounds you can hold while singing a church hymn. In English, this includes A, E, I, O, U, and occasionally Y, as well as AE (as in archaeology) and OE (as in amoeba—a fascinating genus of recently discovered microscopic creatures.) There are fourteen unique vowel sounds created by this combination of letters.

For your first lesson, we will focus on the A sounds, of which there are three: /a/ as in art and talk, /æ/ as in bat and apple and /ei/ as in bait and rain. How many words can you think of that contain these sounds?

I'll also indulge you with an excerpt from Seneca that I agree with wholeheartedly:

"Nothing will ever please me, no matter how excellent or beneficial, if I must retain the knowledge of it to myself.... No good thing is pleasant to possess, without friends to share it."

I eagerly await your reply.

Yours,

Edward Rulloff

———————

Dearest Mister Rulloff,

I whooped and hollared when I got your letter until Aunt Babe smacked me on the ear. I'm glad yer not still mad. I promise to study real hard and make you proud to be my teacher.

I practiced all the A sounds like you said and wrote out pages of words. Aunt Babe only had to help me a little. It was realy fun to sing words and now I know what a vowel is.

Aunt Babe told Pa she hurt her back chopping firewood and needed more help with chores on the farm. I think it was hard for her to say that but she did it so I could study. I spilled the ink bottle and got some on the rug. She was real mad but tried not to be.

I'm sorry your warden is so mean. He sounds like the boys in Ithaca. Do you still have a fever? Aunt Babe makes medicine from poppies to give me when I'm sick. Maybe I could send you some.

What's it like at your jail? Is it bigger than our jail?

Your friend,

Albert

———————

Dearest Albert,

Thank you for the kind offer of your aunt's laudanum, but I assure you I am completely recovered. As to your first lesson, you've done admirable work, and it's clear you spent many hours on the task—perhaps while eating a chicken leg, given the lingering smell on the paper that drew a rather large dose of envy from me upon receipt.

To answer your question, Auburn Prison is large, housing over 500 men. Each inmate is held in a solitary cell, similar in size to those in Ithaca. The only light comes from a soot-covered window and heat from a meager fire two stories below. We spend every night and all day Sunday in our cells, but for a brief church service.

From sunup to sundown, six days a week, we labor in a massive complex of factories—crafting cabinets, building clocks, milling lumber, sharpening knives, cutting stone, and weaving textiles—forbidden from speaking with our fellow prisoners. I am assigned to the nail forge, a disagreeable position, but one which has allowed me to access the materials needed to create the device I am sending with this letter. Meanwhile, I am still working to gain the trust of Mr. Atwater, but I've made much progress in the past weeks.

You will find the enclosed cipher wheel allows us to keep our correspondence confidential moving forward. Jefferson invented this system while minister of France. Each of the wooden disks spooled on the central axis has the 26 letters of the alphabet carved around the outside. I have an identical wheel, kept with your letters in my trunk. If you line up the discs per the coded letters below and rotate the wheel, you'll see another line spells out a message in plain English, referring to the day I am finally able to leave this cage and begin a life of purpose and scholarship.

BZIFM RYS UHOP WV QG HK XKXPGNSIAG?

Dearest Mr. Rulloff,

It was such a fun game to work out your coded message: WOULD YOU LIKE TO BE MY APPRENTICE? I can't imagine anything better in the world. What does an apprentice do?

Last week, Mister Cowan's bull got lost in a late season blizzard and died a mile from his barn. Aunt Babe helped him salt the meat in exchange for the fat trimmings and we spent the day boiling tallow to make heaps of candles so I could study your lessons as late as I want.

Pa isn't doing real good. He won't let me say your name out loud. People mostly stopped spitting on him, though. Two people from the tannery tried to steal some money so we got them in our jail now. They're not nice like you, but at least Pa gets paid so he can buy coffee again and doesn't swear so much in the mornings.

I like your lessons a lot. When I'm not at Aunt Babe's, I go to the woods to practice the sounds. I saw the first green shoots through the snow yesterday.

———————

Dearest Albert,

An apprentice reads books, does research, writes papers, and takes notes. If it's a position of interest, you must diligently continue your studies, and, I'd gently suggest, endeavor to improve your handwriting.

I'm pleased to report a more genial understanding with the warden. He's re-assigned me to the carpet factory. Once he realized my designs were a vast improvement over the artist they'd hired from Paris, they sent him away and provided me with a stack of botany books for inspiration.

Unfortunately, I'm not in a position to view if anything green is growing, outside the vines I've designed into carpets, but the icicles have melted from the window ledges and the light is stronger than last month. When the first trillium blooms, please write me every detail you can of the landscape.

———————

Dearest Mr. Rulloff,

We had a bad week here. A woman died in the secret basement.
She was too heavy to pull up the ladder even with the Negro minister's
help, so we had to dig her out from the outside. It took six days to
tunnel in from behind the poplar tree.

At night, the fireflies swarmed like mad and we buried her on the
hill next to my mama's grave. Her name was Larissa. (The runaway,
not my mama.) We didn't know where she came from, but the minister
spoke of her people back home and how she will be reunited with them
in the embrace of heaven.

I thought if that was true, maybe one day I could meet my
mama in heaven too, but I'm not sure I'd know who she is. Maybe
there's a lot of people with brown hair in heaven. Do you think
she'd recognize me?

Dearest Albert,

You ask of heaven, and while I am tempted to offer platitudes, I will tell
you honestly that I've never believed in that particular concept. Instead,
the Stoic philosophers—Zeno, Seneca, Epictetus, and Marcus Aurelius—
have captured my devotion more than any minister or priest. Many
great men have been Stoicism adherents, including your hero, George
Washington.

Stoicism is not centered around God or religious moralizing
but rests on the principle that nature is rational, that the universe is
governed by the law of reason, and men must resist their emotions
and pursue wisdom, which will engender bravery, insight, and
justice.

You have shown far more bravery than you give yourself credit for,
and are well on your way to acquiring the virtue of wisdom. That said,
I can appreciate the emotional desire to reconnect with your mother,
though my own mother would have a lot to answer for.

Dearest Mr. Rulloff,

What was your mama's name? Did she have brown hair? Aunt Babe says
she knows there's a heaven cause God wouldn't be so cruel as to let
Larissa make it a thousand miles to the edge of freedom, and not find
peace at the end of the journey.

Dearest Albert,

My mother is not a person I desire to think about. Yet, I'm heartened to
hear my brother William has returned to Canada this autumn and
opened a daguerreotype saloon. Perhaps one day he'll allow me to visit
and I'll have a chance to explain things.

Now, on to our lessons. To put what you've learned into context,
let us consider the root sounds themselves, especially the vowels,
moveable liquids L, M, N, and R, and the mutable P, hard C/K, and S.
Any scholar can tell you these sounds exist in all languages. However,
what I alone have discovered, is that the root sounds also hold the same
meaning in all languages.

Consider these four words.

> DIMINISH—English, means to become less
> DIMINUO—Latin, means to lessen
> MIN ÚO—Chinese, means minor
> MINUTHO—Zulu, means nothing

Can you see the import, Albert? If one understands that the root
sound MIN always signifies something inconsequential, suddenly they
can comprehend Zulu, Chinese, and Latin without memorizing a single
word. This is the power of the skeleton key I mentioned, and is the
method I used to teach myself more than two dozen languages in two
years' time.

As you seem to be progressing at a similar pace, I am encouraged
that our studies could provide an opportunity to formalize a curriculum
that could—in 8 years and 11 months—be published as a revolutionary
method of language instruction.

Dearest Mr. Rulloff,

Your roots are real smart, and the secret codes are fun. Not even the rich boys know how to speak Zulu. I'm the luckiest boy in all of Ithaca.

The maple trees started sapping, so me and Aunt Babe loaded twelve buckets on Bailey and took them to the Melton brothers' camp to boil. Yesterday, we got back almost two pints of syrup. People are nicer to me when I'm with Aunt Babe. Stoops Melton even let me dip an icicle in the syrup and eat it like sugar candy.

Dearest Albert,

Albert, it's time to cultivate your rational mind and begin to exercise more self-control over your passions.

Ambitious men must understand that the company of women limits their opportunities. It was my own devastating mistake, and I wish I could have saved my brother from the same, but he's now apparently already ruined himself by wedding a local girl who is with child. So let me be crystal clear with you, Albert, before you find yourself falling into the common trap. You must break free from female company early and forever. That includes resisting the sentimental, time-consuming, and profitless influences of your aunt.

Our project is more important than anything else in the world. I am now convinced we will revolutionize the world with my language method, and we will become—as you say—men worth their salt. But this means you must make studying the greatest priority in your life, to the exclusion of all feminine distractions.

16

Dear Edward,

It's getting harder every day to be stuck in Ithaca, knowing the world outside is so much larger and more interesting. The older boys all talk of the day they can set out west—as your brother did—to the goldfields of California. Meanwhile, all I dream of is the day we can head east, to the books of New York City.

For a glimpse at the outside world, I read the discarded fish wrappings from the flatboats. It makes me feel larger with the knowledge that I can comprehend what others cannot. You'll counsel me, I'm certain, to have greater humility, like Marcus Aurelius, and remind myself that life is ephemeral, that kings die as surely as their mule drivers. I can only say Aurelius was an emperor who had to search for ways to humble himself. I am the gangly, 12-year-old son of the most hated man in town. Life offers me many opportunities each day to practice the virtue of humility.

Pa pushes himself out of bed to teach me to shoot and track, as if that will ever matter. I'm tempted to tell him that his lessons are unnecessary, but it's about the only thing that seems to bring him back to himself these days. Otherwise, he lets his precious bowie grow dull and flaked with rust.

Meanwhile, Aunt Babe has been up to her neck organizing alliances between the Vigilance Society, the Unitarians, and the Quakers since the Negro minister was taken by slave catchers last month. I know you frown upon these efforts, but I've not let my studies lapse, and I've been helping her to write letters protesting the Fugitive Slave Act.

The Negro community here has disappeared overnight. You wouldn't recognize the town. The society took up a collection and hired a boat to take any black folks who wished to go to Canada. Most everyone went. It was down to the minister, Old Pete at Clinton House, and the Duncan's field hand—and now the minister is gone too.

Pa's never been one to disobey an order, but even he grumbled when he got the third letter from Albany in so many months reminding him of the penalties for disobeying that law. I would have thought New York would fight the South harder, but it just shows how much I still have to learn. Aunt Babe says all this evil is our payback for stealing half of Mexico. If so, I wish we could just give all those empty territories back and return to how things were.

———————

Dear Albert,

You may wish for an easier time, but if you are determined to involve yourself in these matters, you must do so with rational wisdom, not unregulated passion.

The fool stamps his feet while the wise man labors to understand his enemy. Let us not be fools, then, and instead look deeply and rationally at our enemy.

Given the South's steadfast defense of slavery, perhaps it may surprise you that, in the days of the Constitutional Convention, there was more ambiguity about the future of the institution. Some leading Southerners actually campaigned for a gradual end to the practice. Thomas Jefferson was one such paradox, who openly called for slavery's eradication, yet owned many slaves, including—if rumor is to be believed—his concubine, by whom he had several children.

George Washington went further and freed his slaves in his will. While it was far from a settled matter, the framers were so certain slavery's end would come they never actually mentioned the word in the Constitution. If you ask me, they kept silent because they didn't want the stain of the practice to be enshrined in such a sacred document, to mention it even in calling for its end.

Soon after the Constitution, many of the same men—leaders from both Northern and Southern states who held slavery to be in conflict with our fledgling country's values—banned the slave trade with Africa and the taking of slaves into the Missouri territories. Had they taken one more crucial step at the federal level to legislate gradual emancipation, as did many individual states, slavery would be gone by now, and our nation would be focused on more productive discussions.

So, what changed between their time and ours to make Southerners so much more entrenched on this issue? Your Aunt may point to the invention of the cotton gin, four million enslaved lives, four billion dollars of economic value, or plantation culture itself, but I submit to you those are merely surface answers.

The most important difference between George Washington's day and ours is that slaveholders can no longer blame the British for "forcing" slavery on the colonies—they can only blame themselves.

Take a moment to imagine the emotional import of this shift.

Tell a man he's done a wrongful act, and he is likely to feel guilty. But tell a man he's a wrongful person, that he's immoral and should be *ashamed*—and you will find he pushes back with an explosive force you could have scarce imagined.

"Ignominy is universally acknowledged to be a worse punishment than death," declared Founding Father Benjamin Rush. Shame causes the most abject suffering a man can experience—greater than grief, anger, despair, and pain put together. If a Southerner can no longer blame an outside enemy for his abhorrent practices, then what choice is available to his psyche—to war with itself? That is suicidal. What then, but to decide those practices are perfectly acceptable, that anyone who says otherwise is his mortal enemy.

Shame a man down to his very soul and beware the consequences.

Do you now understand the futility of moralizing, Albert? It accomplishes the opposite of your intention. Eventually, you must face the fact that there are only two choices left in this tragically procrastinated battle: Compromise your morals or go to war for them, for your enemy will by necessity always choose death to dishonor.

———————

Dear Edward,

I take your point on the senselessness of letter writing, but first, I must focus on achieving peace closer to home. Aunt Babe has declared there will be no more study of "The Latin," as she calls your letters, until I finish reading *Uncle Tom's Cabin* and a stack of pamphlets from her society the size of a hay bale. I will endeavor to get through all of this material in the next two weeks without impacting our studies.

———————

Dear Albert,

Damn it all. Do you fail to fathom what is at stake here? We have only 3 years, 7 months, and 14 days left to prepare for your apprenticeship and our great purpose.

A hundred and fifty years ago, Napoleon's soldiers discovered a fragment of stele—an ancient and mysterious three-sided rock, that came to be known as the Rosetta Stone—carved with hieroglyphics on one side, demotic script on another, and Ancient Greek on the third. Eventually, Jean François Champollion noticed the word *kleopatra* on all three sides. This simple key led not only to the translation of the stone itself, but it allowed linguists to finally decipher Egyptian hieroglyphics that had remained a mystery to scholars since the fall of Alexandria.

Our system of root sounds provides a similar key, except it not only unlocks three languages, but *all* of them. Once written, our *Method for Linguistic Mastery* will soon become far more consequential than *Uncle Tom's Cabin*. Perhaps more than Seneca himself.

To achieve this ambition, however, I require an apprentice with complete dedication. Of course, if your aims go no higher than leather tanner or cabinetmaker, feel free to discontinue our correspondence and make your own path in life.

———————

Dear Edward,

Please don't think I aim so low. I want more than anything to be your apprentice. I'm trying desperately to keep Aunt Babe satisfied, but every few months she wrings her hands and says this whole idea was a mistake from the beginning.

Maybe her feminine passions have led her to disbelieve in your innocence no matter how hard I try to convince her. What would you suggest I say?

Dear Albert,

Do not trouble yourself to vindicate my reputation. As you well know, a core Stoic principle is to ask yourself of each problem: Is this within my control? Your aunt is a very opinionated woman—likely the reason she remains unmarried. I would suggest that her opinion of my character is not within your control. It is our future acts we must focus on.

I sense that aside from her causes, what your aunt cares most about is your future. The more she witnesses you becoming the intelligent scholar that you are, the more she'll see that our letters are the only way to achieve the outcome she desires. You need only demonstrate that to motivate her to continue our lessons.

If her hope is not enough, use the more powerful weapon of fear against her. You're nearly fourteen now—old enough to plan your own future. Remind her of the alternatives by telling her that your father insists you take his place as jailkeeper one day, or that you've seen a mill hand can make good money as long as he doesn't get his arm sawed off.

Dear Edward,

You are as much a genius with people as you are with languages. Your idea worked as well as a snake charmer's flute. I took care not to make any idle-sounding threats, but when I feigned boredom with your latest lesson and mentioned Pa's plan to have me recognized by Tompkins County as his assistant, she said the world had better things in store for her nephew. She sent me right off to work on my studies or there would be no pie.

Dear Albert,

I have had a breakthrough so profound it's left me stunned. The concept is so vital and also so incendiary that I'm not certain it should be shared even via our coded letters. Yet if there is one person on this earth I trust with my ideas, future, and life, it is you. So, I must ask for a solemn promise that these ideas will remain in the strictest confidence between us and not be shared with another soul until we are ready to publish our work.

We know, of course, the root sounds provide a key to comprehending languages. You studied these patterns and easily became fluent in at least two dozen languages. Clearly, this method in itself is revolutionary.

More recently, I've discovered that the subtle differences between the word and the root can hint at the relationships *between languages themselves*.

Do you follow? Just as Linnaeus's Systema Naturae built a taxonomy of all living things based on physical characteristics, roots would allow us the same opportunity with languages. You and I will build a Philology Family Tree—a linguistic version of Kingdom, Class, Order, Genus!

Yet we've still not reached the pinnacle of this discovery. Think of how Georges Cuvier extended the Linnaean system through time by using the fossils of extinct creatures. Could we not do the same with archaic languages? Discover how they spread and cross-pollinated— beyond the limited evidence of a few crumbling documents and tomb artifacts—using the roots within the words themselves? Think of the impact to history, Albert!

Might we even be able to trace these roots back to a single parent language that proves all the accepted racial hierarchies wrong? A shared origin that shows that white, red, yellow, brown, and black are all descended from the same tribe?

The world has not been more shaken since Copernicus. I've barely slept in three days.

To help me accomplish such an ambition, it's critical you understand how one becomes successful in the world of reality, not idealism. To that end, I'm enclosing a copy of Machiavelli's *Il Principe*

that I obtained in exchange for writing sermons for a minister at the
Theological Seminary.

Dear Albert,

Did you receive my last letter? There's been an unusually long gap since
I've heard from you. Are you having trouble with the Italian? If your
studies are delayed, please at least let me know your thoughts on the
phenomenal breakthrough I shared with you. I would have expected it
to drive greater dedication from you, not less.

Albert,

Please let me know whatever impediment has kept you from writing for
so many weeks and I will endeavor to help remove the obstacle. We have
so many vitally important things to accomplish in the next year and
8 months to prepare for writing our manuscript.

Albert, are you there? Are you hurt? As the months drag on with
no letter I'm becoming increasingly concerned.

17

"IT'S ABOUT BEING REALISTIC," I SAID, TRYING TO THINK of a way to simplify the concepts so that Aunt Babe could understand. "Immanuel Kant said morality is rational; thus lying is always immoral. But Machiavelli said people sometimes need to do immoral things for the greater good—that an honest prince is a failed prince."

Babe straightened her apron and sat across from me, turning her soup bowl clockwise as she blew on it. "And what is Albert Jarvis's opinion on morality?"

It struck me as an odd question. "I haven't finished the book yet, Aunt Babe."

I could only imagine what her response might have been if I'd told her of Rulloff's staggering theory.

From the moment I'd decoded his letter, I'd felt a hive of riled up bees in my chest. I couldn't tell anyone his news, so they just kept buzzing around in circles. We'd be famous. Not just men worth their salt but heroes as big as General Washington. We'd give lectures, and Pa would come, and after, he'd say that he should have listened to me. And Charles Curtis would say he was sorry for pelting me with mud balls. And people would be repeating our words for eighteen centuries. Sitting still took all my effort, especially because Aunt Babe's barley bean soup had never been my favorite.

She pursed her lips and nodded, still blowing.

"I see. Well, I'd be very interested to know your thoughts when you finish." She sunk her bread into the soup with her spoon, then sat up suddenly with a finger across her lips. In the silence, I heard baying in the distance.

"Bloodhounds," she said.

She stood up quickly, and I did the same, although I had no idea what to do. There was nobody hiding in the cellar at the moment, but if they found the hidden room, we'd both be sent to prison. Aunt Babe took her rifle out of the pantry and I watched her load it, faster even than Pa.

The dogs got closer, and soon I could see them coming over the hill on the mail road—a half dozen hounds and two men on a wagon bearing a giant empty cage.

"What should I do?"

"Sit down and eat your soup," she said, setting the rifle on the bench, under the skirt of the tablecloth, the barrel pointed toward the door. "Tell me more about Kant."

I couldn't think of anything but the tunnel and the cage and the bloodhounds. I stared at the door to the pantry as if some giant dragon were about to come bursting out of it.

"Albert," Aunt Babe said. "Focus now. We're having our afternoon dinner, talking about your studies. That's all that's happening."

All I could think about was how many times Rulloff had warned me not to get caught by distractions, yet here I was, facing prison, just as he was about to become the next Copernicus.

"Albert. Kant. Now."

I tried to shake away the fear.

"Kant wrote *Critique of Pure Reason*," I said, staring out the window. The wagon drew closer to the house. I could see the two men well now, one was tall with dark hair and the other was a short, heavy man with a thick gray beard. Both sat with their boots on the edge of the wagon box instead of resting on the toe board, leaning back as if the seat were a chaise lounge.

"He was an idealist. Coleridge read him a lot. All the ideas in Emerson's pamphlets started with Kant."

"Good," she said, though instead of listening she opened the kitchen door and peered out at the road.

"Remember how you used to count things when you were afraid? I want you to find something to count while I go see what they want."

Was I supposed to be brave and take her place? To be the man of the house?

I didn't move. I tried desperately to find a place inside me that felt unafraid.

"Count!" Aunt Babe called back as she walked down the steps. She closed the door behind her, but I could still hear everything through the window.

"Hello," she called out, friendlier than I'd expected, but not quite welcoming.

Two bowls of soup. Fourteen jars of tomatoes on the shelf.

"Perhaps you gentlemen are lost," she said.

"Not a bit of it," the shorter man called out in a slow drawl as the swaying wagon took a shortcut toward the door, wheels flattening the new spring grass. The hounds set off, noses to the ground, tracking scents in every direction at once. "Thirsty, though."

Four strings of garlic on the peg. Two mouse turds in the corner.

Aunt Babe walked down the drive and stopped at the edge of the grass, blocking the last ten feet of their intended path. I set one hand on the stock of the gun under the table and tried to practice not looking at the pantry door.

"If you'll keep those hounds away from my chickens, you can help yourself to the water pump," she said, not moving from their path. "Then you can be on your way."

Nine bullets remaining in the box.

The men led their team around Aunt Babe, straight through the crocus buds to the hitching post.

"Mighty kind of you, Ma'am." The taller man seemed to be the one in charge, but both had pistols on their belts that swayed as they sauntered to the pump.

I tried to count the hounds, but they kept running their patterns, sniffing every inch of ground.

After the men had washed their faces and drunk their fill, the taller one leaned back on the heels of his boots.

"There's four fugitives came through these parts," he said, unfolding a paper from his breast pocket. "Have a warrant here to look for 'em. All done and legal. Your husband home?"

"He'll be home soon enough," Aunt Babe lied.

I was surprised enough at her fib that I lost count of the dogs.

"You'd best do whatever it is you're going to do quickly, before he returns. My husband's not a friendly sort."

Whether she realized it or not, she'd just chosen Machiavelli over Kant.

"Oh, it won't take long," the taller one said, and this time the short man laughed.

From the barn, I heard the donkey bray. Probably the dogs had made him nervous.

"You see to the outbuildings," the taller man instructed, taking his hat off to wipe sweat from his brow. "I'll search the house."

I clutched the trigger with my right hand, still hidden under the table.

Would I have reason to use the gun?

The man pushed open the door and walked straight into the kitchen, muddy boots and all.

"Oh," he said when he saw me. "Don't mind me. Interrupted dinner, did I? Eating without your pa, is it?" He had blond hair and a shining green eye. He would have been handsome were it not for a burn scar that covered half his face and a stitched up left eye.

"He's coming back soon."

My lie sounded hollow next to Aunt Babe's. I fingered the scar on my chin.

The man's face didn't register whether he'd noticed.

"We mean no harm to you and your ma. We're just men with a job to do."

Don't look in the pantry. Don't look in the pantry.

The trigger felt cool against my finger. I felt tiny ridges along the mechanism, minute imperfections in the steel. The man's pistol shone from its holster.

"I've a question for you, boy. You know these parts, don't you?"

I nodded. I wasn't certain if I should, but I did.

"Say someone run away and made all the way to Ithaca. Where might they be hidin' out? Still too cold to sleep out a doors, I'da think, ain't it?"

Again I nodded, unsure if I was giving something away.

"Right. Too cold without getting froze. There any folk friendly to Neeegroes round here?" He stretched the word out as if to make a point of saying the less offensive version of the word. "If it was you out there on the run, where'd you go for shelter?"

It was a question I'd never considered.

"I guess I'd make a snow cave," I said, hoping I was being helpful like Aunt Babe, but not too friendly.

He looked at me crossly.

"The hell's a snow cave?"

"Like the trappers and the Indians. If you can't find shelter, you dig into a snow bank and hollow out a space, and it stays warm enough, so you don't freeze as you sleep."

I couldn't understand the look on his face, the way he moved his jaws about until he finally produced a toothpick from his mouth and took it in his fingers. I marveled that the toothpick had been hidden in there the whole time he was talking to me, and I'd never known it.

"Lee side of a hill's the best snow," I said, finally making use of one of Pa's lessons. "In shady spots and behind rocks I bet you could still find enough snow piled up to make a cave."

"You think I'm ignorant, that it, you smug little shit? You think on this, boy. There's a widow in Greenville who'll be turned out of her home if she can't sell the one bit of property her dead husband left her. Then you tell me again about how you don't get froze in the snow."

I wasn't sure what to answer, but the man replaced his toothpick and moved on into the parlor. I could hear him stomping on portions of the carpet, maybe to find a hollow spot, then the hammering of his boots up the stairs. He walked through Aunt Babe's bedroom, then back to the kitchen.

When he opened the door to the pantry, I stopped breathing. It would surely sound hollow if he stomped on the floorboards in there. I couldn't see him behind the door, but he took a long time, way more than he had upstairs.

If he found the tunnel, would I have to shoot him? Was I supposed to wait for him to draw his pistol?

Through the other door I could see Aunt Babe outside by the chicken hutch, shooing the dogs away.

What would Rulloff do?

Finally, he walked out of the pantry with two jars of pickled cucumbers.

"Obliged for the hospitality. Been a day since we et."

He laughed, and gave a shrill whistle as he marched down the stairs with the food I'd helped Aunt Babe brine and can in the heat of last summer. I couldn't tell if the whistle was his way of calling the dogs or his partner. Both returned to the wagon at the same time.

I took my hand off the rifle and held it shaking against my chest, glad that Aunt Babe stayed outside a long time watching them go. When she finally came back in, I waited for her to say everything was okay, that they'd never find the tunnel or the runaways that had left two days ago. I waited for her to ask about Machiavelli.

Instead, she let the door slam against the wall, rattling the pots over the hearth.

"That's it. We've taken too many unnecessary chances. No more smuggling letters to Auburn," she said firmly.

18

SNOWFLAKES FELL HEAVY AS BISCUITS AS WE RODE, clinging to the skeleton branches of poplars, getting trapped in the scarf folds against my neck. Thunder and Eli struggled up the embankment, grunting misty clouds. The rear wheel of the coach slipped on a rock, and for a moment I thought the whole thing might fall backward on top of me in the driver's box.

"Use the whip!" Pa shouted from his horse.

I cracked the whip off to the side and yelled *haw*, but it wasn't the horses' fault we brought a wagon, not a sled. The jailor's coach was sturdy—made from a converted stage—but for the same reason it was also heavy. Four horses would have been better. A summer's day better still. The coach lurched suddenly to the left and stopped, the wheel stuck in a ditch.

"Screw the devil," Pa said. "Fix it, Albert."

I jumped into knee-high snow and trudged around to the side, hoping by some miracle to be able to do as he commanded. I dug in my heels, put my right arm through the bars in the window and heaved my shoulder against the frame, pushing uphill until my bones felt ready to collapse on each other. The coach slipped two feet backward. I had to leap out of the way of the wheels.

"Put all ten pounds behind it, eh?" Thomas set his reins down on the second incarnation of Horse and hopped off. He yanked out a nearby fence post, set it under the back wheel, and pushed the coach out of the ditch as if it were a child's sled. Once clear, the horses strained and the coach lurched forward to the top of the hill. I had to run to catch up.

I got a foot on the step and swung up to the bench. Pa laughed. Not for the first time I wished for more strength—or at least Josiah's wit to joke it off. I angrily swiped the fresh coating of snow from the seat with my glove and swore at myself. I was used to failing Pa's tests, but this time was different. This time, Rulloff's life was in danger.

PA HAD FOUND ME shoveling a path in the snow between the annex and stable and shoved a crumpled piece of paper into my palm.

"Handbills going around," he'd said, his voice oddly light. He'd finally been accepted back into the group at Grant's, and I'd seen him rising early, polishing his bowie. I'd wedged the shovel in the snow so I could take the notice with both hands.

SHALL THE MURDERER GO UNPUNISHED?
KILLER TO BE RELEASED IN A FORTNIGHT!

My stomach dropped to my boots. The notice spoke of Rulloff's release date as the end of the world, not the beginning of a new future.

WILL WE ALLOW OUR WOMEN
AND CHILDREN TO LIVE IN FEAR?
OR SHOW THAT MURDERERS
GET WHAT'S COMING TO THEM?

I shivered, hearing the pounding pitchforks and roaring voices, smelling torch smoke as if surrounded again. They were ready to lynch him for the second time. An innocent man who'd nonetheless served his full sentence in prison. My brilliant teacher and generous friend.

I hadn't been able to write to Rulloff for over twenty-two months, but had counted down the remainder of his sentence every single day with a notch on the beam over the sleeping loft. Selfish friend I was, I'd only wrestled with how I might reconnect with him after his release, trying over and over to craft a plan that let me still participate in his important discovery.

How would I get to New York City alone? If I made it, how could I find him among a half a million people? If I could find him, would he even want to talk to me?

I'd failed to keep Aunt Babe from ruining our project. He probably already had a new apprentice lined up—a smarter one with better handwriting.

Foolish boy. I'd never considered anything could be worse than missing my chance to help prove his theory. But if the mob succeeded, Rulloff would be killed. My chest ached as if I'd breathed ice crystals into my lungs. I was educated in mathematics, philosophy, literature, history, medicine, and linguistic philology, but none of it prepared me one iota for such a situation.

"What do we do, Pa?"

"Governor sent through orders to head to Auburn on the quiet and release the bastard two weeks early. Says he can't let this become a vigilante state. Get your coat. I need a fourth man I can trust to ride up there with me and Thomas and Josiah."

For a moment, I'd swelled with pride, noticing he'd used two magical words: Man and Trust. Then I realized the vigilantes could be listening to our plans even at that moment, putting everyone—especially Rulloff—in grave danger. I ran into the annex and grabbed the musket off the mantle.

The flakes collected on the yoke and melted away. The gathering snow lent a hush to the hurry, leaving a nauseating space for regret. I'd wasted all that time studying, all that energy hoping I could become something better. I'd always be just a Jarvis. A jail-keep's son. My dreams had always been absurd.

You gotta learn what it takes to survive in Ithaca, not some fairy castle where animals drink tea and play hopscotch.

I would grow up and keep the jail, and people would continue to throw mud balls of some form or another all my life—but Rulloff had to get free. If I could help save him from the lynch mob, at least he could do something important with his life. I imagined the luxury of taking a whole new identity, of studying and writing papers in a city overflowing with knowledge—like Astor's new public library where any man, rich or poor, could read one of the eighty thousand books. Maybe once Rulloff published his linguistic masterpiece, every time I emptied a chamber pot, I could know I played a tiny, secret part in something meaningful.

Or could I do more? What if he was still willing to take me on as his apprentice?

"OVER THAT PASS," Pa said, voice raspy, choked by the falling temperature.

"You must think I'm blind as well as dumb." Josiah, wrapped in a blanket in his saddle, was fighting a cold that made his nose red and temper intolerable.

I slapped my hand against my thigh and dug my boots into the toe box to remind myself where dreaming had got me before. I was Albert Jarvis. Nothing more. *Hadn't Seneca's ambition enabled the rise of Nero, and thus the fall of Rome?* All I knew for sure was a mob could be just over the next hill.

On the breeze came the first tang of coal smoke. The steely haze of Auburn grew visible before the city itself—light-gray wood smoke from the houses mixed with black coal soot from the factories and settled in a dense fog over the city.

As we got closer, five tall smokestacks emerged from the roof of a massive stone-and-brick building that looked like a medieval fortress. Around it, wide snowy streets crawled with wagons, carriages, and bundled people.

"Where's the prison?" I asked Thomas.

"Which building you think holds six hundred men?"

"The castle?"

Thomas laughed, then caught himself.

"Bastards inside might be more inclined to call it a dungeon."

Somewhere inside the gargantuan structure was Rulloff.

What would he think of me after all this time?

The horses picked their way carefully down the hillside, each step creaking in the snow. A dozen late-season geese crossed the sky in an undulating V, and Josiah reached for his rifle.

"Don't even think about it," Thomas said. "You draw attention to what we're doing, and I swear I'll point right at you and say you're the baby killer."

19

AFTER A NEARLY SLEEPLESS NIGHT IN A SMALL INN, WE set out for the prison early the next morning. It would be a long trip back to Ithaca, and the weather had closed in overnight.

Pa and Josiah led the way, and had already dismounted as I steered the coach through the gate between the high walls of the fortress. Four guards held their rifles as tight as the scowls on their faces and leaned against a wall that seemed held fast with twisted skeletons of leafless ivy. Ropelike roots climbed the sides with a thousand fingers, toward a statue of a Revolutionary War soldier complete with hat and musket. The flag above whipped around its pole as a loose brass fitting thudded against the wood. It still had only twenty-eight stars.

High windows reflected the watery orange sunrise with a hundred panes of glass. I rubbed my gloved fingers together, trying to get feeling back.

Was Rulloff up there, watching?

Thomas stepped off Horse, then leaned toward Pa with a sour face.

"More snow coming. Best make tracks."

I jumped off the coach seat and slid on the icy cobbles hidden under the blanket of snow.

"Bring your musket," Pa demanded.

I handed the reins to a guardsman and tried to carry the gun like a soldier would have, but it was nearly as tall as me and awkward to hold. I trudged up the stone stair to a heavy iron door flanked by Doric columns, where a hare-lipped guard inspected Pa's papers.

We entered a portico with a massive fireplace and brownstone floor, covered with an intricate plush rug, woven with intersecting flowers.

Rulloff's design?

On the stone mantle sat a curious set of objects—a clock, a small barrel of nails, a polished set of silverware and platters, a doll house complete with furniture, leg irons, a small steam engine, and a painted sign that read, "PRISON WORKSHOP LABOR. INQUIRE HERE."

A man with a neatly trimmed white beard wearing pince-nez sat behind a small desk stacked with pamphlets, looking over an account book. Flaps of skin dangled from his neck like turkey jowls, as if he'd once been fat but had lost weight. He spoke without looking up.

"Are you here for the tour? I'm afraid you're rather early. The first one begins at half past eight, but you're welcome to wait." He glanced at us and took a surprised step back. "Now look here. You can't bring guns into my office."

"I have release papers for Edward Rulloff," Pa said, and produced a letter stamped with the governor's seal.

"Rulloff?" His eyes creased as he blinked, like a man staring at the sun. "That's two weeks early."

"Read the letter," Pa said. "Man murdered women and babies. Everyone with a pepperbox wants him dead. Governor says there's to be no turkey shoot on his watch."

The man hesitated before offering his hand.

"I'm Leonard Atwater, chief of Auburn Prison. May I ask why I didn't receive a telegraph about this?"

Atwater. I recognized the name of the man who'd once tortured Rulloff near to death, before becoming his advocate.

Pa spit on the rug, ignoring the hand.

"I got orders from the governor's what you need to know. You get a wire, maybe I get an ambush."

Atwater sneered and studied the seal, holding his pince-nez steady with his left hand.

"Before I can perform so unprecedented an act, I'm afraid I'm bound to authenticate your letter. I'll send a messenger to Albany. If you can return in two weeks, I'm sure I'll be able to oblige you by then."

I felt like someone had just thrown a rock through a window. Atwater meant to spite Pa, but if we didn't get Rulloff out early, he'd be murdered.

I looked at Pa, Thomas, and Josiah. No one spoke. Pa had made us sound like ruffians.

I cleared my throat, hoping to sound confident, articulate, and poised.

"Sir," I said. "Perhaps we've unintentionally given offense." I glanced at Pa, who'd jerked his head up at the sound of my voice. Even Thomas would never have disrespected Pa by presuming to speak for him in public like that.

To get Atwater to trust me I needed fancy words—exactly the kind of words that would make Pa trust me less. I'd be risking the whole secret I'd kept carefully hidden for more than half my life. Thomas was already looking at me like I had bird shit on my hat. Then I thought of the night before the trial.

I'm afraid I got a bit carried away. There's no need to blame Albert.

Rulloff had not only taken Pa's beating for me, he'd lost his ability to be confident, articulate, and poised—and it had cost him ten years of his life in prison. If I didn't try to help him now, I'd be worse than a namby-pamby. I'd be a traitor.

I fingered the scar on my chin.

"My father didn't mean to imply any improper activity on your part, Sir. It's only that the governor felt secrecy was an absolute imperative. None of us wants to see a man who has diligently served his time be murdered in cold blood. I'm sure you would agree, Mr. Atwater, that this outcome would hardly show the principles of justice at work, much less reflect well on Auburn Prison's innovative system of criminal reformation."

Pa glared at me, head cocked as if I'd started speaking Mandarin.

Atwater repositioned his eyeglasses and looked at me hard.

"I see," he said. "I'm glad to see at least one of you has respect for the importance of this office." He hooked his thumb in the pocket of his vest and broke the seal on the letter. He read it once and then again. Finally, I saw his shoulders fall, and knew I'd been successful.

"You will excuse, I hope, the lack of preparation on our part." Atwater enunciated each syllable, speaking to me, not Pa. He pulled a fancy but fobless gold watch out of his pocket to check the time. "We will find him at work in the rug weavers' building, just the other side of the nail factory."

"Get him and let's go," Pa said to Thomas.

"You'll be wanting his possessions, of course," Atwater said. "He has a trunk, I believe. Spends all of his leisure time writing letters."

Letters.

I was a damn fool for not thinking of that before. Almost nine years of secret correspondence likely sat in that trunk. The contents were coded, but I'd signed my name on each letter, plain as day: "Your loyal friend, Albert Jarvis."

"I'll get his stuff, Pa," I said.

Pa looked as if he was trying to bite through an iron nail. I was in for the worst walloping of my life as soon as he and I were alone. I could only hope by then that I could come up with an explanation that didn't implicate Aunt Babe.

"Come on, you big bug," Thomas said to me. "I've seen what you can lift by yourself."

Atwater led us down a dark corridor flanked with lanterns. When he turned to speak over his shoulder, the light cast ghostly shadows around his head.

"I must ask for complete silence as we cross into the prisoners' barracks," he said. "This is a critical part of the criminal reformation system pioneered at Auburn, which has spread as far as Paris, France."

His words sounded well-rehearsed. We were getting the two-bit tour after all.

Beyond the door, we entered a wide corridor with a hundred-foot ceiling and an overpowering smell. Despite many empty cells, the rank odors of unwashed bodies and the sour stench of excrement and disease clung to the walls. I was used to the strong odor of our jail, but I had to move a gloved hand to my nose to keep from gagging. In the corridor, the liquid in a piss bucket was frozen over.

Rulloff had lived this way for ten years? A man with the intellectual gifts to be running a university, curing tuberculosis—or changing the entire foundation of linguistic scholarship?

We climbed to the third floor and traversed a rickety plank walk-way. Each cell was set deep in stone and the single opening covered with a basket-weave of iron slats that a mouse could barely have crawled through. Atwater stopped at number 319.

Inside was a simple cot, barely wider than a man. A blanket at the end of the bed lay carefully folded, but the inquisitive rat on top refused to be tidied. When I lifted the trunk's lid, I glimpsed candles, an ink bottle, a half dozen books, and a bundle of letters wrapped in twine. I recognized my handwriting straightaway, and slammed it shut.

Thomas picked up one end of the trunk and I grabbed the other handle. As we hefted it down the stairs and out to the coach, I thought about how selfish and cowardly I'd been all along. I'd received every let-ter from Rulloff like a Christmas package, thinking only of my desires. I'd never once imagined him writing with frozen fingers, surrounded by rats, and unable to converse with another human for a decade.

Why had he spent his one respite from factory work writing out Greek lessons for a boy who'd never done anything more than bring him supper and pester him with questions?

Once the trunk was tied to the coach, Atwater led us all through a courtyard and down an impossibly long hallway, then stopped to speak before he opened the door.

"These men ache for work the way other men ache for women," he said. "Give a man employment—quotas to fulfill, daily tallies on which to stay focused—and you've given him self-mastery."

I wondered if the prisoners held the same perspective of their own forced labor.

The rug weaver's room felt like a crypt. The heddles of twenty great looms rose and fell with muffled clacks, tended by men with oilcans and spools of thread. The machines ground out rugs like sausages while pris-oners in striped costumes sewed the two symmetrical halves together to make a whole. Both men and machines moved with lifeless indifference.

A guard led a dozen prisoners across the room—men so shackled and forced into such close proximity, I marveled that they could move at all. Yet they demonstrated a precisely coordinated, shuffling lockstep.

I looked everywhere among the men twisting tension wheels and feeding coal into the steam engine for the massive body and square build I remembered so well. None of them was Rulloff, but I had the unnerving sensation that his eyes were on me.

Pa clipped me on the back of the neck.

"Gun up, Albert. Where's your head?"

The words reverberated through the quiet of the shop. Atwater spun and placed a finger to his mouth, but the words were out, and I knew they'd been heard by my teacher. I flushed to the tips of my ears.

Atwater walked toward a man at a drafting table behind the great looms. He held a ruler and curved drawing plates, tracing precise designs with a pencil. His giant head was unmistakable, but it topped a very different body than I remembered—still tall, but now gaunt as a stick bug. He must have lost fifty pounds since I last saw him. And in place of the top hat and frock coat were dingy stripes.

Here was a modern Sophocles, condemned by men who didn't understand his genius.

Though Rulloff chose not to look up, I could see in his slight hesitation, in the overly practiced way he set down his work, that he was trying to decipher the purpose of our party. I may have even noticed a ripple of fear, carefully disguised in movements that were a bit too deliberate. I wished I could find a way to signal that we were here as friends.

Atwater crossed between the looms, touched Rulloff's shoulder, and gestured for him to follow. Rulloff stood quietly, rolled up his sketching paper, and laid down his pencil.

Pa impatiently pushed Rulloff down the long hallway, as his leg chains limited their speed of progress to the lockstep shuffle. I tried to catch his eye but his visage was that of a walking statue. The only humanity I could detect was when he blinked in the light as we left the building.

When we reached the coach Pa cleared his throat. I was overwhelmed for a moment with visions of what could happen next.

Rulloff might say something that would give away our secret to Pa. Or Rulloff might ignore me, step on a riverboat, and I'd never see him again. Or, maybe, Rulloff would figure out a way to take me with him.

"Edward Rulloff," Pa said, "The governor sought fit to commute your sentence two weeks early. You've served your time for abducting your wife. You are a free man."

I thought Rulloff would at least smile, but he stayed perfectly still, holding Pa's firm gaze, as if he understood something I did not. Atwater stepped forward to remove the shackles, but Pa held up his hand.

"Not finished."

Pa took his time, dark brows twitching like caterpillars above his eyes, enthusiasm bleeding through his words.

"I have another order from the governor, and this one says you're to be arrested for murdering your daughter. You're to stand trial in Ithaca next week."

20

THE WIND DROVE THE ICY CHIPS OF SLEET INTO THE gaps between my gloves and cuffs, under the brim of my hat and straight into my eyes. The weather advanced rapidly toward a blizzard state of unreality—thick whiteness with no shadows, no up or down, not a smell or a sound beside the sinister howl of the wind.

I sat high in the driver's seat, trying to find the road under two days' accumulation of snow, distraught that Rulloff, chained inside, might think I was part of this treachery.

How could Pa be so cruel?

I tried like mad to think of a way to stop the insanity.

What would Rulloff have me do?

The storm pressed down hard, turning the afternoon charcoal dark. Pa rode ahead of the coach, chin tucked deep in his chest. I imagined him stewing over my defiance with Atwater, wrestling with how I knew the fancy words I'd spoken. As soon as we were alone in the annex, the reckoning would come. I'd need believable answers by then.

"Raining butter," Josiah rasped from the left flank.

"Raining grizzlies, more like," Thomas said from the right. "Be a pretty lonesome affair after all this effort."

"Folks'll turn out," Pa called back. I was amazed he could hear them over the whistling wind. "Eph's saved that coil a rope ten years."

"Turn out for what?" I shouted.

"You recall that day, Josiah?" Thomas said. "You were much less ornery back then."

"And you was much better looking," Josiah barked, then coughed, which turned into a hacking fit that lasted several long minutes. When he finally finished, he looked like a leaning mountain in the saddle.

"Keep this up," Thomas said, "and we can bury you and Rulloff at the same time. Save on graveyard expenses."

"Oh, shut your trap." Josiah's chuckle held a grim edge. "You want me dead by Tuesday next, you're just going to have to shoot me yourself. Lose yourself a juror."

The front-left carriage wheel slipped. Thunder and Eli struggled forward, slower than before. It was getting harder to drag the coach through knee-high snow. We were still a dozen miles from home, but I imagined vigilantes behind every tree.

"Tempting," Thomas said. "Just for safety sake, why don't you post up that gold eagle you owe me."

"I ain't that sick, Thomas. And it's a quarter eagle. You know it."

"Josiah, you're from Elmira. How did you get called as a juror in Ithaca?" I asked.

"You just keep an eye out, Albert," Pa answered. "Make sure we ain't ambushed."

The way he said the words, the lie became clear to me. A new trial with a murder charge and stacked jury would hang Rulloff quick. Ithaca would get its revenge, and the governor would avoid vigilante headlines. Facts or no facts, evidence or none, Pa was giving Eph his lynching—giving it to him legally. And as his trusted man, I was helping make it happen.

"Pa—you can't mean to do this."

Pa rode quietly for a time, a slow loping mound of snowdrift. He was a little in front of me and below, so I couldn't see his face, just make out the edge of his dark hat against the driving white. I wanted nothing in the world more than for that hat to turn around, tell me I was mistaken.

"Pa—" My voice broke, so I stopped. I wouldn't have known what to say next anyway.

Finally, he spoke, but still wouldn't face me. His voice carried low against the howl.

"Sometimes a difficult thing needs doing."

"But he's innocent."

Pa said nothing. Thunder paused at the bottom of a small rise and snorted. My shouts couldn't budge him. Only the whip got him moving again—the stress of the bitter cold evident in his halting gait.

Thomas finally broke the silence. "Law ain't always perfect as common sense, Albert."

What logic would Rulloff use to change their minds?

"You can't try a man for the same thing twice," I said to Pa's back. "It's called double jeopardy. It's a fundamental legal principle, *ne bis in idem.*"

Pa rode on. I wondered if he stayed quiet because he was mulling over more fancy words or because I wasn't worth the effort.

"It's been considered, Albert," Thomas said, looking long at Pa as if he was waiting to be stopped. "First trial was for kidnapping his wife. The second is for murdering his daughter. There's no conflict, and no statute of limitations."

The truth of it all burned like raw vinegar in my gut. The fantasy of New York City evaporated, my scholarly career disappeared under the crushing snow. My life would be confined to exactly this—driving prisoners, keeping the jail. My brilliant teacher who'd already spent ten years in hell for no reason—would be executed in cold blood.

All I wanted in the world was the ability to climb into the coach and ask Rulloff what to do. I even thought about posing a question in Arabic or Finnish, hoping he would hear and answer, but there was no way on earth I could explain that to Pa. It would just mean losing my one tiny advantage of being a trusted man.

Aunt Babe's house was just a few miles farther up the road.

"Getting icy out here, don't you think?"

My words were nearly lost in the rush of wind.

"Ain't weather for feeding ducks," Josiah hollered, then coughed for nearly a quarter mile, his hacking now laced with phlegm. When he finally stopped, he looked hollow as an old tree and didn't say another word.

"Warm fire might do him good," I said to Pa.

Pa said nothing.

"Dangerous for the horses," I said.

Pa carried on up the road, face tucked into his collar as the wind blasted from the right. From the set of his shoulders I knew he'd considered and then rejected the idea of stopping at Babe's, without me having to suggest it.

Then Josiah fell off his saddle.

21

BABE BARELY CRACKED THE DOOR, BUT THE RUSH OF the blizzard immediately slammed it against the parlor wall, scattering snow over the rug. On the stoop, Josiah leaned heavily on Pa's shoulder, while Thomas held fast to a shackled Rulloff. Babe's lips pursed in the muddled lantern light as she took in the surprise visit, but she didn't hesitate more than a moment before ushering Pa inside.

"Albert, get the team to the barn," she directed. "I'll fetch the rest of the horses." She wrapped her shawl tight around her shift, grabbed her coat and gloves, then pushed her feet into a pair of boots by the door.

The lantern swung violently, squeaking in protest. Three steps off the porch, I could no longer see the door. Already blinded by the whiteout, I had to find Thunder and Eli by feel, and it was only years of muscle memory that led me back to the porch, where I could follow the rope from the post to the barn.

Inside, the wind whistled through the knotholes. While Babe hung the lantern on a peg, I unhitched the coach and quickly brushed down the horses with purposeful, angry strokes.

"We have a big problem," I spit out, over chattering teeth.

"You don't say." She dug a ball of snow out of Horse's foot with a stick. "These hooves should have been greased." She shook her head, started to speak, and then shook her head again. "What were you all thinking going out in this weather?"

"Pa said it was to save Rulloff from the mob. But it's bad, Aunt Babe. Real bad."

She kept shaking her head until she finally raised it up and looked me so deep in the eye that I drew back.

"You put everything at risk coming here. Do you realize what you've done?"

Her words stabbed at me. I needed her help but here she was again, more worried about her cause than me.

"Your runaways can wait," I shouted back. "Rulloff's in trouble. They're going to put him to death."

"Keep your voice down!" She grabbed my arm hard enough to bruise, wrenching me forward. "They cannot wait, Albert." For the first time in my life I saw fear on Aunt Babe's face. "There are two women in the cellar now and—"

"What, *now?*"

"Yes, now, you foolish, foolish boy. And you brought three lawmen to my door."

Of all the things she could call me, foolish was the most hurtful.

She crouched to sweep the snow from Thunder's forelegs.

"Your Pa's bound to hear something if he stays in the house all night. I can't even get down to the cellar to warn that poor old woman. Lost an eye to the lash."

"I'm sorry for the trouble, but it's Rulloff who needs—"

"Albert, Grace is north of seventy and just *walked* the better part of eight hundred miles in the dead of winter." Aunt Babe's voice quivered. "Can you imagine what she's going through? Hearing all the commotion upstairs, wondering when they'll burst in and drag her off to spend her last remaining days on this earth in chains?"

"I'm sure we'll be able to—"

"And Rebecca is pregnant enough to pop." She banged her fist into the post so hard that Thunder snorted and drew back.

"Aunt Babe," I said, calm as I could manage.

How could she not understand?

"I'm sorry for the risk. I'll help you get Grace and Rebecca to the next station, I promise. But you've got to listen. Pa's going to give Rulloff a fake trial, and then they'll hang him in the square." I tried to wipe the frozen snot off my top lip, but my icy gloves only scratched my face.

Babe pulled her coat tighter around her shoulders. If I was cold in my coat, she must have been freezing in her nightdress.

"Albert, you listen now. Ferrying letters is one thing. Going against your Pa directly is something else entirely. This is his job. He has his weaknesses, but he's not a bad man. You are talking about helping free a prisoner, Albert, and I won't hear another word about it."

Where was the crusader I thought I knew? "How's it any different from helping runaway slaves. They're fugitives too."

She moved on to Eli's hooves, so angry she wouldn't even look at me.

"You listen to me, Albert. This is not your business. This is your Pa's business."

I'd counted on her to tell me what to do, but she looked much older suddenly, her neck as wrinkled as a dried apple head doll.

"You can't mean that. You have to help."

"I don't have to do anything," she said, "except get those exhausted women to the next stop. Your Pa will make his choices."

"So justice only applies to Negroes? That's not fair, Aunt Babe!"

"You hear me now, Albert," she snapped, throwing the stick into the back of the paddock. It was the only time I could remember her stopping work to speak. "There is absolutely *nothing* fair about this world, and you'd better be grateful for that fact every single day because that unfairness works mightily in your favor—more than you can know. Imagine asking Grace and Rebecca in the cellar about 'fair.' All your talk of justice—what you mean is fighting your Pa. You're a smart boy, and one day you'll understand, but right now you've got to believe me: This is bigger than you."

"He's my teacher," I said, sick with memories of the frozen cell where he'd sat and penned ten-page lessons, corrected my grammar, and read my boyish essays week after week. I wished I could tell her the secret about languages, but even if I told Aunt Babe the truth, she wouldn't believe it. She didn't have the background to understand what all those root sounds meant about the past, or to visualize what they could mean about the future. And right now she was too angry to even try.

"Lord," she said, shaking her head at my silence. "I'm not going to argue this with you now. We're going back inside before we freeze to death, and we will not discuss it further, you hear?"

She took the lantern off the peg, and made her way to the door, ignoring me.

"Wait!"

With all Rulloff had done for me, I couldn't let him be betrayed by my family. I opened the trunk lashed to the back of the coach and pulled out a bundle of letters. "These are all addressed to me at *your* farm." I thrust the letters toward her, hand shaking.

She stood in the center of the barn, neither moving nor breathing as she stared me down.

"What are you saying to me?"

"If Pa knew about these, he'd be mad enough to put an end to the whole railroad between here and Auburn. You have to help me, or I'll show him how you went behind his back."

Her mouth fell open, and she looked at me like I'd become some kind of demon.

"You think to *blackmail* me, Albert?"

The word surprised and shamed me.

Was that really what I was doing?

"After everything I've done for you? Where has this cruelty come from? You give me those letters right now."

Lost in an emotional whiteout, I did as I was told. Then I regretted it almost immediately.

Wasn't it her fault I was so desperate?

I wasn't the kind of person to threaten my aunt. I *couldn't* be that kind of person. If she'd only helped me, none of this would have happened. I grew angrier, thinking of how she'd driven me to such a vile act.

"Come inside." She wrapped the letters in the folds of her shawl and picked up the lantern. "Not another word about this tonight, yes?"

"Yes," I agreed, feeling more alone than ever. If Rulloff was to be saved from Pa, and Pa from himself, it was up to me alone.

22

BABE SET THE LANTERN ON THE MANTLE, RUBBED HER hands in front of the fire, then turned to Josiah, sprawled in the rocker. "Why in heaven's name would you all take a man with a violent fever into a blizzard?"

"Josiah's steady as an ox," Pa said, one boot off, struggling to remove the other. His cheeks were scarlet from windburn. "Always has been. He'll be right as rain come morning."

"Like thunder, he will," she said. Josiah's eyes were closed, mouth open. The cane of the chair bulged beneath his weight. "Albert, fetch me the laudanum."

I found the medicine in the pantry, but once I'd grabbed it, my feet refused to move. I cradled the full bottle of red-brown syrup against my chest, trying to use the moment alone to force a plan into my mind.

Once Rulloff got to our jail, the whole town would be watching. There'd be no escape. Within a day, he'd be swinging from the gallows, eyes picked out by crows. Pa would be a hero again at Grant's, but I'd never be able to look at his traitorous face again. And Aunt Babe was no better—so quick to abandon the man she knew had taught me for close to a decade. *If they killed Rulloff, how could I live with myself?* We had to escape together. But if it was ever going to happen, it would have to happen here. Tonight.

But how?

I ran my fingers over the wainscoting of the secret door. The lake was partly frozen, but not yet completely. Rulloff knew the water, and I knew how to get to Mr. L's station. We could bring the runaways, so they'd be safe, like I promised Aunt Babe.

But how could we get away unseen?

Our exit plan was useless as long as Thomas kept hold of his rifle. My jumbled thoughts got me nowhere.

"Hurry, Albert," Babe called.

I found her dabbing Josiah's head with a damp cloth, the way she used to care for me once, before her runaways took all the space in her heart. I tried to shake off the bitterness and focus on what was within my control, which was nothing. She poured two spoonfuls into his slack mouth and I set the bottle on the mantle, between the lantern and the whiskey jug.

Rulloff cleared his throat and spoke for the first time since we'd picked him up.

"If you have burdock root, it could help bring down his fever," he offered.

He sat in the warped side chair by the fire, still in irons. There was a stiffness to his gaunt frame, and his voice sounded quieter and more deferential than I remembered.

"If not, perhaps a tea with garlic and cinnamon."

Aunt Babe ignored him, absorbed in her patient.

"It'll be too hard to get him upstairs," she said, "But we should put him on the settee where he can sleep." Pa nodded and set his arm underneath Josiah's right shoulder.

"Easy there, you big faker," he said. "Thomas, give me a hand, will you?"

Thomas handed me his rifle.

Suddenly—too suddenly—I had my opportunity. Aunt Babe was moving her quilting basket out of the way, Pa and Thomas had their arms full, and Josiah seemed out cold. I was the only one in the room with a gun.

What should I do? I placed my right finger on the trigger of Thomas's rifle and judged the weight of the barrel with my left palm.

Should I tell everyone to stop? Point the rifle at the four of them and say they should be ashamed for trying to kill an innocent man? Then what? Force Pa to hand me the keys to the leg irons and run away into a blizzard in the middle of the night? How much of a head start could we get?

Then my one opportunity ended before it had even begun. Rulloff stood to warm himself, and Thomas eased the rifle out of my hands.

I needed more space to think.

"Should I bring him soup from the pot, Aunt Babe?"

Josiah, who'd I'd thought asleep, bent forward, coughing until he choked. "Well, hell. Now I know I'm a dead man. The kid's playing nursemaid."

"He needs rest, Albert," Aunt Babe said. "He's burning up with fever. If he makes it to morning, we can talk about food."

"Don't let him snow you, Miss Jarvis," Thomas said, forcing an unconvincing grin. "He's fit as a Finnish fiddler, and we're waiting on him hand and foot. You watch what fools he makes of us tomorrow."

"Jolly as a jaybird," Josiah croaked, then fell back into the settee, eyes closed, mouth open.

I slumped back into the chair and stared at the fire, trying to think of something. Rulloff sat back in his chair but still wouldn't catch my eye.

Did he think I was in on this? How could I convince him of my loyalty?

There would be a boat sitting ready by the lake. That could be useful. I let myself be mesmerized by the dancing firelight glistening on the half-empty laudanum bottle. We could replace Rulloff's stripes with clothes meant for runaways, and there would be a hamper of food already made up somewhere, probably in the kitchen.

Why was the laudanum bottle half empty?

I'd chosen a full bottle. *Had I?* I thought back. Yes, definitely a full bottle. Babe had only used a couple of spoonfuls for Josiah.

Where had the rest gone?

Pa brought a glass from the kitchen, set it on the mantle and pulled the stopper out of the whiskey jug. That's when I understood exactly what Rulloff had done.

I jumped reflexively to warn Pa, but tripped on the corner of the rug and banged my knee on the table. Pa scowled at me, eyes rimmed red from the cold.

"You have manners left, Jake?" Babe asked. "You going to offer any to the rest of us?"

I couldn't breathe inside the whirlpool of conflicting loyalties, my intentions thrashing to escape its devastating, silent grip. I wanted Rulloff out of danger—needed him to be free. But as angry as I was at Pa, I didn't want to hurt him either. There would be no forgiveness in Ithaca for the man who let Rulloff get away, twice. He'd be lucky if they didn't take the noose to him instead. Held fast in inaction, I watched with equal parts terror and hope as Pa downed his drink and slammed the glass down hard enough to crack. "It's your house, ain't it?"

"No. It's *our home*," Babe said, a steely edge to her voice. "I've always said that, as you well know. I only set certain conditions."

Pa glared like he wanted to take her head off, but in front of Thomas, he found his self-possession. He filled three more glasses, then handed them around to everyone but Rulloff and Josiah. Then he sat in the rocker and lurched back and forth, as if the chair were a toy.

"Don't you worry," he said. "We'll be out of your house in the morning, and I swear I'll never dirty your threshold again."

I kept my lips closed and pretended to drink my whiskey, too disgraced to look at Pa and too afraid of my optimism to glance at Rulloff. To save one, I had to ruin another.

The silence grew interminable, everyone lost in their private thoughts. Eventually, Thomas became entranced by the woodgrain of his rifle stock. Aunt Babe began singing a soft lullaby to Josiah. I'd never be able to meet Pa's eye again. The only thing left for me was to flee with Rulloff—or die of shame.

The whirr-and-tick, whirr-and-tick of the grandfather clock counted down second by second, interrupted only by the occasional click of the minute hand.

We might get a night or two of shelter in Mr. L's barn before word reached him about the fugitive. *Fugitives*, I corrected myself. Plural. Running away with Rulloff, I would become an outlaw too.

Finally, Aunt Babe dragged herself up to bed, and Thomas fell to snoring on the rug, boots still on. Pa held out the longest, woozy as if on a drunk, but still managing to hold up swollen eyelids that appeared heavy as stones.

I dug deep for the most fleeting hint of courage.

"Do you want me to take a turn, Pa?" I stood over him, a hand on his shoulder. He raised a single tired eye and surprised me with a trusting, loving glance that crushed my heart more surely than his fury would have.

"Minute of shut-eye," he mumbled as I eased the rifle from his hands. He was asleep before I'd sat back down.

I was left alone with Rulloff and a gun.

"Now what?" I asked.

23

ONCE AGAIN, THE CLOCK BROKE THE SILENCE—THIS TIME with a cacophony of chimes. Rulloff allowed all nine bells to echo through the house before answering.

"You've certainly grown tall," he said, then cocked his finger to beckon me closer. "How did that scar on your chin turn out?"

I moved to get up but as soon as I pushed the rifle from my lap, a flash of terror stopped me.

Was this a trap? After Pa's treachery, would he grab the gun and kill us all?

His eyes were sparkly and blue, as kind-looking as ever, but I couldn't hold their gaze. I palmed the rifle with one hand and pointed at the comatose sleepers with the other.

"They'll be all right, won't they?" I asked.

He raised a hand to wave the question off, an elegant gesture that recalled the Rulloff I'd first met—the one in full vigor and fashion, not the emaciated and aged man before me in prison stripes.

"Likely, they'll sleep ten or twelve hours. They won't appreciate the headache in the morning, but I don't think there'll be any permanent damage."

I fought hard against my impulse to fold up inside and let my teacher tell me what to do. His life was in danger, and he had no way to be sure of my loyalty. That could make him a threat.

Would he have stopped me from drinking the laudanum-laced whiskey? Had he planned to immobilize and then kill all of us?

Did he still?

I rested the rifle barrel on my knee and tried to shake away the fear that thumped in my heart like a trapped rabbit. One way or another, my life was now as much at stake as his.

"I didn't mean for any of this," I said, twisting my thumbs into knots. "Aunt Babe stopped the letters. Now Pa's up to no good."

Josiah's wheeze turned into a whistle. Rulloff stared silently at me, his face an emotionless mask.

"I've been studying every day," I added.

A mouse scurried along the baseboard and disappeared into the shadows. Still Rulloff remained silent, waiting.

"I practiced Classical Arabic from your notes and read about the Sumerians from a history book that was left at Clinton House."

I jumped as Thomas snuffled suddenly and rolled onto his side, but Rulloff barely seemed to take note. On the verge of tears, I finally broke down.

"I want to help with your project more than anything in the world. Can I still be your apprentice?"

Rulloff neither smiled nor frowned. He sat quietly, seeming contented, as the grandfather clocked ticked away precious minutes. The wind was dying down, but if we were to head to Mr. L's, we still had nearly thirty miles to row before daylight.

"Do you recall Plato's definition of justice?"

"Is this a test?"

He crossed his legs, a gesture that required dexterity with ankles still shackled, but accomplished without a squeak from the iron linkages.

"It was a principle that became very dear to him after his mentor was executed."

It was a test. Not of memory, but loyalty. I thought of the way Babe broke laws and even commandments to stand up for her version of justice. I nodded, then flush with the growing confidence, spoke out loud.

"He said justice is man's primary duty."

"Then you have a core value from which to make difficult decisions." Rulloff smiled a full set of shiny white teeth.

"The job is yours if you wish it, Albert. It always has been. What happens next is in your hands."

I pressed my back against the chair rails and wondered again for the briefest second whether Rulloff would have warned me against drinking the whiskey, but my distrust passed quickly, buried by the fervor of my desires.

I set down the rifle and crouched over Pa, slumped in the chair—one leg straight, the other buckled. The key to Rulloff's leg irons lay in his inner breast pocket. He'd given me a solemn mission to protect Rulloff from vigilantes, and that's exactly what I was going to do.

I touched Pa's chest with three fingers, then shoved him lightly with my hand, then finally shook him hard. He was as comatose as his worst whiskey nights, and the key slid all too easily from his pocket into my hand. As soon as I held it, I felt its power. My choices would guide us now. If Pa had studied law or philosophy, maybe he would have made a better decision himself, but I'd had the opportunity to gain the greater moral foundation, and I had to take responsibility.

Once I got the shackles off, I fetched a set of clothes for Rulloff and filled a flour sack with food, then I opened the hidden section of wainscoting in the pantry.

"Pa'll have bloodhounds out by afternoon," I said, trying to hurry him up. "A whole posse by nightfall. But with the rowboat, there'll be no trail to follow."

I said a mental goodbye to Aunt Babe, choked up to leave this house that had meant so much to me.

"We have to take two runaways with us to Mr. L's dock at the north end of Cayuga, the only one with two lanterns. Can you still navigate up there with no moonlight?"

"I know Cayuga Lake all too well," he said, folding himself into the void of the panel, then testing the rungs of the ladder for his weight. He took the flour sack from me, then climbed down until all I could see was the top of his head.

I crouched into the opening and set a foot on the ladder above him, but he stopped me with a hand on my ankle.

"It's okay. I can close the latch from the inside," I said, trying to shake him off.

He held firmer.

"Albert, you can't come."

My foot slipped on the rung. The iron door latch felt like ice in my hand as I struggled to breathe.

"You wouldn't *leave* me here?"

"Be rational. It's far easier to hunt down two men traveling together than one alone."

"You can't!" I'd have to face Pa and Babe and Thomas and Josiah. They'd guess. No—they'd *know* I did this.

Rulloff anticipated my terror.

"There's no reason for your father to suspect your involvement. You'll be safe until I can get established in New York. I will send for you."

"Please!" In my awkward overhead position, I struggled to catch his eye beneath me. "I'll do anything you want. I'll—" I struggled to think of a single way I could be helpful.

"This is no time to indulge your passions, Albert. It's critical to be strategic if we're to survive."

For all I tried to imagine what Seneca would do, I was choking on tears, searching for any way to change Rulloff's mind. If I let him go without me, I'd never see him again.

"Aunt Babe knows," I pleaded.

"She could never reveal your involvement," he answered coldly, shutting down my only argument. "She has too much to lose."

The wind rattled the storm shutters on the north side of the house, causing me to jump. "I'm coming with you!" I reached down and grabbed for Rulloff's arm but got only a handful of the overly large canvas jacket he wore, ripping the frayed seam in the shoulder.

"Enough, Albert! Stop being so childish."

He shook off my grip and pushed me away with far greater strength than I would have anticipated from his shrunken frame. I fell out of the doorway and crumpled onto the floor of the pantry, staring at an empty dark hole before me.

I continued to cast about for an argument that would convince him, but the truth of his words grabbed me from deep inside and held me fast to the floor. He was safer without me. I felt the sobs rising in my chest and fought to hold on to them until he was too far away to hear.

But his head reappeared, framed in the miniature doorway, and he cast his shining blue eyes upon me.

"You've been a brave and true friend, Albert, and I will always remember what you've done for me tonight. Know that I am undertaking a very dangerous journey, which is only marginally safer than certain death in Ithaca, but my peril doesn't have to be yours. If they find my body in a snow drift after the spring thaw, your life will continue—no better and no worse. But if I can make it all the way to the city, I will reinvent myself as Professor Leurio, and you and I can work together in Astor's great library."

I sniffled, grateful for his attempt to cheer me up, however impossible. Any attempt I made to contact him, or him to contact me, would put Rulloff in extreme jeopardy. I gave my teacher the closest thing I could approach to an encouraging smile, certain I'd never see him again.

"You promise to get Grace and Rebecca safely to Mr. L?"

"Of course," he said, giving me a wink before he closed the door behind him.

The click of that panel was a torture beyond all imagining.

I dragged myself back to the parlor, imagining all the ways Rulloff would change the world without me. Probably Seneca would have felt magnanimous in my shoes, but I was devastated.

After that, sleep proved impossible, and I spent the entire night wracked with guilt, shame, and loneliness.

Somewhere between midnight and three o'clock, Josiah stopped breathing.

24

PA WAS SHOUTING.

Had I dozed off?

I leapt up as I'd practiced, ready to grab my musket and say, *He can't have got far*, but Pa was yelling at Josiah.

"You bloody fucking fool. How could you get killed by a damn cold?"

He swiped angrily at his eyes, staggered back from the settee, and stumbled over Thomas. The empty lantern crashed to the floor.

Thomas twisted up from the rug to a half-seated position and rubbed his forehead.

"Stop shouting. My head's been run through the mill."

"Wake up, you son of a bitch." Pa kept yelling at Josiah, pushing at his shoulder. "You can't be dead."

"Who's dead?" Then Thomas turned to the settee where Pa was still poking at Josiah's corpse.

"Oh, Jesus, Jesus," Thomas said. "Jesus, Jesus."

"Babe!" Pa shouted.

"Tell me he's sleeping," Pa said to Thomas. "Please tell me he's sleeping."

I'd never seen Pa so distraught. Angry, yes, but the quiet terror in his voice brought tears to my eyes. I had to work to blink them back. All night I'd been angry at how he'd forced me to betray him, how his mess had made me treat Aunt Babe. But seeing such despair dawn on him, all I wanted to do was put an arm on his shoulder.

"Jesus," Thomas said one last time, then lay back against the settee, eyes scrunched into a pained grimace. "All because of that fucker—" Thomas shot up, eyes wide. "Where is he?" He sprung up, grabbed his rifle.

"Jarvis, Rulloff's gone. The fucker's *gone!*"

"He can't have got far," I said, too quickly.

Pa spun around the room like a woozy drunk, then looked back at Josiah. His whole body shook with rage, but it was his open-eyed stare that scared me most. Flat, lost, vulnerable.

"Murdering. Bastard!"

He fixated on Josiah's pale, slack face as if Rulloff had given him the cold and sent him to Auburn in a blizzard.

Thomas flung open the front door, filling the room with an arctic blast and a howling wind that blew snow across the parlor furniture and fanned the fire embers.

"No tracks out front," he shouted. "Must have left through the kitchen." He stumbled to the other side of the house, knocking into an armchair. He didn't even stop to close the front door.

Babe appeared at the top of the stairs, holding a thumb and finger across the arch of her brows, staring me down. She was furious enough she hadn't even stopped to pull on a shawl. I recognized utter disgust in the arch of her shoulders, felt every claw of her hate scratching at my chest. All I wanted was to run and hide, but I knew I had to force myself to meet her eyes.

I'd thought about it all night. I needed her to take pity on a decision already made. Failing that, I needed for her to know that her runaways were with Rulloff, their fate mixed in with his. So I picked myself up off the floor and stood, feet apart, hands on my hips, and dragged my eyes up stair by stair until I saw her face. All my life, she'd been the one to stand up for me, but now I withered under the judgment of her flat green eyes, like a fern in August. I was sick to my stomach but caught her attention, and with a flick of my head drew the invisible line between the cellar and the lake's north shore. I hoped that was enough for her to figure it out, because I couldn't say more until I got her alone.

"No tracks," Thomas returned from the kitchen, finally slamming the front door. Into the quiet left by the silenced wind he bellowed, "Why no tracks?"

"Must've snowed a bushel last night," I said, ready with my answer. "Covered 'em up."

"No," Thomas said. "That's not it. You can still see our tracks coming in yesterday—buried, but visible. I don't get it. Should be at least a trace of that fucker."

"Oh," I said. I'd failed to consider that possibility.

"Son of a bitch," Pa said. He rushed into the kitchen, headed straight for the pantry. *Did he know about the secret room after all?* I yelped as he flung open the door, but then he immediately slammed it closed. "He must be hiding in the house. I'm gonna find that bastard and shoot him straight through the head."

"Jacob!" Babe yelled, then took a long, pitiful glance at me as she descended the stairs. "You calm down and think this through. It's a hard knock, Josiah passing, but you're not doing him any service by destroying my house."

"Don't you dare tell me my business, woman!"

Pa pulled a teacup off the sideboard hook and flung it across the room. It shattered against the far wall in a porcelain explosion. The entire house shook as he pushed Babe out of the way and thudded up the stairs.

Thomas rubbed his eyes hard, as if he was grinding down the sockets, then turned to me.

"We're going to need help. Ride into town and get Eph Schutt. Tell him to bring men. I don't know how Rulloff got out, but he did. If he found a boat, he could be anywhere on the lake by now."

I pulled on my coat, grabbed my musket, and leaned over Babe, who was on her hands and knees picking up shards from the floor.

"They're with him," I said in a low voice. "If he makes it safe, they make it safe. Understand?"

Babe turned to me, mouth mangled in a nasty frown.

"You fool! You've no idea what you've done."

I stomped out the front door. It was the second time she'd called me foolish, but she'd forgive me later. Hell, she'd apologize. It had to happen this way. She and Pa had left me no choice. It was the principle of the thing. Eventually, she'd have to see that. In the barn, I grabbed the halter of Pa's borrowed palomino with my left hand and punched the post with my right. She jumped with a fearful whinny.

What was wrong with me?

When I finally felt the ground grow solid again under my feet, I took my time putting on her bridle and saddle. She was a fast horse, so the longer it took me to get to town, the greater chance I gave Rulloff. But I had other reasons, too. I dreaded facing Eph. Ten years on, he still worked at the tannery and drank his fill at Grant's, but he'd never remarried, and his eyes remained as hollow as I remembered them on the day of the funeral. I could scarce imagine how he'd react to me telling him the man he thought killed his wife, daughter, sister, and niece had escaped the noose—again.

I strapped on my musket and powder horn and led Thunder out to the snow-buried hitching post. Muffled shouts came from the house. I looked up to see Pa throw open the bedroom window. His face was so red, he looked like he might burst from the inside out.

"You ungrateful bastard!"

The palomino pulled against me. "Steady," I said, trying to figure out what Pa was angry about this time.

"You did this? After all I done for you?" He pulled his head inside like a snapping turtle.

I felt a moment of panic but quickly ran through a mental checklist of my secret vulnerabilities. Aunt Babe wouldn't have said anything. I'd closed the door in the pantry and dragged the meat grinder in front of it, had left the empty shackles on the floor, and carefully placed the keys back in Pa's pocket. There was no reason to trace the missing tracks part back to me.

I tried to work out how to talk him out of whatever notion had gotten into his mind. Then Pa reappeared and hurled something out the window. It was white, about the size of a brick, and for a moment, I thought it might be a snowball, until the projectile broke open and rained a cloud of fluttering letters.

"I'll kill you for this, Albert! I swear to God!"

Thunder tugged at me again, but I stood there, mouth agape as Pa pulled his head back inside the window. *How could I have forgotten the letters?* Pa knew every bit of the truth all at once. There was no talking my way out of this one. He was probably coming down to skin me alive.

As I was trying to figure out how to explain, Pa burst out of the window again, this time with his rifle. I watched him pull it to his shoulder. Watched him aim it at me. I watched—unable to move, unable to believe my plan had gone so wrong.

Until a bullet whizzed past my ear.

25

I HEARD MY SCREAM—AS SHRILL AND TERRIFYING AS IF it had come from someone standing beside me. I squinted up at Pa, unbelieving, until I saw his silhouette behind the window glass reloading the rifle. The palomino yanked at the lead, and as soon as I leapt into the saddle, took off at full gallop across the field of new snow.

Another shot kicked up a cloud of snow to my right, and the horse broke left for the trees without any guidance from me.

She took us into the forest, where skeleton branches flew past my face as I tried like mad to think. We were out of rifle range now, but it wouldn't take Pa more than a few minutes to get to the barn, throw a saddle on Horse, and be after me. Maybe less if he skipped the saddle. Still trying to hold on to the palomino, I had to find a way to work through the impossibility of what was happening if I was going to survive.

Where could I go? Hide out at the Snyders'?

Even if I could avoid Pa, word would get around in a flash that I was the one who'd let Rulloff free, and then even Mrs. Snyder would want to see me strung up. The whole town would want me dead—Eph and everyone with the torches, coming for me with that noose. I'd be swinging from the poplar by nightfall.

A branch caught my cheek and sliced it open to my ear.

Ithaca was all I knew.

What else was there? Flee to Canada? To the territories? The snow was too deep this time of year.

I struggled to breathe in the fear and the cold. The palomino had nearly exhausted herself already. I cried out loud, wishing I'd convinced Rulloff to take me with him.

I could still hear shouting, too far away to recognize words but close enough to know Pa wasn't giving up. It was time to make a choice, and it had to be the right one.

What would Pa expect me to do?

He knew me as the namby-pamby son of a jail-keep who *ain't got the sense God gave a toad.* He'd expect to find me easily in a nearby barn, or if I was slightly bolder, hiding out in a wagon or boat headed out of town. He would never think I had it in me to set out alone for a place I'd never been.

Of all the directions I could flee, the least traveled was south. I remembered the map in the telegraph office. There was a rail line from Binghamton to Manhattan, so that could be useful—*if* I could get to Binghamton. The distance was only around fifty miles, and trappers sometimes spoke of a summer trail, but this time of year the snow was deep, the terrain hilly, and to my knowledge, even the Mohawks never dared the trip in winter.

I had a musket, a coat, a hat, gloves, and a horse. No food or water or flint. And if I was going to shake Pa off my trail, my best chance was by getting rid of my horse. I was no trapper and certainly no Mohawk.

Pa was just the other side of the rise, unable to see over the hill. Whatever I was going to do, I had to do it soon. I kicked my heels into the palomino's ribs, doubled back to a small section of the lake where the ice was still gray—not yet frozen solid—and jumped off the horse.

Neither Pa nor the best hounds in Ithaca could follow a trail through water.

Plus, Pa knew I'd not gone near water since that day in the river. He also knew what he'd taught me himself—that this time of year a man would last less than ten minutes in that water before hypothermia set in. He'd never think I had it in me.

The palomino wrenched my arm, yanking the reins from my hand, desperate to keep running. I let go and slapped her backside as she took off. She was the faster of the two horses, and without a rider in the trees, she might be able to stay far enough ahead it would ta hour or more to learn he'd been fooled.

I peered behind me. I could just see the smoke from Aunt Babe's chimney. Inside, that house was warm and dry, the kitchen sweet with the smell of yesterday's griddlecakes, the parlor full of memories. But now and forever, Aunt Babe would despise me. And I would deserve it.

I skidded across the icy shallows until the ice gave way and I plunged into the lake.

FOR THE FIRST few moments, I thought I'd overestimated the impact of the cold. Then the water squeezed through my coat and a thousand needles stabbed me. The familiar beat of Horse's gallop grew closer.

Then from just over the hill I heard Pa shout: "Goddamnit!"

Down I went, under the surface. The ice water ripped my chest apart as if I was drowning all over again. I was ready to jump back out and beg mercy, but I'd never in my life heard Pa kick a horse so furiously. I managed to keep my wail down to a pitiful underwater groan and forced myself to wait as long as I could manage.

When I finally surfaced, I saw that Pa had followed the palomino's tracks into the forest.

I tried to lift myself back onto the ice but my wet clothes felt like they weighed a hundred pounds and I had no strength in my arms. Three times I tried, getting weaker with each one, until in desperation I felt for the bottom, found it just below my knees, and managed to spring with my legs onto ice that, mercifully, held.

Immediately the wind froze the water into ice on the back of my neck, but there was no time to lose. I had to move or die. If I could make it to the Fall Creek dock—*What was that? A quarter mile?*—my footsteps in the snow could belong to anyone. I stumbled back onto shore and lurched forward, but the more I pushed, the more I felt my heart might explode. Hours passed. Maybe minutes.

I began counting my steps, grunting each number aloud as a victory, attacking the ground, the cold, my body to keep moving. Each time I got to ten, I started over. I finally spotted the dock, impossibly far away, and nearly gave up. But I went back to my counting. I couldn't bear to think about more than ten numbers at a time. One through ten. One through ten. Until I could head out toward the hills.

My ordeal had just begun.

26

FOR FOUR WEEKS, I WOUND MY WAY THROUGH THE mazelike valleys—getting lost and doubling back, then getting lost again. I slept in one abandoned barn, several occupied ones, and for one especially bad night, an outhouse. There weren't many farms, but the few I found kept me just on the living side of starvation.

I subsisted on eggs from henhouses, cheese from larders and what I could harvest from a cranberry bog, the meager nutrients leaving my body in stomach-clenching diarrhea. When I was angry at Pa, I pushed forward. Then I'd stop caring and sit down in a quiet place to die. Then my furor at Pa would grow again. There was no way I was going to let him win so easily, so I pushed on. My hair fell out in clumps. I thought of nothing but food.

Limping south on a crude set of snowshoes made of sticks held together with strips from the lining of my coat, I smeared mud over my face to protect it from sunburn. But no matter what I did, my lips cracked and bled. I told myself Rulloff had survived prison and ice baths, all the while correcting my grammar. With each step, I lashed out at Pa—in one of twenty different languages. But nothing stopped my obsessive daydreams of blackberry pies and chicken soup and griddlecakes with syrup. Between farms, I huddled in a snow cave I'd dug with numb hands, and endured endless nightmares—always of drowning.

Finally, on a clear day, I spotted a thin trail of white smoke against a bright blue sky. It took hours to make my way up the ridge but by late morning I'd stood atop a hill overlooking a good-sized town. Which town? Smaller than Auburn, bigger than Ithaca. I carefully traced two rivers—one that came from the north, the other from the east, as they flowed around the edges of town and met in a Y at the eastern end. My heart leapt. That could only be the Susquehanna and the Chenango.

I'd made it to Binghamton alive.

I scanned for railroad tracks. On the far side of town, next to a small office and loading platform, the sun glinted off a massive iron engine. The train to Manhattan. I fell to my knees in disbelief.

Pa would never have suspected I had it in me. I never suspected I had it in me. I fought an uncontrollable urge to run to the telegraph office and tell him his namby-pamby worthless son had just made it to Binghamton in winter. If that didn't make me worth some salt, I don't know what would. Too parched to cry, I managed to laugh out loud.

Then the impossibility of Pa ever knowing of my achievement cut me suddenly, and I felt a desperate ache of loneliness. I'd never feel his pride. I'd never even see him again. Or Aunt Babe. All of Ithaca—everyone I'd ever known—would remember me forever as the traitor who let the murderer free. My name was probably already a curse word at Grant's, uttered only when one could follow it with a hearty spit.

Rulloff was now my only friend on this earth. If he was even alive.

One obstacle at a time. I was still far from safe, and after watching the rail yard for nearly an hour without seeing a single worker or dray loading a crate or box or packet of mail, I despaired that winter had shut down the trains. Then the church bell rang out from the center of town.

Sunday.

I breathed a prayer of thanks, watching as tiny people emerged from their fancy brick houses, drawn by the bell toward the center of town—ladies in colorful bonnets and wide skirts, men in dress coats. Sunday explained why the rail yard was empty.

Sunday might also help me reach the engine unseen, avoiding sticky questions. The train likely only ran once or twice a week, but I could find a good hiding place, and wait it out, maybe my crazy, desperate plan—hatched at full gallop while ducking branches—might just work after all.

I edged down the hill, sticking to the outskirts of town, past scattered timber farmhouses. At some point, to cross the Chenango and reach the rail yard, I would have to risk the center of town. The two-story homes along the river had grandly sloping roofs, with wide wooden porches and bay windows that I hoped were all empty. The streets remained quiet. I could only hope that Binghamton's pastor was long-winded.

The snow on the road had been packed firm by horses and sleighs so walking became easy for the first time in a month. I untied my rickety snowshoes and tucked them in a trash pile in a side yard. My legs grew lighter than they'd felt in weeks, as if my boots could float. I was only a block from the bridge and felt such joy at seeing the signs of people and community across the river that I wanted to shout.

Instead, I read the words of civilization with the reverence normally reserved for Bible verses: J. KENDALL STRAW BONNETS, HALBERT'S FINE FABRICS, HARRIS & SONS DRY GOODS.

Beneath the bridge, the river sparkled like diamonds, the bright white sunlight glinting off every ripple. I was so close. I hazarded a smile and was rewarded with the smell of heaven. Aunt Babe's kitchen. Food. Warmth. Love. Safety.

I shook my head and focused on the river.

Get to the train, Albert. Where's your head?

The smell returned, captivating me. A winter pie warming on a hearth brought shivers stronger than any I'd felt from the freezing cold. I could make out every carrot, every piece of chicken—even the briny scent of chard. I'd been starving for weeks, losing energy every day, and wishing desperately for food. A weak trickle of smoke escaped the chimney. If the breakfast fire was nearly out, maybe no one was home.

The street was still empty, so I climbed the wide front steps and knocked softly, then harder. I waited a solid minute before turning the fancy brass knob and easing myself into a darkened parlor. Silk-draped windows allowed in just enough light to reflect glittering shards of sunshine that danced from a crystal chandelier above and etched glass lamps below. It was as if I was staring at the river again, but this time from underneath.

The smell drew me back to a spartan kitchen where I found a tin-plated box atop an iron stove. Inside was a golden-crusted pie, still releasing steam.

I bent over the pie and broke off an edge of the crust. Flaky, rich heaven. Too desperate to search for a spoon, I cupped my hand and shoveled hot pie into my mouth, burning my fingers and tongue, but I couldn't have stopped if lightning had struck me in the middle of that kitchen.

"What are you doing here?"

It was a young girl's voice.

I panicked like a trapped rabbit, and spun around. She was maybe twelve years old, with raven-black hair and freckles that drifted over sallow, shrunken skin. A bumpy red rash crawled across her neck. She wore only nightclothes, her hands tucked into a green shawl.

"I—" I flew through possible excuses but found none that sufficed. "Good day, Miss," I managed, placing my hands behind my back—both to appear less threatening and hide their shaking. "I was just—"

"You shouldn't be here," she scolded. Her tone was accusatory but not afraid. "Mama made that for supper."

"Yes, I was just. Uh . . . Just . . . Well, good morning, Miss."

She was only a girl. I could push her aside and run. But I was flustered and couldn't think straight.

"Are you alone?"

My words came broken, jumbled. They sounded more predatory than I'd intended.

"I'm sick," she said, and this time I heard the wheeze clearly. She stared me down, head cocked, judging my intentions.

"Janie and Patience died last week. Everyone's at church. Papa made them go pray for me."

"Sick?"

I meant only to keep her occupied while I brought one hand forward at a time, unable to stop licking my fingers. I took a step toward her.

If I ran, would she scream?

She shrugged, as if I'd asked her favorite color.

"Fever."

She shuffled her bare feet, standing on the left and twisting the right underneath her. I could see by her shallow breaths that she was trying to hold off a coughing fit.

I tried to remember Rulloff's remedies for scarlet fever. They wouldn't have astragalus root in the house, and it was the wrong time of year for lemons.

"What's your name?"

"Violet."

"Violet."

"Praying is good, Miss Violet."

I was losing my train of thought.

"Better is to take a big spoonful of apple cider vinegar every morning," I told her. "Your parents, your doctors may think it's mad, but it will make you better, I promise. Sneak it if you must."

She never smiled, but the wrinkle slowly faded from her forehead.

"They'll be home soon," she said. "You should go."

"Yes," I blushed, "Of course. Thank you." A smart squirrel would scamper off, not ask more of the person who released the trap. She stepped out of the doorway, so I could pass, and I caught the strong scent of medicines she had been forced to swallow. I held her gaze and found myself hoping she would beat her fever. I'd been living in my own lonely mind for weeks. Talking to this girl had pulled me back to reality, to human contact.

"Please don't say anything about me being here," I said to the girl. I hesitated, even as I knew I needed to flee. "Say an animal got into the house, maybe, and ate the pie." I probably looked like an animal to her anyway, I realized, thinking of my mud-smeared face and filthy clothes.

"You should get back into bed, stay out of the drafts."

She looked thoughtful but said nothing.

"And don't drink any milk until you're completely well again." Finally, I tore myself away, crossed through the parlor, opened the front door and scurried to the steps.

Up the street, I caught sight of a carriage crossing the bridge. The driver held his hand to his forehead against the glare, staring straight at me. I froze on the bottom step. The man whipped the horses into a run. The bonneted head of the woman next to him bobbed as they bounced over the uneven bridge, straight at me. I had tarried too long. The girl's parents had spotted me.

I took off running, with no idea where to go. I ducked back into snowdrifts between houses. My feet no longer felt light, but heavy as hay bales each time I picked them up. I followed a snow-capped picket fence, then hopped it. A dog barked from inside. A woman ran to the window and shouted for help from someone named Karl. I turned at the laneway trying to find another path to the bridge and ran down the street, but people were returning from church all over.

"You there!" I heard a snort, the clink of a bridle close behind. "You—"

Hooves galloped behind me as I ran down the road and I turned to see a man on horseback, dressed in his Sunday suit. He leapt to the ground and knocked both of us into a snowbank. I found myself staring into the face of an older gentleman with white hair and a black cravat.

He seemed uncertain about what to do next. I read the indecision on his face. He could have punched me but he didn't. I could have punched him and taken off on his horse, but I didn't. He seemed a kind enough man, in pain from the dive off his mare.

I lay in the snow bank, looked up in to the cloudless, crystal blue sky.

How had I let myself believe I could ever succeed? Hadn't I learned how worthless I was by now?

A Canada goose honked and voices grew nearer. Then there was a brief flash before the butt of a man's rifle came down and knocked me out cold.

27

WHEN CONSCIOUSNESS RETURNED, I WISHED IT HADN'T.
My brain banged against the insides of my skull hard as a forge hammer. I rolled to my side and spit blood onto a dark stone floor.

The light of a single candle revealed my surroundings. I was tucked
into the corner of a small room—no, more like crumpled in a jail cell,
trapped by walls of stone and iron. On the far wall, the weak candlelight
danced over a handbill nailed to the back of the door. It didn't take me
long to make out the message—so urgent it screamed in block letters:

REWARD!
$2000 FOR CAPTURE OF MURDERER!

I pulled my hands to my heart, crushing it before it could beat itself
out of my chest. The drawing underneath was a perfect likeness of
that bearded face and large head I knew so well, and the words below
described the reward—an utter fortune—that was being offered by the
governor himself, thanks in part to generous donations by Presbyterians
in seven states.

At the bottom of the handbill was some smaller type I had to squint
to make out, one letter at a time:

MAY BE TRAVELING WITH BOY.

I couldn't take my eyes off the words, even to blink. I was a dead
man, sure as the sun would rise in the morning. Hopefully, they'd get
it over quick—the only mercy I'd ever been able to give the poor rabbits
in Pa's traps. I'd always felt so ill having to dispatch each trembling fur

ball with the bowie. I hated hunting, but Pa would sling the dead rabbit
on his back and say, "Worse to be the prey."

In the jail, a man sat in a simple wood chair beside a small desk,
bending over a bulging waistline to polish his boots, which were still
attached to his feet. His face was bent on his project, so all I could see
was a swirl of shocking red hair and the start of a bald patch. He was
large enough that if someone had built arms on that chair, he might
have been stuck for life. When he finished the left boot, he clapped his
hand on his knee and began whistling a tune whose notes struck me in
a vaguely haunting way.

This man would certainly have figured out the pie-stealing stranger
in his town was on the run, and fired off a telegram to Pa hours ago.
"Traveling with boy caught in Binghamton," would have clicked trium-
phantly across the wires.

"BOY."

The insult brought an unexpectedly bitter wave of anger. Pa would
have chosen the words on the handbill carefully.

But I'd been caught, hadn't I? *Foolish, foolish boy.* The only question
was whether they'd hang me in Binghamton or let Pa drag me back to
the mob in Ithaca.

How long would I have to stare at death before it came?

For now, my only hope was that the kind of man who would whistle
such a mournful song was not the same kind of man who would beat the
tar out of me. I sat up slowly, trying not to groan. An unexpected wave
of dizziness overwhelmed me, and I grabbed a bar for support. That's
when I noticed the man had kindly left my wrists free.

The whistling stopped abruptly.

"Well, good evening to you then," the man said, his voice thick with
a strange accent. I'd heard Pa complain of Irishmen in general, and the
jail-keep in Binghamton in particular, but had never seen one in the flesh.

My mouth filled with blood again, and I had to spit before I spoke.
Rulloff had been gracious when he'd arrived at our jail years ago. I tried
to follow his example.

"Eee." My jaw rung with pain. "Eeev—"

The man chuckled. "Well, you're a polite little bugger, I'll give you that. Now, I'm glad you're up. Good sign, that. Mr. Halbert gave you quite a fat lip. If you can eat, I have a biscuit here with your name on it. No gravy, though. The missus don't believe in gravy. German woman. She says they don't eat gravy where she's from, but I knew a German once who loved his gravy. Don't ever marry a German woman. That's the lesson. But biscuits we got plenty of."

I had no idea how to respond.

Was he taunting me? Leading up to some torment where he'd put food the food just out of reach?

The man leaned toward me, close enough in the small space I could feel his breath.

"You need a cloth for that face a yourn? Looks like that lip's about to split open again on you."

I nodded warily. My mouth tasted sour. The icy chill from the stone floor was seeping directly into my bones. He pulled a clean rag out of the desk drawer, but thrust out his arm first. I flinched, expecting a blow, but he handed me a fleshy palm to shake.

"Phinneas O'Toole."

I couldn't place his age between thirty and fifty, but when he smiled he had young teeth. Cautiously, I grasped his hand. "Al—"

I pulled myself up. If he hadn't yet discovered I was the BOY, I shouldn't make it easier. "—Uh, Ow. Charles Curtis," I lied, trying to absorb the merciless heart of the bully who'd tormented me.

"Pleased to meet you, Charles Curtis." He shook my hand with the fattest, pinkest fingers I'd ever seen, then handed me the rag.

"Now Mr. Curtis, I'm afraid you've found yourself some trouble, you have. Mr. Halbert is an angry fellow. You ask me, it's on account of his young girls passing, God rest their souls." He crossed himself. First time I'd seen that too. "That scarlet fever's a nasty business. Now I can't fault him his anger, but then it wasn't your fault they were taken by fever, was it?"

I held the rag against my bruised face, wondering if one spoke differently to a Papist. This one didn't appear drunk, like the drawings in the newspapers. Most importantly, he hadn't mentioned the handbill. When I took the rag away, it had turned dark with blood from my lip.

"It don't matter how rich a man you are," Phinneas said. "God can still take everything. Lucky then, I ain't a rich man. Not much for God to take from me till Judgment Day. There's the wife, of course, but He can have her if that's His plan. Bring me one who likes her gravy." Phinneas winked and handed me a biscuit.

My ravenous belly overrode the pain in my face. I shoved the biscuit in my mouth with both hands and swallowed almost without chewing. Phinneas handed me another.

"I knew you had the look of hunger about you, Mr. Curtis. Now your Mr. Halbert—well, God took a lot from him recently, and he's not yet in a place of forgiveness."

How long could I keep up the charade?

Rulloff might get free from a trap like this, but I was no Rulloff. I was just foolish Albert Jarvis. I'd never be a scholar—never even be a jail-keep now. A powerful river of shame pinned me down. Even after I was dead, my name would live on as a taunt for the weakest boys in Ithaca, more disgraceful even than Benedict Arnold.

Phinneas handed me a third biscuit.

"Careful not to eat too much too quick. Make you sick, that. One thing I know's about hunger." He ladled water from a bucket into a tin cup and handed it to me. "I tell you, some people measure their lives in words, Mr. Curtis. Others in deeds. Mr. Halbert there, I suspect he measures his life in a ledger at the Bank of Broome County. But you ask me? The only yardstick that matters is people. Up to God if we go to our graves sooner or we go later. Up to us how we treat folks long as we draw breath."

He set his hands on his knees and studied me thoughtfully.

"Mr. Halbert saw you as a man after his silver, but I'll venture you're a man down on his luck. Hungry for certain. Lost, maybe, by the look a you. Man after silver don't stop to eat a pie, is my way of thinking. That about the truth of it?"

I managed a small nod.

"Lesson in that too. You got to steal, do it from poor folks who can grasp what hunger means to a man. Now Miss Violet told me—grown up as a wee lass could be—that you didn't mean any harm. That don't change the law, but it means I ain't gonna make it any easier on 'em to ruin a man's life over an empty belly."

Phinneas pulled a bound book from his desk and uncorked the inkwell. He took as much care with wetting the nib on his tongue as he had with polishing his shoes. "Fourth of Feb-ru-ary, eighteen and fifty-six." He held the pen carefully in his meaty hand and wrote slowly. "Mr. Halbert of River Road returned from church to find Mr. Charles Curtis trying to rob his silver."

"But I wasn't trying to steal any silver."

He ignored me and kept writing.

"Mr. Curtis attempted flight. Pursued by several members of town. Apprehended by Mr. Lee of Fourth Street." Phinneas chuckled, then laughed outright. "Whatever you've done or not done, I tell you old Howard Lee ain't ever going to get over his heroic feat today. You provided that man with the highlight of his life, you did."

"Mr. O'Toole, I was hungry. It was only a pie."

"Now, I need a guilty or innocent from you, Mr. Curtis, do you follow? The charge is trying to steal Mr. Halbert's silver. If you're found guilty of the very *specific* crime you're charged with, you'll get sent off to Auburn Prison."

Auburn. Atwood would recognize me in a heartbeat, and there'd barely be time for ice baths before Pa showed up with the noose.

"I wasn't after silver."

"Excellent. I'll write that down as innocent then. Now it's up to you to convince the judge and not just old Phinneas. You are a fearsome stranger here in Binghamton, and the judge don't have the look of a man who's ever skipped a meal. You got family you can write to? May help to have someone speak for your character."

Aunt Babe? I remembered the last ugly frown she'd given me. *"You fool! You've no idea what you've done."* The biscuits came up in a rush of vomit.

Phinneas calmly emptied the bucket of water over the floor, then sat back at his desk as if it had never happened.

"Got to be someone," he said. "Tomorrow I'll get you a basin and blade. Maybe cleaned up you won't look like such a heathen. But you want to get free, you're gonna need help, Mr. Curtis."

I spoke slowly so Phinneas could scratch the words out—and so that I could choose them carefully.

Professor Leurio
Care of the Astor Library, New York City

Dear Sir,
I hope you've reached your destination successfully. I regret to inform you
that I have been detained in the Binghamton jail over a misunderstanding.
If you are still in need of an apprentice, I would be most grateful for any
assistance you could provide from afar.

Your friend,
Charles Curtis

28

IT TOOK SEVERAL WEEKS BEFORE THEY COULD TRY MY case because the judge had a head cold. Day after excruciating day, I waited for someone to discover I was BOY, but apparently no one did—not Mr. Halbert who came to spit on me, his attorney, or Mrs. O'Toole, who brought broth and schnitzel, but true to form, no gravy.

I never did hear back from Rulloff. He could have died, I told myself. Or sailed for Vienna. Or taken the Oregon Trail. There were a thousand reasons he might not have received my letter, but still, the silence dug a deep hollow into my chest. The handbill remained up, curling at the edges, so he remained at large. I wanted it to be enough that he was free, to feel magnanimous about trading shackles with my teacher. Instead, I was terrified and humiliated—and his silence drove a bitter wedge of loneliness into my heart.

On the morning of my trial, Phinneas entered for the first time without a whistle to announce him. He stared at me hard, as if trying to puzzle his way through a riddle, then fumbled with the key in his sausage fingers. He handed me a slice of fried ham and a biscuit in a cloth, leaving the cell door open.

"I called on the Halberts this morning," he said, ruddy cheeks rising from his all-business face. "Miss Violet is much improved, thanks be to God. She told me her good turn was because a mud-creature told her to drink vinegar. Mr. Halbert called it a dream, and Mrs. Halbert credits an angel, but old Phinneas has some idea who that particular creature may have been."

I grinned through a mouth stuffed with biscuit and Phinneas joined me in joyful a smile, and barked a laugh. Then he got serious again.

"Those Halberts owe you a sizable debt, and that's what I'm going to remember here. That and you were never after the silver." He stared me down, hard as Pastor Isaiah. So, I'm going to wish you good luck and fortune, Mr. Curtis, and hand you over to your attorney." He tipped his hat, then disappeared, leaving both doors open.

I finally swallowed, but now my mind was a blur. *What attorney?*

I ran my fingers over the frame of the open cell door, waiting for someone like the one-armed sod in Ithaca—stinking of whiskey and missing all his teeth—to tell me to change my plea to guilty so he could get back to the pub. Still, I'd have to see the judge. I took another bite of the ham, brushed the dirt off my pant legs and focused on trying to close the one remaining button on my coat with one hand.

"Hello again, Mr. Curtis."

I glanced up at the top-hatted figure of a large man, head bowed in greeting. Beneath a black frock coat I caught sight of a peacock-green vest. Fancy for these parts. When he raised his head, I collapsed against the wall.

Rulloff stood in front of me.

"Steady, Charles. Your ordeal is nearly over."

Edward Rulloff. Stood facing me. In a *jail*.

The ham hit the floor before I'd realized I dropped it.

"I'm glad to find you looking well. I was sorry to hear about your circumstances, but happy to be able to clear up the misunderstanding."

He'd shaved his beard, trimmed his curls, and donned dapper clothing, but to my eyes he was identical to the man on the handbill.

REWARD!
$2000 FOR CAPTURE OF MURDERER!

I was too stunned to speak. Why on earth had Rulloff risked his life to come to Binghamton?

To save me.

I pressed my fist to my mouth to keep from crying out. He was going to defend me in court. I wasn't alone after all.

"Now, I know this is quite a bit to take in, but the train to the city departs in a quarter-hour, so we must hurry."

"What?" Confusion overrode my bursting heart and I barely remembered to swallow. "I can't. My case gets tried this afternoon."

Who could hear us?

I pointed toward the handbill, but it was on the back side of the open door.

Rulloff smiled, calm as if he'd been fishing on an August afternoon.

"Oh, that's taken care of." He waved his hand as if I was referring to a trifle instead of a trial. "I spoke with the judge this morning. He's ruled you innocent. You're free to leave, but if we miss this train home, the next one isn't until Friday."

Rulloff took my arm and led me outside. I blinked back tears in the sunshine.

Home?

WE WALKED PAST a domed courthouse and a blinding white field of snow to the main street that led to the rail yard. The icy cold stung like nettles in my lungs, and I tried to keep my chin tucked away from the few souls who braved the weather. Rulloff didn't appear concerned.

"Morning," he said, tipping his hat to everyone we passed.

TRAVELING WITH BOY had been words before. Now it was truth.

The sweet shop was plastered with handbills. The breeze rustled three of Rulloff's faces at FERBER'S HOES, KNIVES & SHARPENING. A woman exited the baker's so close I could feel the rush of warmth from inside.

"Oh my," she said when she saw us—wide eyes revealing her surprise. "But isn't that a chilly wind."

Certainly, a hundred people had spotted us from the houses and shops lining the block by now. A limping old man brushed past my arm, so close I flinched.

"Pay them no mind," Rulloff said casually. He smiled at strangers occupied with packages and fussing children. "Walk without care, as if we are discussing the weather or the racing scores. The best place to hide is in plain sight."

The steam whistle blew. If we missed the train, we'd be stuck. We'd be recognized. We'd be killed. I started to run, but Rulloff held my arm firmly and refused to alter his pace.

"Listen carefully. On the train we'll need to explain your appearance, so this is the story: You're a young gentleman from Third Avenue, distantly related to the Stuyvesants. I'm the family tutor. After visiting your aunt, a carriage accident killed your driver, and you became lost in the woods. Your family and I have all been worried."

I pulled away from his arm, into the shadow of an alley.

"But I've never even been to Third Avenue! Who are the Stuyvesants? How can I tell that story?"

"Calm down. You won't *tell* the story. That would sound defensive. You'll *live* the story. You remember what I taught you long ago? People will believe anything you say as long as you're—"

"Confident, articulate, and poised."

My racing heart slowed.

"Exactly. *Be* Charles Curtis of Third Avenue and a fugitive will be the furthest thing from their minds." He took my arm again and led me back out into the bright sun. "The key to deception is sloth. Few people make the effort to consider facts by their merit. All you need to do is fill their mind with what you want them to think—the way a magician guides the eyes—and truth becomes whatever you say it is."

As we came upon the train station, I tried to mimic his upright posture. Across the yard, steam from the iron-banded engine billowed across the tracks, shrouding the train in a heavy wet fog. Hazy glimpses revealed its cargo. Instead of the fancy salons I'd expected from newspaper etchings, the cars on the Binghamton line were made from the scavenged parts of unmatched horse carriages.

A man with muddy boots and a chestnut derby made a final dash up a short ladder. "'Board!" the agent shouted with a white puff of breath. I heard a clunk that must have been the release of the brake. With a release of steam, the wheels edged forward. We were still several hundred yards away.

Rulloff held our casual pace, as if we were any two friends who'd known each other a decade. Skipping the station, we wound our way through barrels and crates, then angled toward a red-and-orange carriage. Rulloff waved a set of tickets in the air and the agent motioned us to hurry.

The train edged from walk to a trot. I cinched up my torn trousers to run but Rulloff never wavered. He walked casually, consistently. When we reached the tracks, we had just enough time to hop onto the bottom step of the ladder, open the door underneath the faded PHILADEL-PHIA STAGE lettering, and climb inside.

"How did you manage that?" I asked, stunned at his sense of timing.

"Oldest legal strategy in the book," he said, misunderstanding my question.

29

RULLOFF PULLED THE DOOR CLOSED, AND I SQUEEZED beside him onto a bench upholstered in ripped leather, facing two men. One wore a red silk waistcoat, strained at the buttons. His look was hard to read, but a fuzzy black eyebrow arched into a tense bow over his left eye. The other man adjusted a pair of spectacles and fondled his full white beard. After a long look at my appearance, he crossed his legs in front of a case under the seat.

I became immediately aware of every rip and hole in my filthy clothing. Thanks to Phinneas, I'd been able to clean myself and shave, but I must still look a fright to these strangers. I removed my battered hat and clutched it tightly in my lap.

"Now don't forget you have an appointment with the dean tomorrow." Rulloff turned to face me with a stern look, pried the hat out of my hands, and set it gently on a hat rack I'd not noticed. "I don't want to hear you were out to all hours with the Van Deusinghams at the Century Club. If that accident was good for anything, I hope you now see it's time to get serious about life," he said.

I had a vague recollection of those names from the society pages and guessed Rulloff expected our companions would as well.

"Yes, Professor," I said, chagrined. But my words felt off as I watched the two strangers study my response. The space felt suddenly smaller, claustrophobic. I had to become someone new, and I had to do it quickly.

How would dandy Charles Curtis of Third Avenue behave? He wouldn't give a fig about his teacher's advice, for one. *What would confidence like that feel like? To not worry at every minute what people thought of you? To be able to act as you felt—tired, irritable, petulant—consequences be damned?*

"Heaven forbid," I said, raising my hands in mock surrender, letting my tone edge toward farce. *"Bien sur. Je promets. Pas de cognac ce soir."*

Both wary passengers glanced at me at the same time, then quickly looked away, as if they weren't trying to puzzle out the paradox seated across from them. The man with the red waistcoat made a show of glancing at his gold pocket watch several times, his frown making the dimple in his chin disappear into a tight nest of wrinkles. I dug my too-long fingernails into my fists, and tried to remain poised. Our converted stage moved as if it was sliding on skates across a frozen lake.

"Perhaps one of you gentlemen can aid us," Rulloff said by way of introduction. "I'm afraid my student and I have fallen into a small dis-agreement." He waited until both men met his gaze. "He recalls of course, that Socrates taught Plato and Plato taught Aristotle, but would one of you be so kind as to remind my young friend whom Aristotle himself instructed?"

He ignored their puzzled looks and addressed me directly.

"We're all grateful you survived, Charles, and can't imagine the hor-rors you must have encountered in those woods, but you must learn that such knowledge is far from *humbug*. Let us use adversity to shape our characters, rather than soften our minds, shall we? Now, Aristotle's pupil was—"

The man in the white beard opened his mouth, closed it, then opened it again.

"You mean Alexander the Great?"

"Exactly!" Rulloff exclaimed, snapping his fingers as if he'd discov-ered gold. "Now don't look so disheartened, Charles. It will come back as soon as you're ready to apply yourself."

Rulloff left me to pretend-sulk and introduced himself as Professor Leurio. The one with the beard took one last glance at me then shook Rulloff's hand with an age-spotted fist.

"Almon Richmond," he said. The one with the watch—a Mr. Hornberger—finally relaxed into conversation as well.

The three of them chatted about the Hudson in autumn, the merits of German philosophers, and the outrageous price of French wine.

Rulloff casually dropped in a few details of my life—not a black sheep, really, but perhaps a touch gray, father in shipping, often overseas, mother thought a trip to visit his aunt would do him good.

Faking a scowl, I secretly marveled at the brilliance of his tactics. He left the men intrigued by the mysteries of my accident, tempting them with a few seductive clues—a gelding named Jack, unaccountable fear of squirrels, ice storm—to imagine for themselves the horrible story. So entranced were they in the mystery of what had transpired that neither ever appeared to question if what he said was true.

"Mr. Leurio," Mr. Richmond beamed. "I'm grateful for the opportunity of a professor's opinion on the unique items in my case. Perhaps, Mr. Curtis, you might find these of educational interest as well."

I leaned forward.

Was this a test?

One gap in the conversation and Rulloff had lost control of the magic show.

"I am in the midst of installing a small museum of curiosities in my parlor," Richmond continued. "My own humble *Wünderkammer,* and have just picked up an excellent specimen from a western trader." He laid the case on his lap, opened the buckles and removed a bundle of linen about the size of an acorn squash. He took great care to hold it with both hands, to move with the skating carriage, so as not to jostle the contents.

"Please. Have a look," he said.

Rulloff unwrapped a bleached skull, missing its jaw.

"Ah," he said, holding the item aloft for quite a long time. "An Indian, was he?"

Richmond clapped his hands with glee. "Correct! Very impressive deduction from a skull alone."

How'd he known that?

"See this, Charles?" Rulloff continued, to my amazement. "He received a terrible blow that fractured the temporal bone and the zygomatic process. The lambdoidal suture is almost obliterated. He must have been a man of considerable age."

When had he studied craniometry?

Both Richmond and Hornberger turned their attention to me. They expected a response, but while Rulloff had sent hundreds of letters and several books to Aunt Babe's farm over the years, human bones had never been part of our curriculum. *What could I contribute to such a discussion?* Rulloff had given me an out, I realized. Charles Curtis was a poor student—an educated but lazy rogue. I didn't have to follow their lead at all.

"Alas, poor Yorick," I sighed and rolled my eyes, then turned my gaze out the window so no one could see me smile at my cleverness.

Richmond carefully rewrapped the skull and placed it into his case.

"I'll be sure to include the zygomatic information on the specimen card."

He and Rulloff then fell into discussion of an amethyst geode, a small fly trapped in amber, and the exoskeleton of a massive insect called a *Dryococelus australis*. Each time, Rulloff not only recognized the item but could state some fact about where it originated or how it was formed or its unusual reproductive habits. I had to keep staring out the window so the men wouldn't see the shock on my face. Rulloff may have been playing a role, but he was not some carnival magician. In truth, he was a powerful sorcerer who'd memorized the contents of practically every book he'd ever come in contact with.

The journey took many hours, but Rulloff's show satisfied its audience, and the men accepted our story. As long as daylight lasted, we played whist on Mr. Richmond's upturned case, a fairly simple game whose rules I deciphered easily enough. But as the sun set we took to quietly staring out the window and napping. I could scarce believe the train could continue at full speed in the diminishing light. Soon, I struggled to even make out the spindly shapes of the trees lining the tracks.

Finally, a hollow echo under the carriage caught my attention. We were on a bridge crossing a wide body of water. The moon had risen high enough to shed its ghostly light on a ragged stretch of coastline ahead, lined with low huts, cottage gardens, and hundreds of roaming pigs.

"Welcome home," said Rulloff, and winked at me.

I tried to judge his tone. *Was he joking?* This was as far from my image of New York as could exist—it looked like Mr. Snyder's hog farm—but Rulloff's face held no trace of a smile.

Where were the Chinamen and libraries? The scholars and butterflies pinned to cards?

Mr. Hornberger removed his watch again, squinting to read it in the darkness.

"We'll reach the station more than an hour late. That's the Binghamton line, for you. Now the trains to Philadelphia and Charleston arrive at the very minute."

He clicked his watch closed, his action timed to coincide exactly with the last word of his statement.

As we steamed south under a waxing moon, the coastline gave way to rolling hills, rows of spinach to racing grounds, surveyor sticks to building sites. Finally, I began to see the candlelit windows of larger farmhouses. Rulloff retrieved his hat from the rack, but I couldn't be pulled from the glass. I stared into every window we passed for some novelty, yet even as the houses turned from wood to brick to stone, and grew from two stories to three to five, I saw only families sharing supper on tiny tables in crowded rooms and walls insulated with newspaper as at home. People and animals hustled to get out of the way of the train as we flew down the street.

When we finally pulled up to the platform, a man with a cap turned the handle and opened our carriage door. I'd arrived in New York City! I forced a bored scowl onto my face, even as I took a deep breath to celebrate the full glory of my achievement. My lungs filled with the rotten smell of garbage.

Back in Ithaca, I'd visited Schuyler's Dry Goods store every week to pick up flour, coffee, or molasses, lingering as long as he'd let me to read and reread his *New York City for the Traveler* book. I'd memorized the map etching on pages thirty-six and thirty-seven, but was struggling to put it into use because I didn't know our starting point. I would have liked to ask Rulloff which station we'd arrived at, but there were too many ears nearby to overhear such a naive question.

Instead, I followed him toward a waiting vehicle along with the rest of the passengers, something like an oversized carriage but with a team of eight horses instead of two or four. An omnibus, I realized with a spark of joy. That meant we'd arrived at Rose Hill Station and would be conveyed another dozen or so blocks south to Union Square, where the journey would officially end. Full of glee I read an ornately painted sign near the entry door, but its words brought an unexpected rush of disgust.

NEGROS FORBIDDEN.

Inside, the walls were lined on both sides with velvet-clad benches and decorated with wallpaper, carpet, and flickering wall sconces. It reminded me exactly of the fancy parlor at Clinton House, had Clinton House been set on wheels to convey people down the street. Rulloff moved to help Hornberger with his luggage, but stumbled with the weight and fell practically into the man's lap, apologizing with a hearty laugh.

Had I seen a flash from his pocket?

To keep from looking too eagerly out the brocade-curtained windows like a country rube, I glanced at the handbills that had been shoved into my fist during the short walk between the train and the horsecar by a fleet of young boys.

The first was for a peep show of a live alligator JUST ROUND THE CORNER ON 15TH. Another advertised a Lyceum lecture on the Crimea. The third promised intimate and discreet conversational opportunities at MRS. WHEATLAN'S FINE GENTLEMAN'S PARLOR. I was trying to work out whether that was polite code for a whorehouse, when I came to the fourth handbill.

REWARD!
$2000 FOR CAPTURE OF MURDERER!
MAY BE TRAVELING WITH BOY.

30

WE'D ONLY TRAVELED A HANDFUL OF BLOCKS WHEN, OUT
of the darkness, light exploded all around. An open square gleamed
through the windows, lit so brightly by gas lamps that I could see people strolling around after dark—without lanterns—in a kind of permanent twilight.

Hundreds of women in colored hats and men in stovepipes passed
each other surrounded by glowing, gas-lit snow flurries. They wandered
into shops and restaurants and taverns under light from street lamps,
store windows, and carriages. For all I'd read of the city, I'd never imagined an entire street could feel so alive, hours past sunset.

I had to keep from staring at the marvel when we exited at Union
Square. Rulloff waved goodbye to our companions, then set a firm hand
on my shoulder, hustling me south toward Broadway as I thrilled to
finally explore the beating heart of the city. We pushed into a wild river
of people that stretched as far as I could see. This was no lazy stream
but a storm-tossed tumble of eddies and crosscurrents: Humans and
dogs traveled the stone walks in all directions, blocking each other's
path. Livestock, mounted riders, carriages, wagons, and carts filled the
muddy chasm in between with equal disarray.

A sign on a lamppost stated we were at the corner of 13th Street,
and so oriented, I stared up into the miracle of its flame that burned so
bright it stung my eyes. When I glanced down, I found the corpse of a
dog at its base.

"Don't look back," Rulloff said firmly, but he needn't have bothered.

My eyes were drawn forward to the shops, whose cheery windows
reached nearly from floor to ceiling. With some kind of modern wiz-
ardry, they stood tall as me, without a single wooden pane for support.
As we moved through the crush I saw grand pianos, gold chains, and

fine pistols lit through the glass. One window displayed all varieties of tobacco in great colored bins, ivory-stemmed pipes, and a printed sign promising Turkish cigarettes. Another held brocade settees and silver trays and carved writing desks.

On the corner, Rulloff paused behind a used bookseller's cart and glanced back at the square. I followed his gaze and saw that Hornberger had found himself a policeman. Some unknowable instinct burned in the pit of my stomach, and I knew suddenly that they were hunting for us.

I ducked my head low and busied myself riffling through *Northanger Abbey* on the cart, then a Bible with gilt edging, then something by Dickens. There were more books on that one cart than in any store in Ithaca, and carts like it on every corner. But any joy I might have felt was buried under slick, cold fear. *Had Hornberger read the handbill? Had he recognized us?* My fingers grew icy through the holes in my gloves, and I blew into my hands as the temperature plummeted. I was running for my life again.

"Don't lose sight of me," Rulloff said, then pushed off into the crowd.

Trying to keep eyes on him, I realized how much all the men looked the same—black hat, black broadcloth coat, stiff white collar, and dark trousers. It was as much the uniform of New York gentlemen as the stripes at Auburn were for prisoners. In the anonymity of the sidewalk, I saw how I had to take the measure of each man in a split-second glance. *Friend or foe? Kind or gruff?* I also saw, much to my detriment, that they were doing the same of me.

There was no time to speak French or quote Goethe to establish credentials. My clothes had to speak to the content of my character, and in this place, my wide country hat and tattered brown coat marked me an outcast. Women drew away, men pulled their elbows tight over pocketbooks. My ears were chewed raw by the cold, while somewhere behind me—I didn't dare look back—Hornberger and a policeman were on our tail.

It was only Rulloff's unusually large head that let me pick him out from behind each bonnet and potato wagon as he zigzagged through the crowd. Three blocks down, he stopped next to a young girl to let me catch up. In one outstretched palm, she held out a chipped plate and in the other, a dirty apple from an upturned bucket, both evidently for sale. The snow danced circles around her rag-wrapped feet.

"Not today, I'm afraid," Rulloff told her as I drew up behind.

"How far is it to our rooms?" I asked, expecting Hornberger to spot us at any moment. The frost from my breath caught the light and obscured his face in fog.

"Ah," he said, his voice no longer that of an enthusiastic train companion but an exhausted traveler. He walked the rest of the block in a silent, metered lockstep.

"That requires some explanation," he finally said, stepping into the street. "Follow me."

"I've studied maps." I tried not to sound too proud as I followed. "We're about to cross 9th, am I right?"

I then managed to trip over the rear end of a wayward pig and fall to my knees in the icy mud.

"Watch it, you guttersnipe!"

A man with a gold-tipped cane struck me in the shoulder, then took a swipe at the apple girl for good measure. She jumped out of the way, but her bucket was not as fast and the apples rolled into the street.

I leapt to my feet and looked behind, certain that Hornberger would have noticed the commotion, but he was two blocks behind us, halfway up a set of steps, scanning the crowd. Rulloff, invisible in his gentleman's uniform, would have been much safer to leave me behind, but he waited patiently for me to catch up.

"This way," he said, pulling me by the elbow up a half-flight of marble steps into the massive hall of a great hotel. I counted at least six doormen in red coats with brass buttons who turned to follow my movements, ready to intercede with a rogue who so clearly didn't belong.

In massive, gold-framed mirrors that lined both sides of the hall, I was reminded of why. The boy who stared back in my reflection struck me as even shabbier—more suspect and inappropriate—than I'd imagined. I wouldn't have trusted him for a moment. The boy in that mirror looked so afraid, so improper, and so out of his depth, I was overcome with shame, and on its heels, homesickness.

I tried to shake off such nonsense. Soon enough I would belong in this great place, and provincial Ithaca would be a distant memory. But for now, everyone was watching. And Hornberger was chasing.

From the large hall I heard the patter of a running fountain and—incongruously—birdsong. We walked onto a carpet as large as Babe's kitchen garden. I glanced over at a doorman who fixed his eyes on his shoes, though his ears were clearly following every step.

Over the din of conversation and clack of heels, Rulloff raised his voice.

"Next time, I want your assurances the grain will be shipped separately. All the rat damage is coming out of your pocket, not mine."

He led me to a carved walnut door, opened it, and shoved me inside. Finally, our lodgings! But inside I found only a hallway, leading past several other doors, until it finally opened to an alleyway.

"Soon, Albert, everything will be as we planned."

If this was meant to be comforting, it had the opposite effect.

"Soon?"

Rulloff rolled his eyes, then quickly rearranged his features. "I'd intended to get settled before you joined me. I expected to have more time."

I followed Rulloff back into the cold night air. We'd escaped Hornberger, but I had a growing sense our trials were far from over.

"Any bed will do," I said, hoping to revive his mood.

"Listen to me, Albert. This fine clothing was meant to fool others, not you. We don't have a bed. We don't have a room. Furthermore, we don't have a penny to our names to acquire a room. Every cent I'd managed to acquire is now sitting in the pocket of your judge in Binghamton. That was the price of your freedom."

I took this all in with a shiver. I'd expected bad news, but this was far worse than I'd imagined.

"All we have to keep us from freezing on the street tonight is what we can sell." He withdrew his hand and opened his fist to reveal Hornberger's pocket watch.

I drew back, surprised that I didn't feel more surprised. I *had* seen a flash on the omnibus.

"You *stole* it." I was overcome with gratitude for this chance at survival.

"Of course I stole it," he barked, misunderstanding my tone. "Why shouldn't I? They stole everything from *me*. My freedom, my dignity, my name. They're still trying to take my life!" He set the watch back into his pocket and glared at me. "But what of you? I told you to stay put until I wrote for you. What the hell were you doing in Binghamton?"

Sudden shame hit me like nausea. Rulloff thought I was being completely ungracious when he'd just risked his life for me, was risking it even now.

"You're right. I can never thank you enough. Pa found the letters and he—" The thought of the bullet whizzing past my head made me go cold, and I found myself struggling to speak. "I ran into the hills to get away. I had to steal too. Eggs and cheese from farmers. A pie from a merchant."

"So you traveled to Binghamton on foot? In *February*? Goodness. You *survived*, Albert. You did what you had to do. I hope you feel enormous pride."

"I'll do anything I can to help us," I said, secretly boxing up his awe as a precious gift to hold forever in my heart. He was the only one who would ever know of my accomplishment, who could ever appreciate my tiny moment of courage.

"You must have had a hell of a time of it. Good Lord." He slapped me on the back. "Look, we've had setbacks, certainly, but today marks the beginning of our rise. Seneca would tell us this moment is what we practice privation for. You trust me, don't you Albert?"

"Of course."

I spoke before I could think, but as I reflected, I was mostly sure the answer still felt right.

"Then you must understand. I barely arrived here with my life. I had to beg space in a cramped flophouse in exchange for unloading wine casks. The next night all I could trade were coal fragments I scavenged off the street like an orphaned child. The funds that paid for these clothes and your judge was a one-time opportunity—"

"I'm willing to work hard," I said. "I'll get a job to contribute."

He sighed, then waved away my enthusiasm with a sideways glance that held only pity.

"Look, the first time I came to the city as a young man, I failed because I tried to be an honest worker in a dishonest world. Don't be fooled by the grandness of this city. It is Machiavellian to its core. The game is rigged. The cards marked. We need cunning here just to survive. But if we are to go further—if you and I are to change the world—we must also secure copious time for study. That means adjustments to our principles in service of the greater good. So yes, Albert. We must be thieves for a while."

I took all this in and reminded myself of three essential facts: Rulloff had generously taught me for ten years, he had just risked his life to save mine, and one day he would be as celebrated as Galileo. I was extraordinarily fortunate to be his friend, and as his apprentice, I'd do anything he asked.

"I suppose an honest scholar is not a very successful scholar," I paraphrased, causing Rulloff to laugh heartily.

"That's the very thing!" He put his arm around my shoulder, surprising me with his sudden change of mood. "All right, then. We're currently behind the St. Nicholas Hotel, and unless you want a quick trip to the Tombs, this is not the place to conduct our sordid business. You say you've studied the maps. Do you wish to hazard a guess where we might have the best chance of success selling a stolen watch?"

There was only one answer to this question, and it was infamous even in Ithaca as the den of all depravity, wickedness, and drunkenness. I tried to hide my shivers and reminded myself if I'd had enough grit to survive the past several weeks, surely I could brave a neighborhood in the city.

I swallowed my fear and answered, "We must go to Five Points."

31

EXITING THE ALLEY, WE TURNED BRIEFLY BACK TO
Broadway, and then onto Spring. Before the block ended, the street
lamps had disappeared and darkness overwhelmed the filthy alleys. The
structures were five and six stories tall, but stood barely a cart width
apart. I fought an urge to stand in the center of the street and see if
I could touch the buildings on opposing corners at the same time. On
one corner, a stout woman roasted peanuts on a fire. Opposite, a white-
haired Negro blew into his hands and shuffled down the street. Outside
the dazzle of Broadway, the few people about in this weather looked
even more ragged than I did.

There wasn't a single direction-finding sign here and the careful
mental map I'd followed since Union Square became a hopeless jumble
in the warren of odd-shaped intersections below Canal. From this frozen wasteland, taverns beckoned like churches for the damned, promising light, warmth, and companionship for the hopeless—a category
to which we nearly belonged. Rulloff stopped at a pub across from a
small open square. Above the door, two flickering lanterns illuminated
a small green sign painted with looping O's that spelled out O'BRIENS
ON ORANGE—though someone had scratched out Orange and written
BAXTER.

Three stray dogs followed us inside, as if they could smell the only
human for a mile who'd eaten breakfast. We pushed our way through
a raucous crowd of coffee-colored mulattos, yellow-tinted Chinese, and
red-bearded Irishmen clumped in mixed groups around upturned barrels. I overheard bits of German, Yiddish, and Italian. It felt like the
circus that had arrived in Ithaca one summer on a barge.

Over the drunken din and a mournful fiddle I couldn't see, I
heard the telltale rhythmic thump of a sin parlor overhead. The ceiling

dripped in several places with yellow-green slime. I felt an extraordinary awe to be standing in the heart of Five Points—a place I'd only read about in the temperance essays that lobbied for razing it to the ground.

Rulloff held his hands behind his back, standing tall to see over the betting tables. A steep flight of stairs led up a darkened hallway to the right, blocked by a thin brunette with a bulging growth on her neck and her companion. It took me embarrassingly long to figure out what she was doing, leaning on a black man, her skirts about his shoulders. *Had she fallen?* Then with a start I discovered their activity and nearly lost my composure. Grant's may have had its share of prostitutes, but no one would ever have been so brazen as to commit such acts in public. My face grew hot.

Rulloff elbowed me gently, and I tried to follow his gaze across the bar, past a barely conscious woman with two young children crawling about her feet. A tall man sat in a too-small chair in front of a plate of oysters. When he looked up, I saw a burn scar and stitched up eye. I froze in recognition and turned to run, but he saw us and beckoned with a small flick of his wrist.

Would he remember me?

"Din't 'spect you back," he said to Rulloff by way of greeting. "Or looking so dandy. You're in far finer form than when I saw you last, that's sure. You have more already?"

"Not tonight," Rulloff said, taking a chair across the table from the man. Cautiously I followed and sat to Rulloff's right, realizing too late the chair seat was sticky with spilled beer.

All I could think about was the rifle I'd held under the table while the slave catcher had stomped boot tracks all through Aunt Babe's house, but he didn't even look twice at me.

What possible business could Rulloff have had with—

The man's profession drove a painful spike of realization through my heart. Slave catcher. Runaway slaves. People got paid a handsome reward for information leading to capture. I'd left Grace and Rebecca in Rulloff's care. He'd promised to keep them safe.

"Pity," the slave catcher said, turning his attention back to his oysters. "Bringing the wife back a crate of French porcelain this trip. Woulda loved to get her a necklace and brooch set to go with it. Woman's a true saint, in every sense a the word."

"I'm hoping you might have information for me this time," Rulloff said. "If so, I may be able to pay *you* for your trouble."

"My line a work, one's got to stay motivated, and the wife's mine," the man said. "I keep a mangy old horse for myself, but Euphemia Jane, she is a jewel among women. She has a kitchen slave already, 'course, but I'm saving up for another. I got a plan. Wife's plan, really. We're gonna buy us a mulatto girl, young enough to breed, then sell the babes soon as they're weaned. Euphemia Jane doesn't mind my involvement cause the more light skinned the more profit."

Was he actually talking so casually of raping his slave girl?

Rulloff reached into his vest pocket and discreetly took a peek at the time shown on Hornberger's gold watch.

"I find myself compelled to find a new home for this particularly elegant timepiece," he said, returning the watch and picking up the crumpled green napkin in the center of the table, folding it into a trim rectangle. "I know this isn't your business, and would certainly not make a very romantic gift to your wife, but I'd share ten percent of the proceeds with the man who directed me to a discreet and generous purchaser."

"Soon enough I'll give up this road business, move the family to Savannah, and open me an ice cream saloon. A proper one with papered walls and marble tables and silver spoons that draw people from the finest houses." He waved his arm around the room, "Unlike this Northern filth, you can hand a Southern man a silver spoon to eat from and know he ain't gonna pocket it when he's done. That's the beauty of a place where honor's prized more 'n gold."

"I may not be a Southern gentleman," Rulloff said in the pause that followed, "but I assure you I place a very high value on honor. I am a man who follows through on my word—as you found from our last exchange."

Were Grace and Rebecca locked up somewhere in the city, or had they already been shipped back? Two women equaled a crate of French porcelain like twelve beaver pelts equaled a rifle?

"I degrade myself in this Northern hellhole so that I may purify myself on return to God's country," the man said, "with gifts for the wife. So I've heard names from time to time. For twenty-five percent of your take, and nothing less on your honor—I'll tell you that one of them's called Maggie. Not acquainted with her directly, mind. My business is entirely legal and hers ain't anywhere near it. What I hear, she'd steal a steak right off your plate. On the other hand, she's not like to turn you in 'cause no one on earth is more anti-government than she is. That's worth twenty-five percent, 'cause anyone else's gonna double their money by stealing your stolen watch, then calling in the coppers to pin the theft on you."

Rulloff agreed to the man's terms and listened to his directions, but I couldn't focus on any of it. I bit hard on the inside of my cheek. I wanted to punch the man so hard his one good eye fell out.

32

I FOLLOWED RULLOFF AS HE NAVIGATED A NARROW MUD alley under strings of frozen laundry. In my head, I confronted him about his broken promise. I imagined standing up for my principles, denouncing his treachery and striding away into the night. Kant would have done it. Kant would probably also have frozen to death like that dog on the lamppost. An honest prince is a dead prince in New York City.

The walls on either side of the narrow passageway amplified an infant's wail to an ear-piercing shriek. I suppose I could have found a gentle way to ask Rulloff why he'd betrayed my confidence, but I already knew what he'd say: He needed the money. It was unfortunate but necessary. The real question that burned inside me as I followed him into the dark was a deeper why. A question for which I knew no answer existed.

Why did it have to be necessary? Why did Aunt Babe have to be right?

At the end of the alley we came to a larger street, lined with wooden structures so decayed that most of the windows were missing their shutters. An old woman with a single glove hunched in the darkness, trying to collect the debris from a collapsed staircase into a sack.

Silently, I followed Rulloff through a rotting doorframe and up a sagging staircase, steep as a ladder and pitch black. A freezing wind blew straight through the walls, rippling papers pasted to the sides as insulation. At the fifth-floor landing, I had to duck to fit under the rafters. Rulloff rapped on a tiny door that stood no taller than my chest.

"Got the wrong room," a woman's voice barked. "Girl's one floor down." There was a pause for a moment as Rulloff considered how to respond. "And don't even think of not paying full, or her mother will see you dead in a ditch."

"We're looking for Maggie," Rulloff said. "We were sent by a friend."

After a moment, the door swung open, flooding the dark landing with candlelight, so I had to squint to see the woman inside. She was large as a cart horse, with auburn hair and several chins. Behind her, I glimpsed an attic room, the shape of which suggested a sloping roof with dormer windows. I could only guess, though because I couldn't see past a hundred bags of flour, sacks of potatoes, and barrels of who-knows-what that lined every square inch of the plank floor.

Maggie looked us up and down, easier for her than us since we stood in light and she in shadow. Her sideways stance felt aggressive: One hand still clutched the door handle. The other perched angrily on the back of her hip.

"Who the hell are you pair a contraries, then? Mister Crystal Palace an' Farmer Frank? You say one word trying to sell me on your religion, and I'll send you both straight to hell by the staircase."

Rulloff smiled in the face of her threats, something I was unable to do.

"We have a certain item of value," he said. "We'd like to offer you the opportunity to profit from its sale."

Smoke billowed through the open door and burned my eyes. There was no fireplace, but she had chiseled a few bricks out of the chimney to warm the room. Other than the grocery goods, a heap of straw, a stool, and a soup pot were the only items I could see.

"And you are?"

"Professor Leurio at your service," he said. I thought he might bow and was glad when he didn't go that far. "My colleague and I find that we—"

"You." She turned to face me. "Name." Before I could think of what to say she pulled her hand from her hip and leveled a short-barreled pistol at my face. "Now!"

"Albert," I squeaked, barely recognizing I'd answered wrong.

"His name is Charles *Albert* Curtis," Rulloff corrected gruffly. "He occasionally goes by his middle name. A terrible habit, in my opinion." He frowned at me.

Maggie seemed to be considering something as she took all this in, holding the gun pointed at me all the while. She looked at both of us closely, but especially Rulloff, and I thought I caught the hint of a smile behind her pursed lips.

"Well then, Mr. *Leurio* and Mr. *Curtis*," she said "I'll be the judge of any item of value. Hand it over."

"I'm afraid we can do no such thing," Rulloff said. "Until that pistol is put where it belongs."

"This is where it belongs," she said flatly, "till I decide any different."

I couldn't take my eyes off Maggie or the pistol, but to my left I felt Rulloff—the picture of calm—remove the watch from his vest pocket and hold it low to catch the lantern light. He clicked it open and closed, then set it back inside his pocket.

"You could steal it from me, of course," he said. "You have me at a disadvantage with your weapon, but then you'd miss the chance for a long-term partnership."

I kept waiting for him to grab her arm and save me.

What long-term partnership?

Maggie cocked her head but said nothing, as if daring him to continue.

"We both know the uniqueness of this particular item will make it risky to sell," Rulloff said, "Too easily recognized. The wrong buyer may get the idea that a reward could outweigh its value. It's a regrettable beginning to our partnership, I admit, yet it's what we have to offer for the moment."

I continued to stare into the black hole of the gun, trying to will myself first to breathe and second to not piss myself. Maggie didn't move it from my head, but as she listened to Rulloff, its target slowly shifted from my temple to my right ear.

"If you decide not to waste your bullets," he continued as if he didn't care either way on the outcome, "the watch is yours in return for a very minor request of a floor to sleep on and a meal or two. Within a week's time, once Mr. Curtis and I are established, we propose to begin delivery every month of three dozen bolts of pure, uncut, and *untraceable* silk—at a very reasonable price."

WE SPENT THE NIGHT on Maggie's floor, stuffed between barrels marked SALT COD. Despite my exhaustion, I tossed and turned through a nearly sleepless night. In my few brief dreams, Hornberger led a mob after me as I ran down a maze of streets that grew smaller and smaller. In the quiet of my waking hours, I tried to puzzle out how Broadway and BAXTER could exist in the same city, and to work out how silk thief had become my profession.

In the morning, Maggie's manner was no kinder, but she did offer us two biscuits apiece from a tin. She ate six.

I attempted to break through her hostility with a smile, but failed.

"Your name," I said, "like Wild Maggie from the stories?"

"Not one a you," she said, snapping the lid on her tin. "Tell me you don't go in for that sentimental Proddy claptrap. Same shite they said all through the famine—we were fools who deserved our lot 'cause a drink."

She grew quiet and gnawed on biscuit number seven, then suddenly got full of passion and pointed toward the street.

"What you see around here, eh? Take away liquor, you get fewer drunks. Do you get wages enough for a floor that doesn't flood all winter long? Or to buy a blanket for your children? You get treated like you're worth a damn?"

She turned toward me and her eyes bore straight into mine, all the way down to the secret places inside me.

"You smart enough to read them papers, you best know this: Ain't whiskey makes women sell their daughters—that's desperation. Whiskey blunts the pain's all. All them stories of women declarin' *I'd rather die than lose my virtue!*—all of 'em written by men. Protestant. Fucking. Men."

I struggled with how to respond. It had never occurred to me that women were capable of swearing. As for temperance, all I knew was what I'd read—which was apparently worthless.

"Be that as it may," Rulloff said, "I suspect some of those same Protestant men might rather face death than shame, themselves."

After he spoke, his silence grew uncomfortable, so I tried to change the subject.

"You were there for the famine?" I asked. "In Ireland, I mean?"

Rulloff caught my eye and shot me a disapproving frown.

Maggie made the sourest face I'd yet seen on her and crossed both hands on top of the biscuit tin like I was trying to pry it way from her.

"Sligo," she said, rapping a finger so hard I wondered if she would cause a dent. "You read stories about that too, smart boy? Think you know something of that, do ye?"

What did I know? The worst of the famine had happened the summer Rulloff was in our jail. Ten years ago, though every week or two an essay still got published somewhere, arguing either that the British response was immoral or the whole catastrophe was God's judgment on the lazy, filthy Papists. So, I knew Sligo was Lord Palmerston's territory, that it may have been the hardest-hit county of all, and that knew none of this knowledge would endear me to Maggie. I focused on the cracks of light squeezing through the floor planks.

"You know so much, sure you know 'twas only the potato crop that failed."

She must have read the confusion on my face because she pointed at me victoriously, as if she'd scored points in a card game.

"Your newspapers dint tell you there were bags and bags of flour piled high in villages while folk starved? Acres of wheat, tilled by *our* hands, taken by the lord for rent? *Stolen* from mothers thin as skeletons, from babes with green faces, bellies bloated from choking on grass when there weren't no food? Your newspapers didn't tell you what it's like to watch the last act of your pa to be crawling on all fours to beg scraps on the road. To *watch* him die there, face in the mud. I bet your papers dint tell you how a starved body bloats up like a bad fish when there's no one strong enough to drag him to a grave."

Maggie pried open the tin and shoved another biscuit in her mouth, chewing and speaking.

"You gonna read them temperance stories, you know this: The only reason Maggie Graham is alive today's thanks to whiskey."

She paused to finish chewing and swallow.

"All the folk they sent to America in the ships? It weren't the workers strong enough to survive nor the worthy ones that begged for a ticket. They filled ships with the ones they dint want no more. The weaklings and the whiskey-brewing troublemakers."

She took one more biscuit, then set the empty tin on the floor between the flour sacks and pointed her powerful finger at her own massive chest.

"I weren't ever a weakling, but Lord knows I was one hell of a troublemaker."

33

LATER THAT MORNING, IN THE GRAYISH DAYLIGHT, I followed Rulloff into streets full of bustling strangers and goods for sale in every window, but I wasn't exploring the city of my dreams. I fingered the scar on my chin and glanced furtively around every corner, expecting Hornberger to appear with his policeman.

"What are you going to tell the slave catcher?" I asked. "We didn't get any money for the watch."

"There will be plenty of money to keep everyone happy soon enough," he said, and grabbed my hand in front of a theater draped with yellow pennants.

"Besides, he already has a seed-pearl bracelet for his beloved wife, thanks to me."

I wasn't going to speak. Then I couldn't help it.

"Because you gave him Grace and Rebecca."

"What? Who? The runaways? I left them with your Mr. L., though I did steal his donkey. No—because of the jewelry store I robbed."

"Jewelry store?"

"Funny story, actually. I was in Connecticut, on my way to New York, when I was arrested on suspicion of robbing a jewelry store."

"You were *arrested*?"

"Yes, but only on suspicion."

"So you didn't rob the store?"

"No, of course I robbed the store. Keep up now. But I'd hidden the take under a log across the street, and when a neighborhood boy found the goods and the owner got them back, the sheriff decided there wasn't enough evidence to hold me, so he let me go."

I thought of all the wanted posters up and down the state.

"I don't understand. How did they not *recognize* you?"

"Ah," he said. "I spoke German and pretended to have the numb palsy." He paused long enough to demonstrate a tremor on the left side of his body, then he laughed. "Lucky for you that on my way out of town I robbed the same jewelry store, and also that the slave catcher's wife is fond of seed pearls, or you'd still be sitting behind bars in Binghamton."

Smiling jauntily, he led me two doors farther on, underneath a black awning and through a set of double doors into an elegant tailor's shop.

"Allow yourself to enjoy this," he whispered.

Glimmering, crystal-draped chandeliers glowed bright with gas, warming the room despite the cloudy day outside. The back wall shimmered with a hundred shades of fabric stacked in cabinets. Heaps of crimson, mustard, and purple silks lay draped over tables. One side of the shop was designed for women, with cloaks hung from pegs, and piles of feathers, lace, and ribbons in silver bowls. The men's half was only slightly more subdued. Brown, gray, and black wool were common enough, but the silk cravats and vests sparkled in such an array of colors that I counted at least four shades of green and three of purple.

I looked for a mat to wipe my muddy feet. A tall man with wide lips and a peaked forehead introduced himself as Potts, and welcomed Rulloff heartily. But he stopped short when he saw me.

"I'd like to commission a suit for my student, Mr. Charles Curtis," Rulloff said. "Your very best. Anything to get him out of these awful rags and back to work at the bank. He's finally learned he was not born to be Meriwether Lewis."

"Ah!" The man snapped to attention and offered us both a cup of tea. "I see you are an adventurous sort," he smiled as he hung up my worn coat and frontier hat. "I must admit to being quite a fan of the *Leatherstocking Tales*."

I wondered if during all the years I'd spent dreaming of New York City, Potts had been reading Cooper and penny dreadfuls, dreaming of open plains, a horse, and a pistol.

He led me to a small dais in front of a standing mirror as tall as I was.

"Are we looking for a day suit or evening?"

Potts had a curious habit of ending his sentences with a small wheeze.

I looked into that glass, surprised at my rough form. I didn't recognize either Albert Jarvis *or* Charles Curtis in that mirror.

Whatever I might decide about my future, this moment demanded that I step into character once again. Mister Charles Curtis of Third Avenue, distantly related to the Stuyvesants. Where might I wear this fictional suit? Ah, but the Astor Library, of course.

"Day, please." I almost called him Sir, then remembered my station was superior.

Rulloff slunk away, and I understood his purpose in coming here. He was evaluating the silks while I kept the proprietor busy.

"Marvelous." Potts's mustache stretched over a wide smile. He walked in a grand circle around me, studying my form as if I was a piece of art.

I stood as straight as I could. Chest out. Chin down.

"What is your opinion of blue, Sir?"

"Blue?"

Potts draped a sheet of midnight blue wool over my shoulder.

"We could go with a standard black suit, if that's your preference."

I inhaled the clean new scent, and ran my fingers over a weave so fine I'd have slept on it for a pillow.

"It would please your father at the bank, no doubt. I'll only add an outsider's observation that you come across as a man of class, obviously, but perhaps also one who is a touch more daring than your peers. One who may wish to feel less rigorously defined by his garments."

He placed a tall beaver-skin hat on my head.

I looked into his colossal mirror, draped in the fantasies of that fabric, and suddenly, I saw a scholar—a man who could raise a hand and have a carriage stop, who could send the doormen scrambling to welcome him in any hotel, who would not have to explain his presence in a train carriage or on a street corner. My heart soared. I saw a man who *belonged.*

"The blue is very intriguing."

"Excellent." He disappeared and returned with a bolt of purple silk. "A royal color, perhaps, for the vest," he said.

He ran a tape down across my back and down my arm. Behind me in the mirror, I caught a glimpse of Rulloff removing a bolt of fabric from the wall and judging its weight. The fantasy collapsed as I was reminded of our true errand.

"Are you the owner of this shop?" I asked Potts.

"Four years in the present location, three on Water Street. And you? You've been West, I see," he said, wheezing again. I began to wonder whether the sound was some form of laugh, or perhaps an illness.

"Some of my clients set out for California." He leaned in and whispered, "I must admit I've considered it myself. Is it as hard as they say out there?"

"It's rough," I said, tempted to make up stories of Indians attacking wagons or pistol fights over gold claims, but Potts had read more novels than I had. I chose to keep some mystery about my fake adventure, as Rulloff had done on the train. Meanwhile, I stared into Potts's magic mirror far longer than necessary, trying to regain that fragile investiture of power, but it was gone. I remained quiet as Rulloff completed his research and busied himself in a newspaper. Potts finished his work a few minutes later.

Outside I stuffed my fingers in my pockets against the cold. If we went forward with Rulloff's plan and were successful, Potts would lose everything it had taken him seven years to build. If we failed, we'd lose everything—starting with our lives.

"How trustworthy is that map in your head? Can you find your way back to Maggie's from here?" Rulloff asked.

Surprised and suddenly terrified, I tried to remember the path we'd taken, but realized I'd been too deep in thought to pay attention.

Why was he leaving me?

"Head south on Centre and east on Walker," Rulloff said. "If you get lost, ask a sweeper—actually, don't ask anyone, or you'll likely end up in a back alley with a knife at your throat. When you get to Mulberry, you'll recognize the building."

"Where are you going?"

He tipped his hat.

"I have a funeral to attend," he said, then disappeared around the corner.

I LEFT THE FASHION PARADE of Broadway and took a short walk down Prince, then turned south on Centre. I got used to the cold quickly enough. It was the rotting garbage I still couldn't adjust to. A dozen people on both sides of the street dug through the overflowing rubbish piles.

Centre was a wide street, lined with factories. Wagons loaded and unloaded goods in front of upholsterers' shops and soap makers and glove factories. Teams of strong horses filled the frozen air with steamy breath as they came and went. Some buildings had no signage, but I could hear the din of machinery operating inside—steam grinders, bandsaws, metal drills. *Building chairs, maybe? Or wagon wheels?*

In front of each factory, groups of men waited quietly, huddled, backs against the wall near the boiler vents for warmth, some sharing a word or two, but mostly keeping to themselves.

All these businesses must need lots of workers.

I was a hard worker.

I may not be as strong as Pa or Thomas, but I could be patient and wait my turn. Why shouldn't I get a job in a factory instead of becoming a thief? Rulloff was already experienced making nails and carpets. Was that not a better path? Especially with the law already after us?

We could be scholars in the evenings until we could save enough to do it full time. I breathed deep, forgetting about the garbage for the first time. There were jobs everywhere. This street alone was packed with places needing workers. We'd just have to disappoint Maggie. I smiled. We could have an honorable future.

I was getting ready to turn onto Canal when I heard a shout, then another. The crowd surged on the sidewalk and shoved me out of their way, against a brick wall. A man in torn overalls appeared in the door of a false teeth factory and pointed to the first strong man he saw.

"You. Station twenty-one," the man said.

After he'd disappeared, two other men exited through the doorway, carrying a third man who was bleeding profusely from the arm. His head lolled back, unconscious, blood from his arm dripping all over the shirt of the man to his right. My stomach turned as the crowd grew quiet, certainly whispering a prayer similar to mine, hoping that the man lived, that he didn't lose his arm, and thanking God that his fate was not theirs today. Perhaps not in that order. The surreal quiet spread as hammers stopped on neighboring streets in a collective gasp of pity.

Then the hammers started up again, and the men outside the factory pushed in tighter, shouting louder, knowing that another position had suddenly become available. Just another day on Centre Street.

My seductive fantasy of an easy, honest life lay in a thousand bloody pieces. As I reached Mulberry and spotted Maggie's dormer window, I knew—it was either me or Potts.

Two nights later, under a moonless sky, Rulloff broke the lock on a livery stable door with an iron bar.

34

"WHAT'S THE PENALTY FOR STEALING A HORSE IN THIS town?" I whispered. I could just see the top of the Tombs prison looming over Bottle Alley.

"Not stealing," he said, and pushed the door open slowly. The creaks from the runners echoed off every building on the block. Even the stars seemed to press down with a million watching eyes.

"Borrowing."

I leaned back against the planks of a liquor grocery to look more at ease, but soon realized I'd leaned into fresh urine and stood back up.

Though I was better at hitching horses than Rulloff, it was his idea that I keep watch. He wanted me to learn how to work in the dark. "That's where slow-witted thieves go wrong," he'd said. "Someone always sees the lantern moving where it shouldn't be."

We would succeed because we'd do everything in the blackest night, skilled as phantoms.

A gunshot rang out in the dark—somewhere close. I blew into my hands. I sure didn't feel like a phantom.

Finally, Rulloff emerged with a wagon and two horses, one of them droopy-eyed. He closed the stable door and we climbed aboard. All along Franklin, then Elm, above each dark tobacco shop and hardware store we passed, lay three or four stories of sleeping men.

"Clerks, ledger keepers, newspapermen, and political flunkies," Rulloff pointed out. "Thin layer of strivers, separating the gilt from the gutter."

Even now he was still my teacher, trying to help me understand the hidden structure of the city. Yet all I could think was that it meant a dozen men might wonder why a wagon was creaking past their

window—too late for a delivery, too early for the milk run. I was grateful the cobblestone streets down here were coated in filth, for the horse
shoes didn't make a single sound.

I fingered my scar as I steered the horses into a pitch-black service
alley off Spring, behind Potts's Emporium. Rulloff jumped down in the
blackness, eyes like a cat, but it took a full minute for me to distinguish
the back of the theater from the tailor's shop. Finally, I stepped down
and counted my steps as I'd practiced until I found the hitching post in
the dark.

Suddenly, the back door of the theater flung open, stabbing the alley
with light.

I ducked behind the cart's wheel. We'd waited three hours after the
performance ended, but when I peered through the spokes, two men in
togas and greasepaint sat on the stoop, passing a bottle. If they chose to
look up and wonder at a hitched wagon in the middle of the night, we
were finished.

"I tell you, she had eyes on you," the taller one said, his voice a drunken
octave too high, echoing off every stone in the alley. "I could see it all the
way from the wings."

"You're dreaming." The other voice was quieter, sadder.

Rulloff walked across the alley as if it were middle of the day, in full
view of the actors if they'd chosen to look beyond their shoes. I could
barely breathe as he used the light cast by the open door to break the
store's lock with a fireplace poker.

"If I was dreaming, would it be that she was after *your* tickle tail,
you dolt?"

"I don't want to talk about it." The second man's voice was steely
edged.

Rulloff disappeared into the darkened store, leaving the door open a
crack for me. The men grew quiet, sucking from the bottle. Three rats
scampered across the alley, then a fourth. A cold wind pushed through
the air and I found myself shaking.

Was I supposed to walk right in front of them?

"I'm a goddamn actor, man. She's a glove wearer."

I forced myself to stand, partly shadowed by the cart, desperately trying to look like I belonged at three in the morning.

Confident. Articulate. Poised.

"By all means. Sell yourself short and give me a go at her instead."

"I'm not listening to your crap anymore. We have the noon show tomorrow. I'm going to bed."

"Pig shit. You're going to Bridget's to find a tall brunette who'll put on a pair a gloves and let you ride her to high heaven."

The door swung closed with a thud, and I heard the latch click. I took a deep breath and ran across the alley, wondering how many of the people in beds above had been awakened, people who could at any minute glance out their window and wonder about two men loading a cart in the middle of the night. I plunged into the blackness of the store.

Rulloff stood behind a large square table, a dark shape tying bolts of silk up in bundles of shirting. I ran my hand over one of the bolts on the table. It felt like Cayuga Lake on a windless day.

"Shhh," he whispered, and I realized I'd been breathing heavily through my mouth.

He tied the bundle and handed me the end. I grabbed it, anticipating the weight of a heap of laundry, but it barely budged. How heavy could silk be? I had to position my body underneath the table and pull it onto my shoulder. Bowed like a beggar, I felt like I was dragging a wrapped corpse. I stumbled to the left and knocked into the bonnet table, scraping the legs against the parquet floor.

"Steady."

I threaded the narrow space between the tables, wishing Potts had chosen to lay them out in a clear grid to make my work easier. My shoulder burned and my hands grew slippery with sweat. The bundle knocked into a rack of furs to my left and I barely grabbed it before it toppled. I wouldn't have survived ten minutes in a false-teeth factory.

When I got back from the wagon, Rulloff had a second bundle ready to go.

I panted, sweat streaming down my face. "How many more?"

"A few dozen."

My arms already felt useless.

"You want to take it all?"

"Fortune sides with him who dares," Rulloff said.

My frayed nerves got the better of me and I spit on the ground, wondering how Virgil would have felt about being quoted in such a context. Until now, this had seemed like a daring adventure, but silk was really heavy. Thievery wasn't just risky, it was truly hard work.

I grabbed the next bundle. And then the next. It took more than an hour to get everything loaded, but when we were done, we'd cleaned Potts out entirely. I turned, looking for Rulloff to help me lift the last bundle into the wagon, but he'd disappeared. As the minutes dragged on, I began to worry he'd gotten himself in trouble. So I was grateful when he appeared around the corner and threw one last lumpy bundle onto the pile. I unhitched the horses and climbed onto the driver's bench beside Rulloff just as a woman's voice echoed clear into the night.

"Wake up, you son of a drunk!"

I glimpsed her as we edged out onto Broadway, lunging forward under the street lamps, arms wrapped around the body of a man with a wooden leg. "I ain't going to carry you the whole way. Ain't my fault your dog lost."

Matches flared behind lacy window curtains.

"We should run," I whispered.

Rulloff shook his head.

"Stay calm."

I heard someone rap on a windowsill, then a voice.

"I won't be woken by a whore at sparrow's fart."

"I got a right to earn a living same as you," she yelled hoarsely.

I tried to focus on driving the horses, but she shrieked—a shrill sound that bounced off every brick and must have woken everyone for a mile. I turned to see the man in the window holding his chamber pot upside down.

"You black-footed bastard!" she screamed. Lantern light burst from every window in the alley.

"I'll slice your prick right off and eat it for breakfast."

"This is a respectable neighborhood. Go wag your snatch south of Canal."

"Heartless bastards live here," she shouted. "You think I won't remember where you live? I'll knock you into a cocked hat. Wake up and defend me, you drunken slob," she shouted. A shrill whistle echoed down the empty street.

"She's brought the police," I said, ready to leap out of the wagon.

Rulloff grabbed me hard by the collar and forced me back down on the seat with a grip that was far from gentle.

"Don't make that mistake again. Running proves your guilt."

I was about to argue that a wagon full of stolen silks would just as easily prove our guilt, but he kept his fist at my throat and spit in the foot box.

"Grow the *fuck* up. Now!"

I was too surprised to argue. I guided the overfilled wagon off Broadway and onto Broome.

"Stay calm," he said. "With luck, she'll keep them busy."

For a moment, luck seemed to be on our side, but then the whistle brought another copper running down Broome. He ran smack into our wagon.

"Sorry," he said automatically. He was young and nervous.

I held the reins so tight my fingernails pressed into my palm.

"Quite a row." Rulloff said.

"Broadway's the hardest beat in the city," the young lawman said, catching his breath. I hoped he would rush off to the disturbance, but he didn't move. He seemed to be testing out a twisted ankle.

"Bowery sounds harder, but it's not. Down there, everyone's wretched and no one gives a damn if they murder each other. Down there, job's more like judging a boxing match. Up here, rule's always changing."

"Must be hard," Rulloff said.

The boy shrugged, put his full weight on his ankle and seemed to find he was no worse for the wear.

"We all have our part in the Punch and Judy show," he said, then laughed at his joke. In the growing twilight, I could see he was no older than me. "Gentlemen have money—gentlemen get what they please." He smiled and tipped his hat to Rulloff. "Sun'll be up in an hour." The boy scanned the sky over the rooftops. "Then I can get a proper meal."

"Good luck to you then," Rulloff said amiably.

"And you as well. Working hard in the middle of the night we both are, eh? Before the milk run, even." He paused after saying this and the hairs on my arms stood up. "What is it brings you men out in the middle of the night, anyway?"

"Laundry," I said too quickly.

"Aah," he said.

I raised the reins to move on, but he laid a hand on the side of the wagon. One of the bundles had broken open, revealing a pile of crimson silk. "Pretty fine laundry."

Beside me, I felt Rulloff shift his weight. In the palm of his hand I glimpsed the barrel of Maggie's miniature pistol.

"Who is it needs silks washed in the middle of the night, exactly?"

I heard a click in the dark. The police boy had cocked his pistol.

I sat squarely in front of the gun, sweat running in my eyes.

Confident.

"Theater," I said, hoping my voice didn't break.

Articulate.

"Cast was drinking after the show. Couldn't get them to change out of their costumes." I threw up my arms, and shifted into the story as I made it up.

Poised.

"Actors sometimes they think they *are* the royalty they play on stage, you know? Make us wait till all hours and still want everything ready by the noon show tomorrow. I tell you, if we get a drop of rain, those boozy thespians are going to be stuck with soggy drawers—and I won't shed a tear. The worst performance of Euripides you've ever seen."

The boy looked at Rulloff, then me, then the wagon, then back at me. Finally, he laughed again.

"Go on about your business then," he said, then added with a wink, "I'll pray for rain."

The boy had moved on. Rulloff trembled beside me. As he pocketed the pistol, I realized he wasn't trembling, but laughing.

"Costumes for the theater," he croaked. "Brilliant."

The cold wind rippled across the tops of the bundles behind me. New York City truly was a place where anything was possible. Albert Jarvis, the indecisive weakling, was dead. In his place, Charles Curtis was born. A man who conquered, conned, and took whatever he desired.

35

SLUMPED AGAINST MAGGIE'S WARM CHIMNEY, I STARED at the mountain of bundles we'd piled atop the sacks and barrels. I'd dragged a few of them but most had made it up five flights thanks to a tireless Rulloff. Thirty-four in all. They reached the rafters.

Maggie unwrapped the bundles one at a time, letting them slide open until the blues, greens, and blacks undulated and sparkled in the candlelight. She ran her fingers over the soft folds of silk, caressing the fabric with a delicacy I hadn't expected.

"Pure crêpe de chine." She turned to us and didn't even try to suppress the grin that blossomed on her face.

Something in her look reminded me of the butterfly I'd watched emerge from a chrysalis behind Aunt Babe's barn, and I smiled. It was short lived. Thinking about Aunt Babe was a sour note, but not enough to douse the glow of all my accomplishments. I pushed the thought away and forced the smile back till my cheeks hurt.

"How long will it take you to sell this?" Rulloff asked.

"Lotta rich ladies, want to look like richer ladies," Maggie said, pointing at me as if she knew I wasn't from around here. "Lot of 'em got kitchen help from Sligo—women I go back a long way with. Women with an ear open for all them dances and weddings, for a family all a sudden needs a full set a mourning clothes done up, and can suggest how wider skirts and longer trains can be had for less cash. Won't take long, 'cause if they got a Sligo maid, however fancy their house may look outside, they ain't got enough money on the inside to hire *Protestant* help."

I marveled at how, in the same breath, Maggie had not only explained her ingenious way to fence the silks but made a point that it would only work through her. Unless we'd known those maids all the way back to Sligo, there was no point in us getting any ideas about cutting her out. She trusted us, and also she didn't.

Exactly how I felt.

"Slower start, I reckon, but it'll pick up fast. I'll pay for one bundle at a time, sell it, and buy the next. Stock gets low, you fill it back up. Lotta funeral black and debutante white, but for them ball gowns, they'll expect a choice of every color you can imagine and twice as many you can't."

Maggie put her boot on the chair and reached her right hand deep under her skirt. I was too shocked to look away in time, so I glimpsed her naked knee when she withdrew her purse and blushed to the tips of my ears. She counted out a roll of banknotes into Rulloff's palm.

"Fifty dollars," she said, and placed the empty purse on the table. "Just think how many people that'd feed."

Rulloff counted out the cash, then handed me my half: *Twenty-five dollars'* worth of banknotes. I'd never held more than three in my life. I studied one after the other: an orange-and-black bill edged with loops and scrolls from the Augusta Insurance and Banking Company, a bright green two-dollar bond scrip from South Carolina. The letters of the Canal & Banking Company of New Orleans were shaped into nymphs. The cash was as colorful as the silks it had been traded for. Then I noticed Maggie watching me and shoved the bills in my pocket, as if it was no big deal.

Just a *fortune.*

In my pocket was more money than Pa made in half a year, and then only if the jail was full. Twenty-five dollars as *one* payment for *one* night's work. There were thirty-three more piles of colorful banknotes waiting for me after this one. I thought about all the crap Pa'd had to take, all the backbreaking labor Aunt Babe did at the farm. Here I was—sixteen years old, and I'd never have to work again.

"First thing you'll be needing to do with that money is to buy a pistol," Maggie said. "Go to the shop on Canal. They got good prices on Colts. You'll waste your money in the avenues."

Light began to spill into the sky outside the windows. Rulloff excused himself for a moment, and I assumed he'd headed to the outhouse in the courtyard, but he returned a moment later carrying the lumpy last bundle from the store.

"This one's not for sale," he said to Maggie, then handed the pile to me.

I couldn't read the glint in his eyes, but when I unwrapped the shirting I found my midnight blue suit, complete but for the cuffs, along with Potts's sample stovepipe. I laughed out loud, pulled on the jacket and hat, and did a little jig right there on the floor.

Maggie managed a half smile that proved better than any mirror. "You two look the part, sure," she said. "Call yourselves whatever you wish, but go to the shop on Canal. Even aristocrats carry guns in *this* town, Edward Rulloff and Albert Jarvis."

36

I PASSED MY SECOND SLEEPLESS NIGHT, WAITING FOR the inevitable crisis.

Would the police bang down the door in the middle of the night? Would Rulloff move to silence Maggie with some violent act? Both? He'd barely reacted to her statement, and I couldn't for the life of me decipher his casual attitude.

The morning brought a gray dawn and fatigue but no clarity. Rulloff took me downstairs where a woman on the third floor finished my suit in less than an hour. She almost fainted when I handed her a dollar for her troubles.

"Almost a week's wages," Rulloff said under his breath, but I didn't care. I doubted I'd be alive by the end of the day.

It wasn't until I was dressed in the same costume as Rulloff and we were headed uptown that I finally had a chance to speak openly, albeit quietly around packs of strangers.

"What will we do about Maggie knowing who we are? We can't go back to Mulberry. Could we catch a stage, do you think? Or a ship? Do we have enough money to book passage for London?"

Rulloff listened for a while with no comment, then finally rolled his eyes.

"Think rationally. What advantage would it be for her to turn us in?"

I was mystified by his indifference.

"There's a two thousand dollar reward!" I spoke much too loud and reverted to a whisper to repeat myself. "Two *thousand* dollars is quite a rational advantage."

"This is true," Rulloff said. "But what else is true?"

I stopped walking, confused by his question.

"We followed through on the—" I caught myself from speaking of silks out loud, "the delivery as promised."

"Exactly so." Rulloff continued walking, and I had to hasten my step to keep up. "Not only might it be challenging to explain the goods in her possession, you also must do arithmetic, as she surely has. She could have turned us in at any point over the past several days, but chose to wager on our success instead. If I tell you she will sell the items for at least three times her cost, what value have we delivered by remaining free?"

I was used to working out sums on a board, but after a while came up with an answer I doubted very much, so I reworked it twice in my head. "Five thousand dollars?"

"Yes. Five thousand dollars. Crime pays a far sight better than the law. As long as we keep delivering, we're worth more to her free than caught, so mathematically, we are perfectly safe. But we will not be so lucky with everyone. You must never use that name again."

"No," I said, with the utmost gravity. "That will never happen again."

As we walked, it slowly dawned on me that despite all my fears of the night before, we were in no immediate danger. I had money in my pocket. I had anonymity to protect me from enemies. I had someone wiser and more experienced to guide me. An unfamiliar feeling grew in my chest, one I last remembered from that day in Aunt Babe's rocker.

I was *safe*.

A joyful exuberance took hold and I almost felt giddy. My clothing marked me as a man of stature. A chimney sweep on the sidewalk said pardon as I passed, and stepped out of my way. Albert Jarvis was a ghost now to everyone but Maggie. For increasingly long and glorious stretches of time, I could believe I *was* Charles Curtis.

I followed Rulloff into a shop on Canal. He walked straight past the displays of Colt Sidehammers and dueling pistols and some type of revolving carbine. At the counter he inquired about custom designs and then asked for a piece of paper. He began to sketch something I'd never seen before.

came up with this invention in—in Auburn," he said. "Though I
: have the chance to manufacture it at the time. Think about this:
What is the biggest problem with pistols?"

"There are many problems with pistols. Starting with why we need
one."

Rulloff continued to sketch.

"Unlike with a rifle, which has a long barrel to guide the ball, you
never know where the cartridge that is fired from a small hand gun will
actually go. You shoot. You miss. Maybe you die. But see here?"

He tapped a finger on the unique aspect of his completed design.

"Three barrels. Doesn't make it any more accurate, but at least one of
them will hit the right damn place."

WITH A THICK COATING of snow on everything, the noises of the
city were quieter and even the air smelled fresh. When we reached
Third Avenue, we veered off onto streets lined with stately residences
that were fronted with skeleton trees. In a bold harbinger of spring, the
first thumb-sized buds burst through the tips of each branch, looking
like a swarm of grasshoppers had landed.

Just past 11th Street, Rulloff stopped in front of a five-story, redbrick
home trimmed with ebony shutters and a carved stone portico. A light
well revealed a belowground room where a root cellar should be, except
I glimpsed elegant furniture through the window.

He unbuttoned his coat and turned to face me with a barely con-
cealed grin.

"How would you like to live here?"

The shock stopped me cold.

"*Here?*"

I didn't need to mention the obvious contrast between this graceful
residence and the warped pine floor in Maggie's attic—as different as
my new suit was from my ragged old clothes.

"I've started the process, but I need your help to finish it," he said.

I followed him up the stone steps, where a young woman in a bl.. dress and white apron opened the door. Rulloff took a card from his pocket.

"Welcome, Professor Leurio," she said after reading the card. "You must be Mr. Curtis," she said to me. "Mrs. Jacobs is waiting for you in the family room, but asked that I give you a tour of the home first."

"How do you do?" I held out my hand.

She gave me a puzzled look, then took my hand in an uncertain shake that confirmed my blunder. I'd have to watch Rulloff more closely.

"This way, please," she said as she led us down a long, narrow hallway. "I'm Patience. I do the cleaning and laundry. Sarah Catherine does the cooking. Breakfast is served at nine, dinner at one. Mrs. Jacobs likes to do dinner as a big affair with the silver and porcelain here in the parlor."

She opened a set of double doors into a room as long and wide as our courthouse in Ithaca, but taller. I could have stood on Rulloff's shoulders and still not touched the ceiling. Heavy velvet drapes with tasseled fringe hung over the front and rear windows. A grand piano in the corner awaited the delicate fingers of a musician, and carved furniture covered in red brocade suggested parties of twenty or forty people could be made comfortable as one played. The window light glittered from two massive cut-glass chandeliers, suggesting the splendor of the room in its full glory, but black serge hung over what I assumed must be four massive mirrors in the room.

"At least that's what she wanted when Mr. Jacobs was alive," Patience continued. "I don't know what it will be like now it's just her in the house." I caught a downcast look on her face when I turned back to where she stood in the doorway. "Truth is, dinners have gotten smaller every year as the children got married or sailed away for the business."

She smoothed her apron, and then headed up a narrow flight of stairs with a carved ebony banister. "The room for the two of you to share is up this way," she said as we followed, first Rulloff then me. "Mrs. Jacobs also takes tea and cakes at four ever since she came back from London. And we put out a soup or cold meats at eight. We've always done that, but since she came back from Paris we're supposed to call it *souper*. Everything but dinner is served in the family room downstairs."

At the landing she turned, and I glimpsed another flight of stairs heading up.

"Children's rooms are up there," she explained, "Though of course they're empty now. Sarah Catherine and I are in the attic, of course." We followed her down a short hall into a large room facing the street. "This belonged to the late Mr. Jacobs," Patience said. "Mrs. Jacobs stays in the one across the hall, facing the garden."

A massive four-poster bed covered with a red velvet canopy sat against the wall, looking as if it could easily fit a half-dozen sleeping men. The underside of the canopy was lined with waves of red silk, drawn to a circular knot in the center. Across from the bed stood a fireplace. The marble mantle held an etched glass lamp and a blue vase filled with vibrant yellow tulips, petals yawning.

Behind another door lay an office with a large walnut desk and a window facing the street. A crystal inkstand above the blotter held an assortment of writing pens and a full inkwell.

"We'd get another chair, of course," she said, "If you wish to work on your studies together."

Our studies. I barely managed to believe this was *our* room. For the first time since arriving in the city I could imagine doing what I dreamed about all along—reading books, researching languages, writing our manuscript. I may not have loved all of Rulloff's methods, but I had to admit they were incredibly effective.

"Queen Victoria can't possibly live in a place more glorious than this," I whispered to Rulloff.

Potts's ruin lay vaguely on my conscience, but I would make up for it with extraordinarily hard work. Once Rulloff and I changed the world, my conscience could be clean again.

Downstairs, we were led to the simple, belowground room I'd glimpsed from outside, cozy and low-ceilinged. A woman of about sixty sat on a sofa, wearing a black silk dress and ebony necklace, straining to make out the stitches in her needlework. Behind her stood a tall wire cage on a wrought iron stand. Inside, a bright yellow bird hopped cheer-lessly back and forth on his short perch. From some other room I could smell a pie in the warmer and knew I'd do anything to live in this house.

"Ah," she looked up. "Welcome, gentlemen. Please forgive me for not meeting you upstairs, but I find this room so much easier to keep warm in the winter, and full of memories of the children at play." She beckoned me with her finger. "Just like my Thomas, isn't he, Marshall? Come, Mr. Curtis. Stand here. In the light, if you don't mind."

I stepped forward, looking around the room for someone named Marshall.

"I'm terribly sorry about your father," she said. "My youngest son is barely older than you. Left for Singapore just a month ago. Poor Thomas doesn't even know his father has passed yet. My heart breaks with worry every day he's gone, doesn't it, Marshall?"

This time I saw her turn toward the bird when she asked the ques-tion. I managed a weak smile.

"I'm very sorry about your husband, as well," I said.

"Now I understand that you two scholars are working on a book of languages," she said, changing the subject from grief almost by force. "That sounds fascinating."

"Mr. Curtis is a serious young man," Rulloff spoke up. "Not one for drinking, gambling, or distractions. I can assure you, his study habits are excellent."

Patience entered with an armful of logs.

"Do we need more firewood, Marshall? Yes, I'd say so." She raised her voice, so it was impossible for Patience to ignore her grumbling. "I'm unclear why one must be forced to ask for service in one's own house."

She turned to Rulloff.

"All of my friends tell me to install coal grates," she said, "But to me, coal seems like such dirty, factory heat. Don't you think? Perhaps you'll say I've become too sentimental. No, no. You'd be right." She waved her hand at an imagined expression. "Last season, my home welcomed the Schermerhorns and Mrs. Hamilton Fish. Now, I'm a widow, the sophisticated people are all moving north of 25th, and even fireplaces are no longer *à la mode*. It's a cruel point in life when you discover the best moments of your life are behind you."

"I admit I'm more focused on the future," Rulloff said.

"Just wait. It will happen to you as well. Wishing you could go back—" She waved off her nostalgia and got to the point. "Anyway, I can at least offer Croton water, gas lighting, water closets, and bathing facilities. Is the room to your liking?"

"It will do quite nicely," Rulloff said. "Charles and I are headed to the attorney's office to transfer his father's assets. Apparently it's a touch complicated because of relations to the Stuyvesants through his late mother, but I'm assured it will all be sorted soon."

Mrs. Jacobs finally smiled. "What great luck to have met you at the funeral," she said. "I hadn't even realized my husband had such a scholarly acquaintance. And with all this extra space in the house now, it will be so nice to have some life back between these walls. Of course, renting the room is not about the money—"

"Certainly not."

"But still, to keep the ledgers neat, you'll make sure to provide the twenty dollars in advance, won't you?"

"Absolutely."

Had she said twenty dollars? For a month of lodging? Our fortune wouldn't even last until spring at that rate.

"Yes," Rulloff agreed. "Twenty a week. Tell you what, as soon as the inheritance comes through, we'll pay four weeks in advance. Would cash be acceptable?"

Twenty per week? Stealing silks was not a one-time event that set us up for good. I set a hand on a table to steady myself. We'd have to rob a store every few months to keep living in this place.

Mrs. Jacobs smiled.

"That will be just fine, Professor Leurio." Then she turned to me. "Welcome to the house, dear boy. I'm sure your father would be very proud."

PERSEVERARE
AUTEM DIABOLICUM

1860

37

"TO HELL WITH THE SUMERIANS!" SWEAT SOAKED Rulloff's collar as he closed yet another book with a thud and set it on the pile that began on the Oriental carpet and reached impressively toward the Astor Library's skylight. "I'm going back to Hebrew and Aramaic. We can outflank Fisher if we start with the Tower of Babel."

Had he lost his senses?

After years of exhausting study, we'd built a lexicon of all the major languages on earth, word by word. Our scribbled pages wallpapered the office at Mrs. Jacobs's, covered the desk, and spilled out into stacks throughout the bedroom. But without the unifying key to break the code they added up to nothing more than a mountain of puzzle pieces that we couldn't fit together. Humanity's original language was quite literally on the tips of our tongues, but the fundamental connection between Hebrew, Akkadian, Chaldean, Assyrian, Aramaic, Arabic, Persian, Greek, Latin, and so many others, eluded us.

We'd studied right through the Dead Rabbits riot, the Panic of '57, John Brown's uprising, and Lincoln's debates with Douglas—along with everything else that happened in the world irrelevant to our purpose. No butterflies or dragon dances for us. Our feverish pace allowed for little more than a cursory glance at the *Tribune* with our tea and toast. All except one news item.

When Darwin's book arrived this side of the Atlantic, Rulloff started having nightmares about being upstaged—waking up in cold sweats and frightening me with the wild look in his eyes. A shopkeeper told him there wasn't a copy left to be bought in New York, so he'd emptied the entire contents of his pockets on the counter. Within ten minutes we owned a scuffed volume of *On the Origin of Species*, bookmarked with a pink ribbon and labeled "From the Library of Mrs. R. T. Knowles."

"We'll find that key," he'd vowed that night, slamming the book closed. "And write the greatest story the world has ever known. No one will give a fig for Darwin's finch when we reveal the first words ever spoken by man."

This thought buoyed us for a while, and Rulloff began planning to sell the manuscript for the unprecedented price of five hundred thousand dollars. While this seemed an impossible amount to me, certainly we'd make a large enough sum to end our illicit dealings with Maggie, and buy Mrs. Jacobs's house—or one like it. But when he received a rejection letter from the first National Philology Conference in Poughkeepsie, he stopped shaving. Then bathing.

"There's no time," he snapped. "Nothing else matters!" He began glancing behind him every block or two, sure he was being followed by people who wanted to steal our ideas.

The first time Rulloff thought he'd discovered the key I was ecstatic, but when we tried to apply it, our carefully woven web fell into a heap. The second time I was hopeful. By the fifteenth, I was disenchanted.

"We need more time," I said. "We're pushing too hard. If the answer isn't there, we can't force it."

"Darwin's stealing our fame right out from underneath us," became his hourly refrain. To say we worked tirelessly would be inaccurate. I grew exhausted beyond measure, while Rulloff worked with a frenzy bordering on hysteria. Meanwhile, frequent dispatches from Maggie described a growing discontent with the dwindling stocks in her attic and ended with a concerning postscript: "ER & AJ."

IN THE LIBRARY, thunder boomed and a summer shower quickly built to an all-out rainstorm that drummed a vigorous march on the skylight, echoed by three floors of balconies surrounding the circular reading room. The architecture reminded me of Auburn Prison, though the inmates here ran to the likes of Herodotus, Euripides, and Aeschylus, along with tactics of naval warfare, planting tables for wheat, flax, and tobacco, instruction manuals for producing vulcanized rubber and—most critically for our purposes—the largest linguistics collection in the Americas.

I leaned back in the armchair and counted the angels, putti, and heavenly virtues painted on the ceiling, trying to figure out the response with the least chance of triggering Rulloff's increasingly explosive temper.

"The conference is two weeks away," I nudged gently. "Are you sure you want to rewrite the whole manuscript? You don't even believe in the Bible."

"Blame Darwin." He ran his finger down an index page. "His book should have opened the door for our congruent theory. Instead, alarm over the idea of racial equality has caused every portal, gate, and window to be nailed shut and boarded over as if the Mongols are set to invade. You remember Fisher in Putnam's. He called the concept of man developing language himself ludicrous. Practically blasphemous. Of course, he's wrong, but he's also influential. How else are we going to get a special reading at Poughkeepsie? The Bible is our Trojan Horse."

This felt less like the world-changing project I'd signed up for every day.

"Why not add in a conspiracy of priests and publish it as a novel?" I muttered under my breath, moody from lack of sleep. The words danced on the page before me until I finally had to close my eyes.

"WAKE UP!" Rulloff cried, and I snapped open my eyes, almost surprised to find myself still in the library.

He said nothing more, but his blue eyes virtually glowed with a quiet confidence that told me this time was radically different.

"You've found the key," I said.

I felt a rush of nauseating shame for doubting him. As he'd promised, we wouldn't just be great; they would carve our images into busts and revere our names for thousands of years. We'd be heroes.

"Kappa alpha rho—beta alpha nu," he said. "Our fucking finch."

He scribbled the letters on a scrap of paper that he handed to m
he was slipping me state secrets.

"Take this back to the office and start pulling the pieces together. There's no time to lose. You'll find it makes everything fall into place now. I have an errand to complete, but will join you as soon as I'm able."

He set his hat on his head, trapping the black curl of hair that always slipped over his ear, then stopped me short with a stern look. "Whatever you do, stay on your guard. The men at the lumberyard across the street have been watching our every move. I'm certain they're planning to steal our work."

38

EXHAUSTED AS I WAS FROM THE DELIRIUM OF THE PAST
two weeks, I had to smile when our destination appeared outside the
train window. Poughkeepsie was so layered in red, white, and blue bun-
ting that it seemed a stiff wind might blow the whole town away. A ban-
ner hung from each end of the station building welcoming MEMBERS
OF THE AMERICAN PHILOLOGICAL ASSOCIATION.

Over the hiss and squeal of the arriving engine, came the sound of
fiddles. Their resonance was so harmonic and gay that my heart swelled
again with the importance of our mission. All the society's luminaries
were here at the same time—the people who would be most excited
to publish our earth-shattering discovery as soon as they understood
its import. The next such event wouldn't happen for four more years—
a lifetime away. Our telegrams requesting a private audience had gone
unanswered, so we'd have to improvise some method to achieve a special manuscript review in three days or all our hard work and soul-
destroying sacrifices could be for naught. Yet, I felt destiny was on our
side, as if anything was possible.

On the platform, a man in a broad-brimmed derby held his arm out
as if he could personally shake the hands of every arriving passenger—a
feat that would have taken hours. Luckily, engrossed in excited linguistic debate and a chaos of bags, coats, umbrellas, and Greek proverbs,
no one paid him any mind. I took pity on the man and grabbed for his
gloved hand.

"How do you do, Sir?

He started momentarily, but when he regained his composure his
smile so overwhelmed his face that I could see nothing but teeth and
whiskers.

"Welcome to Poughkeepsie! We're honored to host you folks here. Mayor Ezekiel Thornbush. Here to serve."

I was about to compliment his colorful town when Rulloff thrust me aside.

"Ah, *Mayor*. What an honor. Wonderful to make your acquaintance. Quite a welcome you've rolled out." He tipped his hat. "Tell me," he raised an eyebrow of conspiratorial connection, "Are you a linguist yourself?"

"Well," Thornbush beamed, "Nothing like our esteemed visitors, but I've been known to dust off the books from time to time." He stood straighter. "I believe it's my sacred duty as a Christian to be able to read the Bible in its native language, I've been working on my Latin for several decades."

I cringed for the poor man and waited for Rulloff to launch into one of his withering tirades: *Which native language did you say? The Classical Hebrew and Aramaic of the Old Testament or the Koine Greek of the New? Maybe you mean to read only the Gospel of Mark, in which case that one section may have originally been penned in Latin, but of course—*

"That's wonderful," Rulloff said, beaming. "What dedication you have to seek a more comprehensive understanding of Our Lord's intent. I'm certain that—hosted by a man of your stature—the conference will prove to be a spectacular success."

"Ah," sweat shone on Thornbush's pale cheeks as he labored to conceal his grin, "you are too kind, Sir."

"Thank you for your time, Mayor," I broke in, anxious to free the unfortunate mouse from the cat's paw.

Rulloff refused to be dissuaded.

"Since you are so well educated on our topic at hand, Mayor, perhaps you know Mr. Simmons and Mr. Patrick of the organizing committee?"

Rulloff looked away to adjust his grip on the leather satchel in his hand. He was a master at planting a seed of intrigue with a seeming nonchalance that left me breathless with awe each time. It also left me a touch queasy.

"Yes!" Thornbush beamed. "I'm honored to say that Mr. Patrick is lodging at my very own home during his stay."

I felt guilty but grateful that Rulloff was so adept at convincing anyone to do anything, because I still preferred to stay out of the business of lying as much as possible. I focused my attention instead on the manuscript inside the satchel, the greatest accomplishment of my life, finally complete. So many pages I'd had to stand on the bag to close the buckles.

In the fourteen days since Rulloff's epiphany, with barely a wink of sleep, we'd used his key to unlock the cipher and trace twenty-seven different languages back in time, step-by-step, the same way Darwin had traced bees and ants, ostriches and beans to the "one primordial form, into which life was first breathed."

One original language.

A linguistic proof that even the most "rigorously scientific" of racial classifications was nothing more than a house of cards in the wind. That all the world's races shared a single, original parent language. And if that was so, it meant all human beings had once belonged to a single tribe. And to take it one step more, if that was true, the only conclusion was earthshaking: God had created all men as intellectual equals.

Beyond making a mockery of slavery, our work begged an even more shocking question: If racial hierarchies were imaginary, might servant and master even be capable of exchanging roles?

It was a thing of almost mystical beauty.

Surely society would listen this time.

For all of Darwin's carefully crafted scientific arguments, the suggestion that the white race could be related to the Hottentots had been ridiculed beyond belief. Even of those who bothered to read the book, most used the opportunity to find fault, rather than revelation.

Rulloff had said it years ago: Human beings were rational creatures only in theory. Lately, Lincoln, on the stump, had been asserting that men had no right to mislead others who have less access to history and less leisure to study it.

What had happened to the world where such a thing actually needed to be said?

His words fell on purposefully deaf ears.

I was desperate that all our sacrifices, all the lives we'd ruined, had to mean something in the end. Maybe faced with enough overwhelming evidence, men's minds could evolve as much as their bodies had.

"Are the words not beautiful?" Rulloff had said. "*Beleza inischia mot nuvat lorongimo.* The original perfect language. Can you not hear the harmony in the syllables?"

Rulloff looked both ways along the Poughkeepsie platform as if someone might still be following us.

Was that part of his act for Thornbush or more of his paranoia?

"Wonderful, wonderful," he said, grabbing Thornbush's arm and walking him to a quiet corner.

"Our newly completed opera house will host the formal ceremonies, of course," Thornbush began. "And we will have—"

"I see. Good man," Rulloff interrupted. "I'm terribly sorry to ask this, but could you tell me, as one intellectual to another, whether you find Mr. Simmons and Mr. Patrick to be *trustworthy*?"

"Well, on my word," Thornbush pulled at the sleeves of his coat, "most certainly. Why only yesterday I saw Mr. Patrick correct a young man at the bakery who'd given him too much change."

"Excellent!" Rulloff glanced around again. "Because we must present the contents of this satchel only to the most discreet of men. Only those who can be trusted. You see, Mr. Thornbush, we've brought to Poughkeepsie the most monumental book in the history of philology."

"Well," Thornbush stood back, solemnly taking on the weight of our efforts.

"Perhaps you would be so kind as to facilitate an introduction?"

"I'll do better than that," Thornbush beamed. "I'll deliver your work into their hands myself and invite you to supper at my house to discuss the particulars."

39

THREE NIGHTS LATER, I SHIFTED ON MR. THORNBUSH'S brocade settee next to the head of the Philology Institute of Philadelphia, while we waited for Mr. Simmons and Mr. Patrick to arrive.

"I must congratulate you on a splendid conference," a delegate from Rhode Island said to Thornbush.

For the first time since I'd known him, Rulloff didn't take the opportunity to win over the room with wit or flattery, nor even participate in the small talk. Instead of his normally beaming smile, an agitated grin barely clung to his face, and his left hand remained clenched in a tight fist.

With our precious manuscript in the hands of the delegates, he hadn't ceased moving for two days, certain the delay was because the chairman and secretary of the American Philological Society had employed copyists to steal our life's work and publish it under their names. I hadn't been able to calm him in the least on this point, and was having even less success doing so now that they were more than twenty minutes late for our supper.

Suffocating in the airless parlor, I asked Mr. Thornbush to point me toward the privy, hoping a little solitude would calm my jitters.

Outside, the last rays of sun illuminated the crowns of locust trees on the far side of the wall. I paused to appreciate the arial ballet of a murmuration of starlings set against the salmon sky.

"You must admit, it's painstakingly researched," I heard a man say in a hushed voice, from the street side of the wall. I recognized the deep voice of Mr. Patrick from his speeches.

I felt a dizzying surge of pride.

Were they discussing our manuscript?

My head filled with visions of speaking tours and honors and packed lecture halls.

"I'll admit it's beautifully written. Eight hundred pages, yet I read the entirety in an evening," answered Mr. Simmons. "Can you imagine the sheer volume of history, archaeology, and etymology required to draw so many connections between civilizations? There are near a thousand fascinating ideas I intend to investigate further."

"It certainly is explosive. I am grateful you reached out to me for a second opinion."

Mr. Simmons cleared his throat.

"It left me utterly speechless. Can you imagine the response?"

The dance complete, the starlings settled in the trees as the night pressed in. I drew nearer to the wall, crouching between a heavily perfumed lilac hedge and an espaliered apple tree.

"We'd lose every dime of our funding," said Mr. Patrick.

My stomach lurched.

"Good heavens, yes. If we weren't first murdered in our beds," said Simmons. "God delivered a set of languages to meet the differing conceptual needs of the races. Everyone knows that. The entire field of philology would be forever tainted if Leurio's blasphemous lunacy gets out—tied to the equally absurd notion that we were once monkeys."

"What do you think drove that odd Leurio fellow? If his conclusion wasn't as insane as Darwin's, I might say there is a touch of genius in his reasoning."

"Oh, I think he is an utter madman, pure and simple. He quotes the Bible, yet flouts God's intended role for the Caucasian race. We can't let any legitimate publisher in the country come near this dangerous work. I've drawn up a list of like-minded colleagues we'll have to petition beginning first thing tomorrow."

"Agreed," said Mr. Patrick. "However, after such a fine conference, I see nothing but a spoiled evening resulting from the truth. Do you think we could avoid such an unfortunate battle on our last night in Poughkeepsie?"

"Why don't we put it down to a budget issue and defer him to the Charleston meeting in '64? With any luck, we'll be dead by then."

Mr. Patrick laughed heartily.

I collapsed against the ensnared apple branches, trying to fathom what this tragic news meant for my hopes. Four years of work—day and night—wasted. But that was nothing. I'd traded my very soul for the promise of making an unprecedented difference in the world. For the dream of becoming the Seneca of 1860.

In the process, I'd ruined Pa's life and Aunt Babe's. Also, Potts's and a dozen other shop owners like him. Each time I'd walked away from Maggie's attic with my pockets bursting, I'd kept the heaves of shame at bay with the notion of greater good.

All the lies, all the stealing wasn't for my benefit, I'd told myself. I was fighting for justice in the war of racial equality.

It was easy enough to believe—because for all Aunt Babe's efforts, only a few dozen people had achieved freedom through her cellar.

Couldn't I make a far greater difference? Not as a poor foot soldier in the cause, but as the apprentice to a general? And if the tactics were unfortunate, hadn't Machiavelli proven dishonesty was the only path to success? Didn't I owe it to Pa and Aunt Babe and Potts to make their sacrifices add up to something meaningful?

The thing was, each time there had been more names to add to the list of people whom I owed. The levels of debt were becoming impossible, and I never came any closer to paying any of it off.

Slumped in the garden, the greater lie became clear. Machiavelli may have been right about success, but Kant was right about the soul. Not only was our manuscript beyond saving, but so was I. With nothing to give back to those I'd hurt, my only choice was to stop the madness and walk away. Crawl away, more like. Rulloff didn't need me anymore. I'd find work in a mill somewhere, or as a ranch hand, till God finally decided to end my miserable life.

Up to God if we go to our graves sooner or we go later. Up to us how we treat folks long as we draw breath.

Whatever was left of my ruined life, all I had left to offer was how I treated folks from here on out. It didn't feel like nearly enough.

When I returned to the smoke-filled gathering, I drank myself silly. I watched Rulloff through dinner as if studying a man who'd been shot but did not yet know he was dead. I barely touched the kidney pie, but made liberal use of the brandy, wine, and port.

"Did you find the discussion of the Egyptian panel enlightening, Mr. Curtis?"

"Fascinating," I said, swinging my arm to toast, but knocking the fork off my plate instead. "Oops," I said, laughing so hard I began to snort. Rulloff shot me a look across the table, and I held up my glass. "To revealing hidden secrets," I said. The table grew silent, and I realized I'd interrupted the bald man with the silver cufflinks. "Sorry. Please continue, Mr. Cufflinks."

Rulloff eyed me warily, but consumed his dessert, holding his glass in the air to toast the Carthaginians, then the Phoenicians. He still thought he had a chance of being respected among colleagues, on the verge of realizing his dreams.

The candles on the table flickered over paste porcelain. A servant who was really the dressed-up cook kept our glasses filled. I heard the delegate from Michigan agree on a point with Mr. Simmons, and having watched a master manipulator for years, I could easily spot his amateur flattery as the hope of favoritism. Meanwhile, Mr. Patrick was especially hard on the youngest attendee to reinforce his leadership status. This was no intellectual congress of brilliant linguists but a group of pandering children, all trying to advance their agendas. As they lit their cigars, I ground my teeth to hold my tongue, to keep from spitting out how detestable we all were.

"What was your opinion of our new opera house?" Mr. Thornbush asked.

"Remarkable," Rulloff said. "And if I may redirect our attention, there is the matter of the manuscript—"

"Brilliant conceit," I said, liking the way my head nodded. "A tower of vanity. *Vanité. Vanitate. Eitelkeit. Hiúság.*"

"That's quite enough, Charles."

If we'd been dining in its fifth-floor balcony, I might have jumped.

"It's been quite a week," Mr. Patrick said. "Perhaps we're nearing the end of the evening for all of us."

"Then surely it is time to discuss the primary matter at hand," Rulloff said. "I must tell you up front, I'm quite firm on the publication fee, but I'm happy to negotiate on the particulars of distribution."

"Ah," said Mr. Patrick. "I can certainly understand your position, given the extensive research that went into the work." He eyed Mr. Simmons.

"It must have taken years of study. Where did you find the time?"

"We were quite dedicated to the cause," Rulloff sat straighter.

How was he not picking up on their hesitation? He was always so astute about these things.

"I'm afraid the unfortunate truth is that our budget limitations cannot stretch far enough to bring your work under our catalog this year."

"We'll take less," I said.

"Charles—"

"I can't say I'd advise that," Mr. Patrick said. "After such considerable effort on your part. We're quite sorry that we're unable to meet your financial expectations." His eyes darted again to Mr. Simmons.

"Perhaps at the next convention we can—"

"What if we sell it for ten dollars?" I said, trying to stay steady as the floor swayed. "Would you publish it then?"

"He's a bit excited with the conference and the drink," Rulloff said. "He doesn't know what he's saying."

"Hell, I'll pay you ten dollars to print it." I pulled the notes out of my pocket and threw them on the table. "How about that? Surely, you'd be willing to accept the manuscript then."

"I'm afraid it's not quite that simple," Mr. Simmons began.

"Thank you for your time, gentlemen. I believe we must be going." Rulloff grabbed the leather satchel holding the manuscript and dragged me out of the house, where I promptly vomited on Mr. Thornbush's holly hedge.

"Have you taken leave of your senses? What in the hell is the matter with you?" he said.

"It's over." I wiped my mouth, as we stumbled along the street leading back to the hotel. "All that sacrifice, all that terrible—" I careened off a tree trunk. "Unforgivable stuff we did. All for nothing."

"Of course it's not over. Don't you see what's going on? Didn't you notice the way they looked at each other? They're planning to steal our ideas for themselves, and come out with their book."

I tripped over a rut in the street. Rulloff set his arm under me and brought me back to my feet.

"We need to move faster. To get our work out before theirs. We'll publish it ourselves and make ten times the profit. When you sober up, we'll need a plan to secure funds quickly before they beat us to the first printing."

"More bundles for Maggie," I said, too loud.

"Hush, Charles," Rulloff warned. "And I'm afraid Maggie's no longer an option."

"Ah, she's finally decided we're rubbish," I said.

"No, you foolish boy. Once we stopped delivering silks, she would have ruthlessly exposed us unless we paid outrageous sums for silence— especially once we became famous for our scholarship."

Foolish boy I may have been, but even with the world spinning around me, something in his voice registered.

"What do you mean *would* have?" I pressed him with a hard look.

"You needn't worry. Maggie's dead."

40

IN THE MORNING MY HEAD WAS FULL OF BLUE DEVILS and I deserved every bit of it.

Rulloff hustled me out of the hotel and onto a waiting train so fast he barely paused for the ink to dry when the agent scratched out our tickets. It took every bit of my focus to not vomit on anyone nearby so I was surprised to discover he'd purchased all six seats of a first-class compartment. At first, I was glad for the privacy, then immediately sorry to spend the entire journey alone with him. But unable to do anything more than survive one moment to the next, I folded myself onto the crimson velvet seat and fell into a nightmarish slumber.

When I awoke, the sun had already reached its afternoon slide. I had what Pa would have called bust-head, and my mouth tasted like pig shit, but as the trees rolled by the window I found some of my long-lost senses returning. Unfortunately, they also brought memories. I lay my head in my hands, unable to look at him.

"How?"

After all our years together, Rulloff knew exactly what I meant.

"She didn't suffer." He took a deep breath and lay back against the corner of the compartment. "It was respectful. I'm sure it was how Maggie would have chosen to go. Biscuits baked with opium powder."

"Is that supposed to make me feel better?"

Rulloff sighed, then folded his hands into his lap.

"I understand this comes as a surprise, but you must be rational about the threat she posed."

"Surprise? Is that what you call finding out I'm apprenticed to a *murderer?*"

"You need to keep your voice down."

"And what of your wife?" I spat out. "Was that a *respectful* murder as well?"

I hadn't planned such an accusation, but my mouth spoke truth even before my heart was ready to accept what I must have known all along.

Rulloff seemed to shrink into himself, and in his glance I saw a terrified nine-year-old hiding inside a six-foot body. Still, he managed to keep his voice on an even keel. He even used my real name, which he hadn't done once since leaving Aunt Babe's.

"If you will calm yourself and lower your voice, Albert, I will tell you that story. I will leave out no detail. And when it is done, we will never speak of it again."

I wouldn't have thought there was a thing on earth he could have said to calm me in that moment, but he was ever a genius at engineering attention. I would hear his confession, and as soon as the train pulled into New York, I'd part company with him forever.

"Agreed."

Rulloff settled himself, confidently crossing his legs—except I knew his moves by now. I saw the magician's trick for diverting my eyes from his trembling hand. He paused as if searching for the beginning.

"I was your age," he said. "A year or two older. And as you know, loneliness had led me to a series of catastrophic decisions. Harriet had smiled at me, seen me, not as her instructor but as a man. I allowed myself to be seduced by the fantasy that she was the one person on earth who believed in me, who saw me not as the poor teacher I was, but as the far greater man I knew I could become.

"Instead, I found myself stuck in a miserable marriage in a miserable town with no foreseeable way out. For all my skill as a physician, how could I earn a living when payment came in the form of farm animals and secondhand clothing? What reputation could an earnest doctor build in a village that persisted in believing tuberculosis to be caused by vampires?

"I was beyond desperate to escape, and wrote letters across the country. The new Medical College at Chicago was intrigued by my badger studies—such as the poultice we used on your stitches—and offered me a position at the college. Obviously, I was ecstatic, but Harriet set herself against the move from the very beginning, vowing she'd never leave her family or Ithaca.

"She was young and immune to logic, so I tried to be patient with her moods. She was with child at the time, and, thinking I could slowly break down her obstinance, I convinced the college to give me a deferment until the baby was born. I spent six onerous months, laboriously explaining the advantages of the move, the possibility it offered to help develop national medical standards and build a curriculum for practitioners. I told her of the growing town of Chicago, soon to be connected by canal, railroad, and telegraph to her precious family.

"Finally, Priscilla was born. But if anything, the child further set Harriet's mind against leaving her family, especially, she said, her brother's wife Amelia, who was due to give birth as well. I tell you, the fights I had with Harriet were torture. She would never admit the person she really didn't want to leave was her precious Doc Bull."

He shook his head.

"I don't know. I grew up in a world where a woman was bound by marriage, where they took a mighty firm stance against adultery. But Harriet's family only encouraged her faithlessness.

"By then, the medical college had written that my post would go to another if I could not take it. I was desperate to find a solution—when an opportunity presented itself. Eph's wife came down with childbed fever—as you well know, an almost impossible condition to treat. She and her baby would likely die—they were quite desperately ill— in which case Harriet would have no more excuses to delay our move to Chicago. On the other hand, if I could discover a novel method to cure their condition, how grandly would I be received in Chicago then?

"I recalled that ancient Persians had used copper to cure blood disorders and was curious whether the treatment might prove useful in other applications. I devised a protocol and meticulously documented the results, hoping they could become the basis of a prominent paper. Unfortunately, the results were not as I'd hoped, making the paper impossible, but at least Harriet's bonds to Ithaca could be severed."

It took me a minute to realize that what he meant by "severed bonds" was their deaths. I recalled the funeral so many years ago—the tedium of the long sermon in the searing summer heat, the shock when Harriet smacked me for kicking my heels against the pews.

"You *experimented* on them?"

"Don't use that tone with me. They would have died anyway, most likely, and that would have been for nothing. What would you have me do?"

"What about *first do no harm?*"

He clenched his fist.

"Albert, if you're going to hear this story, you must consider the full context. This was well over a decade ago. There were no such moral guideposts for physicians. In war, do generals not make strategic choices to risk the lives of a few soldiers in one area to save many in another? How different was my work? It had a real chance of saving thousands. People like your mother."

He shut me up good with that statement. *How different would my life have been if my mother had lived? How much more love would I have felt? How much less pain?*

"The outcome—" Rulloff paused to make sure I was with him, "—should have made things simpler, but Harriet was inconsolable, with mood swings that verged on lunacy, from excessive crying to disoriented rants. One morning she'd let the baby wail for hours, neither soothing nor feeding it. Another, she wouldn't let it out of her arms even to use the privy. I hadn't slept a wink in days between the crying and ranting and worries about arriving at my post in Chicago with a raving wife. I began to consider leaving her and the baby in the care of her family as the only option, regardless of their proximity to that rube, Doc Bull.

"But as I was packing to leave, she found the copper experiment notes. She'd been ranting for weeks, and suddenly, she looked at me like *I* was the lunatic. As if I was a *monster* for trying to improve the treatment options for such a common and devastating condition? *Oh, that look. That dreadful hour.* To have someone think you so hideous, so

unfit for belonging on this earth—it's not possible. It's not allowab...
The psyche—"

He uncrossed his legs. He was no longer trying to hide the shaking.

"I'd thought I was being helpful, but was I callous about their treatment? Did not grieving their loss reveal something *wrong* with me? The very way you're looking at me now. What penitence should I have done?

"What can I say to make you understand? When all your life you've carefully crafted supports and structures to hold the tortured parts of your soul together, and instantly it threatens to collapse. To allow someone to hold up a mirror of your deeds in a wholly different light from your intentions? To see reflected in their very eyes the unworthiness you'd managed to bury so deep. The very one who is supposed to care for you threatening to expose your most vulnerable self to the entire world, where your choices will be misinterpreted, and once again you will be pilloried? That moment was life or death for me, no different than if she'd held a knife to my breast. Worse than death—*dishonor.*

"I meant only to stop her from talking. To shut up her accusations and threats and judgments, to escape the shame she was drowning me in. Her neck was small. My hands large. It felt only a moment that I held her, trying to stop her tortured screaming, trying to halt the horrified way she looked at me. I was not a monster! I needed her to understand that.

"After it was over, I tried to bring her back. If you are to know the story, you are to know it all. Do not think me unfeeling. Weeping for my ruined life, I tried everything I knew to restore her spirit to her body. But it was done. The specter of failure I'd striven my whole life to avoid, the fate worse than death, was upon me. I was done for. I deserved to be done for. Those supports for my soul came tumbling down all around me in a pile of ash. I was worthless."

Rulloff drew his long limbs into his chest like a small child. He looked withered and beaten, ghostly pale. He continued to speak, softly, as if sheer momentum alone carried him, as if he was a moving train without the will to either create steam or apply brakes.

"I collapsed on the floor next to her body, cursing God and the world and everything that had brought me to that moment, but it did no good. I knew the fault lay within. An irredeemable flaw in my soul that made me exactly the abject monster I had tried to hide from her. There was no path forward. For all my talents and work, all was lost. The devastation was total. As I lay on the floor, bereft, I could see no choice but to take my life too. A tincture of opium would be the easiest method. I would slowly drift into a dream state of unreality where my body would simply forget to breathe.

"I'd procured the vial when the baby began to cry. The baby! Good Lord, I'd forgotten the baby. Would I leave her on the neighbor's door-step before ending my life? What if she cried and woke them before I could complete the act? And what future had I left tiny Priscilla, with a story of such parents to stalk her throughout life? I could see nothing but heartbreak, ridicule, and taunts. Better for her to join her mother and me in peaceful rest, was it not? I was so gentle with the eye drop-per, and her cries faded, faded, faded—till she lay quiet. And I felt her beautiful tiny heartbeat with my finger until it lay still.

"I set her in her mother's arms and lay beside them, bringing the vial to my lips. When they discovered our bodies, there would be no sign of struggle, no hint of remorse. Nothing to indicate that we hadn't all chosen this path as a family. Our tale would be a sad one, but not tragic. I would not be a monster.

Couldn't he see that's exactly what he was? A horrific monster who killed his wife and child and was so blind he didn't even realize how unforgivable it was?

"Then I remembered my notes on the copper experiment. Someone might read them, might see what had happened here and—well, they might get the wrong idea. I had to burn the notes, which I did, but it took time. The fire had gone cold—Harriet's neglected duties—and I needed more wood from the shed to make sure there would be nothing left but ashes.

"By the time it was done, their bodies had grown cold to the touch. Clammy, almost waxy. They felt so *dead*, so abhorrently dead. I tried a dozen times to bring that vial to my lips, but logic had returned as master of the debate in my head. It's as if I woke up from a trance. What had happened was terrible, but need we all die in vain? Could I not make up for my horrific deed in some way? Vow to make their deaths meaningful?

"It occurred to me, then, that there was nothing left to hold me back from the post in Chicago. You will think it so obvious, but until that very moment it had entirely escaped my notice. I thought—if I put all of my talents and knowledge in service of the greater good, and one day managed to change the world—wouldn't that be a better way to honor Harriet and Priscilla than merely taking my life?

I could hold my impassive face no longer.

"How could you do something so terrible?"

"Judge me as you will, Albert Jarvis, but first ask yourself how different your choices have been from mine."

All the rage, all the judgment I aimed at him, suddenly turned and came straight back at me like a runaway horse. Hadn't I told myself a similar story? My slide into the abyss had begun so subtly, so effortlessly, yet built to a massive fall, and a point of no return. I hadn't murdered anyone directly, but wasn't I responsible for ruining Pa and Aunt Babe, Potts, and dozens of others? Wasn't I the one who gave away our identities to Maggie? Hadn't my actions led to her death as surely as the hand that replaced her biscuit tin? Rulloff wasn't a world apart from me. He was just a shade away.

"This has to end," I struggled to breathe. "You can have the manuscript, take all the credit. I'll keep your secret in the strictest confidence, but I can't do this anymore. As soon as we arrive in New York, I'll find another path. I don't know what. I don't know if it even matters."

"You'll do no such thing," Rulloff said.

I looked at him in shock.

"I still need your help to secure funds to publish the book," he said. "I just told you this is the most important thing in the world— the reason I'm still alive, the world-changing manuscript my wife and daughter died for. I can't refuse to honor their sacrifice because the jealous twits in Poughkeepsie want it for their own, or because my partner can't stand to look at my face."

"You expect me to steal more silks? Ruin more shop owners? After all this?"

"Just this once. I only need enough to pay a publisher for the initial print run. If you must leave after that, I'll be disappointed, but I will allow it."

"Well forget it. I don't have it in me. Hell, you're right. I'm near as wretched as you, but I'm not doing another thing. Do what you will to me. I deserve it well enough. If you've a bottle of opium in your pocket, hand it over, and I'll save you the trouble."

"Oh, Albert," Rulloff said gently. "After so many years together, you must know I could never harm you. You're my only friend on this earth. I couldn't do what you're saying even if it were in my best interests. Even if my life was at stake. I promise."

"Then you'll let me leave?"

"Of course not. I told you I need your help. But one last job, and I'll wish you the best of luck on your journey."

"Not going to happen," I said flatly, gathering my hat as the train slowed, finally coming into the city. "If you're not going to kill me, you're going to have to let me go."

He took my arm firmly in his right hand and picked up the satchel with his left.

"I cannot make the same promise about your dear Aunt Babe," he said and dragged me out of the compartment, onto the platform.

My head spun with revelations and threats, and I struggled to get my bearings. The surrounding streets were only vaguely familiar and in my woozy state I wondered if I'd been drugged. Had we come into Rose Hill or Eleventh Avenue? I looked at the station house for direction and stopped short when I read the sign.

BINGHAMTON.

41

THE TOWN HAD GROWN IN THE YEARS SINCE RULLOFF
had freed me from its jail. Many of the small homes with open yards
had been replaced by brick houses with fences, and a cigar factory
loomed across the river. The jailhouse was exactly where I remembered
it, but they'd built a courthouse alongside, with a bright copper dome
oxidizing in streaks of pigeon-crap green.

Was Phinneas still shining his shoes in that chair, eating biscuits
without gravy?

"Clearly you have a plan," I grumbled. "Feel like telling me what it
is?" I tried to force my splitting head to figure a way out of this mess.

The late afternoon sun illuminated Rulloff's face in a vibrant glow.

"As you may have anticipated, we can't operate in New York anymore without risking a connection to Maggie's death." He cradled the
satchel protectively against his body as if it were filled with diamonds.

What were the chances he'd actually let me go as promised? Not until
he had money for the job. Then not until the manuscript was published.
Then not until the reviews had been written. Then not until the speaking
tours were complete. Then—never. I knew the man too well. Aunt Babe
wouldn't be safe unless I could find a way to stop Rulloff completely.

"I'm sure you recall I worked on the canal boats once. We can take
the goods from Binghamton to Baltimore straight down the Susquehanna, then sell them to a merchant at too good a price for questions.
The whole process will take two weeks at most."

When had he worked all this out?

"I can't argue with the logic, save for two small problems I could
point out—if I may."

"By all means."

Was his three-barreled pistol in the satchel or his pocket?

"First, we don't have any goods, and second, we don't have a boat."
Rulloff laughed.

Did he believe I was playing his game or suspect I was stalling?

"The second is easy enough to solve. I'll find a vessel. Something older, not yet upgraded to steam, so we can operate in silence. The first is also quite feasible. When we were here four years ago, we passed a fancy little shop downtown, right on the river. Do you recall?"

"Halbert's," I realized with a start.

"Yes, the very one. Of course, it's also a wonderful opportunity for revenge on the man who put you in jail." He shot me a playful smile, as if this was a grand joke, as if Aunt Babe's life and Halbert's livelihood didn't hang in the balance.

I tried my best to return the grin and buy time.

If he set the satchel down, how long would it take me to extract the gun if it was in there?

We stopped in front of a four-story brick building with arched windows on Court Street, two doors from the river. A kelly-green awning helped conceal sight lines to the front door. It had become second nature for us to stroll casually past a display window, taking in the layout and merchandise. As Rulloff had anticipated, we found finely carved cases lining the walls, filled with silks. Halbert must have been doing well for himself—his stocks rivaled some of the city's finest.

A getaway would be risky, though. If anything went wrong, rivers blocked our exit in three of four directions. The few narrow bridges could all too easily be barricaded by people on the far banks. In the town itself, dozens of apartments sat over the shops.

If I did find the gun in the satchel and managed to get it out, could I make myself use it?

I followed Rulloff off the road and slid on my soles down a sodden, grassy bank toward the river, muddying the cuffs of my pants. At the bottom, Rulloff leaned his back against a willow and looked up at the sky. His feet slipped slightly underneath him, the tree cracking from his weight. Then he stood, yawned, and ambled to the next one, testing its strength.

A giggle drew my attention to a young woman a short distance down the river path, standing next to a young man. I recognized her raven-black hair immediately. *What was she now? Sixteen?* Miss Violet Halbert. Her companion was roughly her age, with sandy curls and an apron the same kelly green as the awning. Both had the shy smiles and perpetually angled heads of sweethearts. He stood at the edge of the water skipping rocks with the shy confidence I'd always wanted to have at his age. The setting sun reflected off the ripples in a magical tangerine color, but when I looked up, charcoal clouds were sweeping in from the horizon.

Rulloff wiped his palms together, then faced the river and seemed to take careful note of its contours. Then he motioned for me to follow him the opposite way along the river path. I was grateful not to interrupt Miss Violet or the boy who courted her affections. I felt the prickle of goosebumps.

She'd made it through scarlet fever and grown up. If I'd played any part in that outcome, it was the one thing I'd done right in my life.

I smiled to myself, then realized I was about to bankrupt her father.

About a mile upstream, Rulloff stepped down a ramp to a floating dock alongside the river. A half dozen vessels were tied up, and he walked slowly by each one, calling hallo to a captain here, a deckhand there, passing each of the steamers. Finally, he squeezed past a team of two oxen tied to the dock and stopped at a large flat-bottomed boat with no boiler. A canvas tarp stretched across the housing. Under the canopy, the boat's hold sat empty.

"Good evening to you, Sir," Rulloff said to the captain. "I wonder if you might have a moment to hear about Sullivan's new steam engines. They can be retrofitted to near any vessel and will have you running up and down the river in half the time."

The old captain merely scratched at the white beard on his neck.

"I look like the kind of man can afford a steamer? You think I wouldn't rather have my Irishman load coal 'stead a whipping those smelly beasts?"

Rulloff laughed.

"Permission for a poor salesman to come aboard, Sir? I haven't been on one of these since the early forties."

I leaned tentatively on a tarred post. *If the pistol was in his coat, would it be the inside left pocket or the outside right pocket?*

"You a captain?"

"No," Rulloff stepped off the ramp into the boat and ran his hand lovingly against the gunnel. "Never more than a lowly deckhand," he laughed. "In my younger days."

"You run this river? You look familiar," the captain said.

I looked around for the fastest way off the dock, poised to run if he recognized Rulloff's infamous face.

"I was up north along the Erie. Did the city to Buffalo run mostly." The sun ducked behind the willow trees.

"Locks and channels," the captain said. "Always wanted to have a look at 'em, but here I am. Chenango to the Susquehanna to the Chesapeake. That's my route."

"Where's your Irishman tonight?" Rulloff asked. "Not out drinking, I hope."

The captain gestured for Rulloff to sit on an upturned crate.

"No. He's a good enough lad. We're stopped for a few days waiting on cigars to head south. He has a cousin, lives next town over, so he's gone for a visit."

Rulloff accepted the crate and carefully placed the satchel between his knees as he sat, then smiled wide and mysterious.

"Susquehanna men don't happen to play dice, do they?"

I guessed the gun must be inside with the manuscript after all.

The captain pulled a half-empty bottle of rum out from under his seat. "I can see you're determined to pick my pockets any way you can," he said. "But I'll play you a game of dice."

It grew dark. I could smell the clouds roll in, heard the willows buck in the growing wind. The captain lit a small, squeaking oil lamp hanging above his head. The boat rocked in the current while I waited on the dock, pressing a knob of tar between my thumb and finger.

If I ran, what were the chances I could reach Aunt Babe before Rulloff? If I could, then what? Tell her she'd have to leave the farm forever?

"My assistant and I are meeting a few friends at the American Hotel later," Rulloff said to the captain. "You're welcome to join us."

Why invite the man for drinks? I tried to work out the con, but he was way ahead of me. I looked for some kind of weapon on the boat I might grab.

The crowbar? If I were fast enough to hit Rulloff over the head, what would the captain do? Call for help. Throw me in jail. As soon as Rulloff recovered, Aunt Babe would be dead.

"Thank you kindly, but there's the beasts to look after. You understand."

"I certainly do," Rulloff said, and peeked under his dice cup, placing a five-dollar note in the center of the table. "Nice low draft you have on this boat. Three twos."

The captain raised his eyes at the size of the note. He looked under his cup, then off to the side. Finally, he dug into his pockets and pulled out a small pile of coins. "Four twos. They pay you well at this steamship company, I see."

He passed Rulloff the bottle.

"Ah, yes. More than I can spend, really, traveling as much as I do. But I'll tell you I do miss being on the water. Five twos."

The captain sat back with surprise that caught my attention. I hadn't tried to follow the rules of this game, much less understand what Rulloff was doing playing dice, but I knew enough to know his plan was in motion. "I'll have to challenge you there," said the captain.

Rulloff shrugged his shoulders, then tilted his head into his acting role. "I have just the one die on my side," he said. "You looked pretty sure of yourself. I was guessing you had more."

This was illogical enough I could see he was losing on purpose, but to what end?

The captain removed his cup to reveal only two twos, then scooped the money into his cap.

"One more game?" he asked.

"Oh, why not," Rulloff said, taking a swig and handing the bottle back. "Does this boat run with a rudder or just oars, then?"

"Dual rudders. Work like a charm," the captain said. "It has been a while since you've been on a boat. You're practically leaning on the tiller there."

"Yes, yes, of course." He placed a ten-dollar note on the table.

"You know, I was on a boat very much like this once. Spent an entire summer taking soundings up and down Cayuga Lake for a steamship company. Can you believe there's parts of that lake more than four-hundred-feet deep?" Rulloff shook his head, smiled, relaxed. "Boggles the mind. So deep, when we pulled up the lead weights, they'd be nearly cold as ice." He laughed. "Young men we were, we'd arm wrestle for the chance to touch something so cold on those steamy August days."

I leaned hard on the post.

How cold? Less than forty-one degrees?

I'd studied enough medicine to know those temperatures would keep a body from rotting. If Rulloff had locked his wife and daughter in a trunk, weighted it with irons, and dropped it at the right spot, it could have sunk four hundred feet to the bottom. That would have been well past the reach of all the lake dragging done before his trial. If I was right, Rulloff's wife and daughter would remain at the bottom of Cayuga Lake forever. *Eyes wide open.*

Rulloff intentionally lost another three games, while I tried and failed to come up with a way to stop him that didn't result in Aunt Babe's death. Finally, he tipped his hat to the captain, and I followed him back toward the American Hotel.

"Mark my words," Rulloff said. "That captain's off to turn easy money into easy drink at the Bedford Arms."

"Why? You invited him to the American."

"Yes, and if you just won forty dollars, would you want to spend it in front of the man you'd just defeated, or go somewhere to toast your fortune where you didn't have to feel bad for another man's losses?"

"Well played," I said.

Maybe if I could get some drink in him?

"Shall we go into the American then until he leaves? I'll buy you a brandy."

But a shadow passed, hunched along the road, and I recognized the boat captain's wool coat and white beard in the tavern's glow. Off to spend his winnings on drink, exactly as predicted. I spit into the bushes.

"No time to lose," Rulloff said.

42

I STEPPED INTO THE BOAT AND TOOK A POSITION BY THE gunwale, underneath the canvas tarp that smelled of bird droppings and mildew. The night air turned crisp.

In the moonless dark, Rulloff cast off. While I could see little, after all these years together I knew his every move even on an unfamiliar boat—where his hand would be, where his foot would fall. Without speaking, I knew that he would pilot and I would pole, I knew, as if we shared the same mind, how hard to press at the muck-covered river bottom as he steered. The wood was worn smooth against my palm by decades of an honest boatman's labor.

Could I use it to knock him out of the boat and into the river? What were the chances he would survive?

He was a boatman. Probably knew how to handle himself in the water.

On the black void of the river, night seemed to squeeze out even the air. I inched nearer to the satchel, but Rulloff had it right at his feet and was working the buckles with one hand while he piloted with the other. The current carried us downriver swiftly, fed by the rain.

"There," he said. "Halbert's." He worked the tiller at a sharp angle, as if he wanted to ram us into the shore, then he gave the rudder a final shove and brought the boat parallel to the bank with a practiced ease. He handed me a heavy coil of line affixed to the stern cleat, and I leaped into the shallows. The cold bite of the river surprised me, given the warmth of the night.

I climbed the bank, struggling to get traction on the slope while playing out the rope, but managed to wrap the line around the willow trunk Rulloff indicated. The boat drifted slowly past, until the heavy line ran taut and the tree shuddered. I heard a splash, and a minute later Rulloff secured the bow to another tree.

Maybe I could find a way to stop him after the theft. Up here, Phinneas was sure to recognize us both, but down south I could tip off the Baltimore police. Let them catch us with stolen goods that could be returned to Violet's father. Instead of fugitives, with luck they'd see two simple thieves. We'd get prison time, but maybe that would be enough for Aunt Babe to live out the rest of her life in peace.

I crept as quietly as I could to the back alley, where I found that Halbert's lock was trickier than I'd expected. In addition to the old thumb latch, he'd installed a hefty padlock, still shiny. Had someone tried to rob him before? Poor Halbert didn't realize I'd become a thief skilled enough to pick most anything but a Herring's safe—but picking a lock required tools we didn't have with us. I shivered in my soaked trousers.

Rulloff stepped in with the crowbar from the boat. I stood, alert for any noise that could wake the sleeping neighbors. He knew it was important to give the door steady pressure so that it broke with a light click instead of a loud clatter. But when he pulled on the crowbar the door only groaned. He tried again, his impatience growing.

"Hell with it," he said, and threw his whole weight against the bar. The solid oak of the doorframe snapped and the door flung open in a loud, splintering pop. A piece of the brass bolt clattered to the stone below, echoing into the silence.

I waited, breathless in the dark, but no lantern light pierced the dark and no sudden glow lit the surrounding windows. After a minute, I knew we'd been lucky. We were always lucky.

We entered a black hallway—Rulloff first, then me. The drips from my trousers soaked the wooden floor. I let my eyes adjust to the dark and noticed the faintest outline of a steep staircase to my right. A floorboard creaked. Then it creaked again.

I turned and saw the glow of a match light the stairwell, then flare out. The next thing I knew, I was flying across the hall. My head bashed into the wall and I slumped to the floor.

I pressed myself backward to find leverage, but in the darkness could barely tell up from down. A body was on top of me. I kicked out but struck the wall. The pain in my foot drew my rage and I kicked again, connecting with flesh. I heard a groan. Then a sharp pain sliced through my rib and I screamed.

"Don't move!"

The voice broke. It was the voice of a boy, not a man. A strong boy. My belly grew warm. I smelled blood.

The boy pressed his knee into my left shoulder, pinning me painfully against the ground. My rage turned to terror. I swung a fist blindly into the air, but connected only with his shoulder. I felt the knife plunge into me again. The pain knocked the breath out of me.

"Help! Help at Halbert's!" The boy shouted through the open door into the night.

My whole body vibrated with agony.

Was this my end? Stabbed to death on the floor of a Binghamton hallway?

I reached up to grab the boy's neck, but my hands were too weak to press on his windpipe. I grew more exhausted by the second, and tried to force myself to think.

Rulloff would slip quietly out the front door and escape on the boat. In the darkness, even the boy would never know there had been more than one thief.

I stopped fighting and surrendered to the moment. He'd have no reason to hurt Aunt Babe now. The relief felt exquisite as I let the end come, appreciating each final detail. The wet wool of my trousers, the iron-rich smell of my blood, the hot breath of the boy. A shaft of moonlight grew strong enough I could see the boy's sandy curls and frightened eyes.

Violet's sweetheart.

Then I saw a flash, heard a trio of explosions, and was suddenly showered in sticky heat. The knee slid off my shoulder and the boy collapsed on top of me, the knife flat against my chest. Rulloff threw his gun down on the floor and pushed the boy's body out of the way. The moonlight revealed he no longer had a face.

Rulloff cradled me in his arms.

"I've got you. Hang on."

He threw me over his shoulder as he ran out the back door. Every bounce jostled my organs and felt like another stab wound.

"Stay with me, Albert" he gasped.

The panicked clang of the church bell reverberated through the night. The rush of the river grew closer, and I became woozy. A hundred different stars moved on the ground nearby. *Or were they demons?*

"Why?" I pleaded. "He was just a boy."

"Shhh," Rulloff said to me. "Save your strength."

Far off, I heard a man shout: "Murder!" He sounded as panicked as the bell. More torches flared. A strange kind of dawn.

Why hadn't he left me behind?

Rulloff slid on the bank. The grass leaped up and smacked me hard on the shoulder. The pain was intense.

"Stay here," he said and ran to untie the bow line.

Frigid water shocked me back into the moment. I must have passed out. The icy current grabbed at my trouser legs, but Rulloff held me solid on his shoulder, squeezing his arm around my waist. Then I crashed into something wooden. The cockpit of the boat.

"I'll be right back," he said and ran up the bank to untie the stern line. Even shallow breaths made me hack, and each cough felt like I was being stabbed all over again. I held my palm tight against my belly and struggled to gulp at the air.

He was going to get away. If he got away, he wouldn't stop. He'd keep doing this as long as he lived—killing people to advance his ambitions— adding links to his heavy chain of sin, on the hope that achievement would magically free him from the unbearable weight.

Rulloff trudged up the bank to the willow tree, where he worked to untie the line that ran to the stern cleat. The river tugged hard at the bottom of the vessel, and the boat pulled in turn, as if it wanted to be free of land.

Maggie was dead. A boy had no face. Eph's wife and baby were in their graves. And somewhere at the bottom of Cayuga Lake, Rulloff's wife and daughter stared at each other, open-eyed forever.

"Keep pressure on the wound, Albert," he called over his shoulder. "I'll be right there. We'll be down river before they even know there was a boat."

He'd saved me from loneliness as a child and ignorance as a young man. He'd risked his life to save me from jail in Binghamton, and now he was doing it all over again. For all he spoke of rationalism, his actions proved the depth of his heart.

He'd worked the line free and was holding the heavy boat purely with his strong frame, pulling it toward the bank where he could leap aboard. He was right. The lanterns wouldn't arrive in time. We'd slip away from the boy with no face like ghosts in the night.

I recalled Plato. *Justice is man's primary duty.*

I pushed myself up on one arm with the last of my strength and unwound the stern line from the cleat.

The boat lurched away from the shore, finding the center of the fast-moving current, driven downstream unguided. Rulloff stood on the bank, backlit by the growing torchlight, trapped with a limp piece of rope. His silhouette shrank rapidly, but the slump of his shoulders was clear enough.

As he processed my betrayal he broke my dying heart.

43

I STRETCHED MY ARM ABOVE MY HEAD. A SHARP PAIN seared through my belly.

"Fuck!" I flung open my eyes and saw the sky and part of a tent—no, a tarp. The night before came rushing back. I'd been stabbed. The boy had no face. I'd trapped Rulloff on the bank.

Apparently, a quick death was too easy. I was to die slowly—tortured by memories of the suffering I'd caused: Aunt Babe and Pa, scores of merchants, Maggie, Miss Violet's suitor with his sandy curls. The excruciating shame was far more painful than death. I couldn't forgive myself for any of it, but loathed myself especially because, for all my unforgivable sins, the feeling that sickened me most was how I'd betrayed my only friend.

I turned over and a searing pain mercifully blocked out such soul-wrenching thoughts. Still, I pushed myself up to a sitting position, biting my lip, and slumped against a crate. The boat had come to rest on a muddy bank, held fast by an eddy. A mile down the way a steeple punctured the line of trees. My shirt stuck to my skin with a crust of blood that I dissolved slowly in muddy bilge water, to get a look. When I saw the dirty slash across my belly, my raw pink guts trying to spill out, my hands began to shake.

Rulloff would have said it could have been worse. The knife hadn't stabbed so much as slashed. Two gashes had sliced open my belly, just above my belt, and a couple of inches to the right.

I tried to recall anatomy diagrams from books. If my stomach had been penetrated, the acids would have poured out, and I would never have made it through the night. My spleen was on the other side, so that was untouched. Kidneys were back farther, bladder lower. I was breathing, so my diaphragm had been spared. That meant the holes were in my bowels.

Death would come, but it would take its time about it. I'd start to ooze pus by nightfall, but would likely remain lucid the better part of the day—wracked with memories more painful than the wound—before a blissful fever brought on incoherence. A few days more before I'd become a corpse.

What did one do on his last clear-headed day on the earth? Stare at the sky? Seek out a pastor? Find a quiet place to die? I wanted to ask Rulloff. Then I wanted to kill him for what he'd done.

When the answer came to me, it had two parts.

The satchel sat right where Rulloff had left it, buckles open but manuscript safe and sound, as if a world apart from the nightmares it had caused. I removed the stack of pages and ran a blood-smeared finger over the delicate, looped handwriting of the introduction, the chapter explaining the root sounds, the etymologies I'd spent so many years painstakingly crafting in the office on Third Avenue, while the whale oil burned and Rulloff pushed for ever-deeper connections.

On the Origin of Language—our linguistic companion to Darwin's biology. Full of research that proved God had not chosen some and demoted others. The man banned from the omnibus was as worthy and intelligent as the one who sat behind a mahogany desk, the Sligo maid as deserving as the Protestant one, the Chinaman on Bottle Alley as exceptional as Queen Victoria in her palace.

For those inclined to listen, our manuscript proved these things. But that was the problem exactly. The people who most needed to be convinced of its concepts were the last ones who would read it with an open mind. Even the titans of philology had been unable to comprehend something their minds had made impossible from the start.

What was the likelihood our meticulously researched and cross-indexed manuscript could ever have the slightest influence on banning slavery in the territories?

Nothing about its existence could make up for Rulloff killing his wife and child, or the Schutts, or Maggie, or the boy. Nothing about its existence made the world a better place for me being in it.

It took only the slightest push for the trail of pages to flutter over the gunwale like cherry blossom petals on a gentle breeze. They floated peacefully downstream for a short while, until they were sucked below the surface into the dark belly of the river.

Part one accomplished.

Part two would be much harder.

My shirt front was black with dried blood, even as fresh crimson continued to seep through. My trousers and jacket displayed a sheen of gore, but its deep blue color provided some camouflage. I fastened the coat buttons to cover the worst of the stains and washed my face and hands the best I could in the bilge water. Into one pocket I set a box of bullets and into the other, the captain's half bottle of rum.

I had to rest for ten minutes after this effort, holding my palm tight against my belly, which was bleeding again. Then I pulled myself out of the boat and staggered through the underbrush until I found a path through the woods. I walked with a hunch, elbow pressed into the wound, gritting my teeth against the burn of my belly. Every step was excruciating, but the hardest part was making sure the dizziness didn't turn to faint.

As I got closer to town, I tried to stand straighter, pinning my arm against the fraying wool where the knife had penetrated. It was more of an outpost than a town, really. Dirt streets, plank walks. The air thick and sweet with the unmistakable scent of a blackberry pie. I almost laughed.

Always, always a pie.

My shabby suit and mud-stained cuffs would have earned scornful glances in the city, but in this town, the two men who stood in the long afternoon shadows nodded hello. A woman with a basket of green beans, wearing a rag for a kerchief, smiled at me. A couple young boys tried to convince a beagle pup to chase a lizard.

No one here needed to change the world or put their name in the history books. They wanted enough rain to water the crop without drowning it, for their pregnant daughter to give birth safely, for their wife to lay off about fixing the shed roof, for a sick horse to pull through.

Ambition meant a full hay crop. They weren't heroes, maybe, but they certainly weren't villains.

Across the street sat the post office, complete with a telegraph machine several years past its prime. The attendant seemed distracted with his newspaper, so I took a pencil from the cup and wrote on a form stamped Halstead Telegraph Office.

Deliver to:

    Beatrice Jarvis, Jarvis Farm, Ithaca

Message:

    I'm sorry, Aunt Babe.

Stop

After the attendant sent the telegram, he sat down and opened his newspaper. MURDERER CAUGHT IN BINGHAMTON, shouted the headline. I had no interest in reading further, no need to study the description of the murderer's partner still at large—six foot, black hair, wounded in the belly—it would say. They'd find me soon enough, but I'd managed to complete part two. *Now I could die.*

I left the office, found the nearest hotel, and paid in advance for four days at the Liberty Inn. I estimated I'd be dead in three.

The man behind the counter looked at me curiously when I asked for a glass of milk, a pair of pliers, sewing needle, and a newspaper, but I'd set a ten-dollar note on the counter, and he cheered right up.

In the room, while consciousness remained, I did as I'd learned— more as a matter of training than aiming for any desired outcome. I removed the gunpowder from the bullets with the pliers and threaded the needle. Propping myself up against the headboard, with the newspaper underneath to catch the blood, I unbuttoned my shirt and examined the wound.

We're going to hold the two edges tight together, alright?

I took a long swig of the rum with my left hand and pressed the flaps of skin together with my right until they pushed out like a frown.

You see, we're taking care now to penetrate the skin at the perpendicular, to minimize the entry wound and help you grow up to be a handsome boy with a character-building scar.

I pushed the needle through the skin. Blood oozed out the center of the gash and into my trousers. I gritted my teeth and made a stitch, then another, until I had counted out twenty-six. Then I covered the wound with the gunpowder poultice and fell into a nightmarish slumber.

The first time I awoke, my head hurt as much as my stomach. I rolled up to a seated position, just enough to piss in the pot and close the curtains. The second time I awoke in darkness, black enough that it must have been night. Past that, the fever grew and nothing made sense anymore. Spiders the size of horses dropped from the ceiling. The room filled with boiling river water. Rulloff came to me, devastated by my betrayal, his blue eyes turning black.

With the first stabs of lucidity, I had to blink back daylight. A maid must have opened the curtains and emptied the pot. The ceiling plaster was chipped in three places, the wallpaper stained brown from some sort of leak. I pulled up my shirt, saw the seam of black stitches running across my stomach, and clenched my teeth. I pressed at the wound under the poultice and felt a dull ache, but not a sharp pain, and I observed no bleeding under the skin or other signs of blood poison.

Death had rejected me for now, sent me back to live my few remaining days tortured with self-abasement. Still, for all my desire to die on that river, I found myself grateful for the pain, the thirst, the brightness that seared my eyes. For an additional breath, the cracked ceiling, and itchy blanket. For a day or two before the sheriff came looking for the murderer's partner and led me to the noose. I pushed myself up against the headboard and rubbed my face with my hands.

The maid had left newspapers, neatly stacked on the bedside table. Three days' worth.

BINGHAMTON MURDERER DISCOVERED TO BE NOTORIOUS ITHACA BABY KILLER!

I forced myself to read the article through several times, pressing my finger against the page to remain focused. The faceless boy had a name: Fredrick Merrick. The newspaper praised his courage in defending his employer's shop against an intruder, but all I could think was that he was dead. He'd taken on two robbers and lost his life for a few bolts of fabric that didn't even belong to him.

A list of Rulloff's previous misdeeds and escapes followed, along with a shocking etching of him battering his wife with a heavy iron pestle.

A fictional representation, perhaps, but was the truth any less offensive?

I searched every page of every paper for the description he would have provided to help police capture the partner who'd so cruelly betrayed him. There was none. While some writers were skeptical on this point, Rulloff's confession about the Halbert's robbery had included a key point—he'd been working alone.

Despite my betrayal, Rulloff had once again saved my life.

Over the next few weeks, the newspapers kept coming. For a while, Rulloff was more talked about than President Grant. The pages filled with etchings of him studying in his cell at Auburn Prison, copies of his handwriting, talk of a lost manuscript about languages. He'd achieved the fame he'd so long desired—not as a brilliant linguist but as the grisly "Educated Murderer." His intelligence had been tested by multiple experts, some of whom proclaimed him to be of remarkable, almost impossible, intellect. Others put his ideas down to trickery. They didn't need evidence beyond the obvious. How could someone educated enough to read New Testament Greek miss the moral lessons enclosed within its text?

Ultimately, the papers got some facts right and some facts wrong, but they never came close to answering the question everyone was asking: Why had a man with such a towering intellect turned to crime?

Yet if his past was murky, his future was even more problematic. Did one kill a genius or allow him to continue with his intellectual works while preventing his immoral ones? His case became a cause célèbre and an argument against capital punishment. Papers filled afresh with opinion pieces about whether the death penalty was barbaric, whether it represented cruel and unusual punishment. Some claimed his education should exempt him, others that it made him more culpable. Mark Twain satirically suggested the state hang an imbecile in his place so that all could be happy with the result.

The courts of New York State, however, paid the newspapers no attention, and the trial was over quickly. Rulloff had escaped the hangman's noose twice already. Nothing would prevent his final date with it.

My stomach grew queasy as the day neared. The man who'd been loyal to me all my life was to die virtually by my hand. I hated Rulloff, yet I loved him. I owed him my education, my liberty, and my life—but in exchange I'd allowed him to corrode my soul. I was alive and could not manage to change that fact. As Rulloff discovered early on, the body rebels against suicide. I could no more refrain from saving mine than I could refuse to breathe. Yet, I wished I'd never entered the world, had never had the chance to stain it with my disgrace, my ignominy.

Living without self-respect was not living at all.

So, what of my sentence? If I wasn't to be hung or imprisoned, if the courts were not to decide my fate, I would have to act as my own judge and jury. That was the cruelest and most unusual punishment of all, because I knew exactly the penalty I most feared. And this was the exact wrath I cast upon myself—the harshest possible castigation.

I would have to face up to my shameful acts in front of those I'd wronged—starting with Rulloff.

44

A KINDLY-LOOKING OLDER COUPLE LET ME RIDE IN their cart as they traveled to Binghamton for the hanging, as long as I promised to keep the peace between their two boys, who were otherwise inclined to beat on each other. I lay back in the wagon and marveled that the sky still had the heart to be so blue.

"They say he's a real monster," the older boy said to the younger. "With fangs."

"Is not."

The older boy, who probably had patience for nothing else in life, found it in torture. He took his time with the story, blowing his bangs from his eyes.

"Is so," he said, "and red eyes."

The younger one looked at me expectantly, with a crease across his forehead that said he was determined not to believe his brother but would anyway.

"That's enough," said their mother, who shot me a disapproving look, as if I should have been able to stop boys from being boys. "We're taking this trip to show you what happens if you don't learn to be good."

"He killed hundreds of people," whispered the older boy.

The creaking wheel hit a rut and I tried not to wince at the pain in my belly.

"Did not," said the younger boy proudly, happy to have a fact in his possession. "Five." He counted them off, one for each finger. "The lady, her baby, the other lady, her baby and the stock boy."

"Five they know about," his brother corrected him.

The younger boy pulled at my sleeve. "Tell him there was five."

I watched the wind come up in the trees, the clouds drawing in the chill that would soon blow all through September, straight on till harvest. Reluctantly I thought of Maggie, who made six, but also Pa and Aunt Babe, Josiah, Eph, Hornberger, Potts, Thornbush and scores of merchants, all done in by the monstrous team of Rulloff and Jarvis.

"Hundreds of victims," I said.

Even the older boy stayed quiet after that.

THE GRASSY SQUARE by the Binghamton Courthouse had been transformed into an outdoor theater for the live production of a Shakespearean-level tragedy. A gallery on either side of the green promised comfortable seating for a few dozen important people. In the center of the stage towered the gallows, built tall enough to be visible from the far side of the square, so no one would miss tomorrow's show. Several enterprising families had already staked out the territory closest to the scaffold and, judging by the remnants of cook fires, had been waiting several days for the main event.

The jailhouse itself was still tiny, but now it was guarded by a dozen men with rifles. Just before sunset, Phinneas followed his routine and headed home for supper. I watched his satisfied, loping gait shrink into the distance—until even the faintest sound of his whistle had disappeared on the breeze.

Up to God if we go to our graves sooner, or we go later. Up to us how we treat folks long as we draw breath.

By trying too hard to become a hero, I'd become a villain. I was in deep deficit on my life's account books, and there was only one way forward—to treat people the best I could from here on out—especially the ones who mattered most.

I buttoned my coat, took a deep breath and marched straight up to the guard who seemed to be in charge—confident, articulate, and poised.

"There is a last-minute development I must discuss with my client," I said, pointing to the empty satchel on my shoulder.

The guard shook his head.

"You reporters have been trying every trick in the book to get in there for a story," he said. "I ain't buying it."

"This could be critical to his case," I continued. "You don't want to be responsible for a gross miscarriage of justice."

The man cradled his rifle stock and looked quietly, casually threatening.

The next step felt like suicide.

"If you don't believe I'm his attorney, just take me in there and ask him," I said.

I had no idea how he would react. Face-to-face with his executioner, would Rulloff change his mind and implicate me?

The guard thought for a moment, then a spark of curiosity crossed his eye. He opened the door and dragged me through by the arm. Rulloff sat with his head down, cross-legged and shackled to the stone floor.

"This one your lawyer?"

Rulloff glanced up with slow fatigue, then stared an extra minute when he saw me. I was drowning again, unable to breathe, unable to kick or flail or pull myself out. Surely, his word along with my stab wound would be proof enough to ensure the stage on the green stayed up long enough for a second show.

"He is my attorney," Rulloff said finally. Nothing more.

Once the disappointed guard left, Rulloff made no attempt to move, so I squatted down to his level, too overwhelmed with guilt to speak.

"You survived," he said.

I swallowed, took up my shirt and unwrapped the muslin to show him the wound.

"Thanks to your poultice."

He allowed himself a small smile.

"Stitches make it look like a bear got after you."

I looked about the room for anything to comment on, but could think of nothing beyond the question smoldering in my heart.

"Why didn't you send them after me?"

Rulloff blinked slowly and failed to contain a sigh.

"I don't suppose you actually have a pardon in that satchel," he s

"Why?" I pressed.

"A vial of opium? You know hanging is the most excruciating form of death."

I sat on the floor cross-legged in front of him, emotions draining out of me like lifeblood. I began to understand that Rulloff's slow-eyed movements were due to the physical crash of despair. Wretched sorrow is what was left after the dam burst and all the secrets flowed out. I swallowed again, waited.

"To what end? You were dead or you were alive. I told you I could never harm you. You're my—" He placed a shaking hand under his knee. "They say your neck breaks from the drop but rarely is such a precise outcome achieved—if it is even desired. If the rope's too thin, the hanged man is decapitated. If it's too short, strangulation can take fifteen minutes or more. Either of those outcomes is a better crowd-pleaser than a simple broken neck."

I didn't fill the silence that followed. With all the discipline I could muster, I sat and waited in the discomfort. I let the awkwardness act as bait for the real truths that must be spoken. A trick I'd learned, of course, from him.

"You're my only friend on this earth."

He drew his arms across his chest and grasped his elbows as if he was forcibly trying to keep his heart from bursting from his chest.

"Is anyone else outside asking for me? A telegram boy?"

This was unexpected.

"The telegram office closed hours ago," I said, trying to work through my confusion. "We're you hoping the governor—"

"My brother," he said. "Ridiculous, I know, but I was hoping for a word." He was a deflated balloon who still managed to quiver in the slightest wind. "I sent William a telegram twenty-two days ago, but the linkages haven't been completed yet. It could only go by wire as far as Missouri. Then another ten days for the Pony Express to Sacramento, then it still has to get to San Francisco, I believe by boat. How many days is that?"

"Too many," I said. I would have said the same regardless of the arithmetic. "I'm sure a reply is on its way, though."

"Maybe. I think not."

"Is there something you'd like me to write to him?"

"I can't write it out in a letter, you understand. Not the one— Anything I write could be stolen, could be printed in the papers, could ruin him even faster than his disgraceful relationship to me, were that to be discovered." He wrung his hands, perhaps without realizing it. "He's become established now, you see. He has a family. A photographic business. This is why he won't write me. But he needs to know why—"

A spark of anger grew in his hollow eyes.

"Still he refuses to forgive. Can he not understand what it was like for me? He knows the depths of shame we endured. He was there! I was sixteen, and he was five, but at five you remember, don't you? Something so atrocious as your own mother—"

A sneer twisted his features into a gruesome frown.

"Paraded through the town. They'd call it barbaric now. It was exceptional even then—a leftover from the Puritans. Nothing so subtle as a scarlet letter for them. Adultery was sin enough, but for *money?*" His voice went low, a tremor took hold of the right side of his face. His eyes bore into mine, but I couldn't tell if he was seeing Albert or his brother or a scene from his past.

"To stand in the street, surrounded by boys who already hated me for being smart, who already taunted me for our poverty—as if we hadn't come from one of the best families before my father died! To have to watch my *mother.*" His breath grew ragged, as if in a nightmare. "To watch them force her onto that beast and slice her braid off with a kitchen knife. Then to spit and jeer all along the cobblestones, tearing at her clothes. Our entire community, hundreds of people, each with the bucket of rotten food saved for a week to throw at her. A *donkey* rider!

"They grew so vicious. She'd washed their laundry and made funny faces with their children and sewed costumes for the winter festival, but now someone shouted 'Radish her!' And the call went up all along the street, and they dragged her off the donkey and into an alley.

"Because my stepfather refused to pay for someone as high and mighty as me to go to law school. Because she was desperate to raise funds. Because—" He wept openly now, trying to breathe between choking sobs. "Because of *me*. Because I'd called him an ignorant ass. Because I couldn't set aside my pride to beg his help, she did."

But the story had stopped for me on a point of confusion.

"DID YOU SAY *RADISH*?"

"I couldn't look at her. It was too painful. I couldn't look at anyone. I stole fabric for the suit so I could at least appear like I had some dignity left. When I got caught, the shop owner wanted a public apology. A *public* apology. After what those same people had just done to my mother? After that, it wasn't two *hours* before I was at that store torch in hand, burning it to the ground. Burning all of it to the ground.

"I *wanted* to go to jail. I *craved* it. I was so dirty inside, so abhorrent to myself. It didn't matter that she refused to visit me. But my brother was different. He was old enough to write—I'd taught him all his letters— but he didn't write. Even after her death, he blamed me. Blames me still, I'm sure of it.

"I just want to die well, Albert. With honor. You'll see to it that the manuscript gets published somehow, won't you? That despite this disgraceful end—that one day my legacy will mean more than this?"

I held the empty satchel at my side, remembering my relief as each page of the manuscript had been sucked to the dark bottom of the river. Kant and Machiavelli boxed in my brain until both were bloody and bruised and meaningless.

"I promise," I lied.

Rulloff nodded with appreciation and looked around the jail cell, appearing to take notes on all the little details of life that would soon be gone to him. I followed his gaze to Phinneas's chair, set slightly back from the desk, to the teeming summer vines clinging to the window bars, to the palms of his hands, and finally back to me.

"Radishing is no longer practiced in civilized society," he said. His voice no longer held any trace of emotion, but his breath came out forced, carefully squeezed from his lungs like a set of bellows.

"It involves molesting with vegetables. Reenacting the sin in question."

45

BY MIDMORNING, THE CROWDS HAD GROWN SO THICK that even six blocks away it would have been hard to slip a playing card between one person and the next. I spent an hour pushing through sweaty bodies to gain a position on the second-floor bank balcony for a clear view, though I kept my hat low on my head. Phinneas was out there somewhere.

The noose waited on the gallows for the noon chimes, though I doubted anyone would hear them over the din of the crowd. The viewing platform filled with officials in suits and ladies in their finery. In the shadow of the scaffold, I recognized Mr. Halbert helping his wife and daughter onto the platform, all of them wearing black. The way they greeted the man and woman next to them—and the couple's bowed heads and slumped shoulders—made me think the latter were Merrick's parents.

I fingered the scar on my chin. The arms of the courthouse clock twisted closer to noon. The crowd grew restless in the growing heat.

"Get a move on!" they shouted. "Hang the filthy bastard."

I wondered how many of them had no sins on their heads. Surely Rulloff could hear the roar of people calling for his demise.

It must sound familiar to him.

If I'd known of his hidden wounds, could I have helped avoid this end? Was there a poultice to keep the rot from growing on one's soul?

Then the door swung open, and the crowd's roar grew so loud I had to cover my ears. People didn't just shout, they screamed and banged on every pot for miles around. A half dozen members of a drum corps were beating on their instruments, but I wondered if even they could hear their rhythm over the tumult.

Rulloff exited the building standing tall and straight, determined it appeared to display his manners to the last. A large vegetable hit him hard on the shoulder. A cabbage? Then two eggs. Then a hunk of shit, though there was no telling from what kind of animal.

If healing him had been impossible, and if he had to be stopped—wouldn't it have been more merciful if I'd had the courage to shoot him myself?

Sweat rolled down the back of my neck.

"Hang the bastard!"

My hands were shaking so much I had to clasp them behind my back. It was the lynch mob from so many years ago, but grown massive in scale. Hideous. Raging. *Murderous.*

I thought of all the hours Rulloff and I had spent crafting etymologies— the way he'd encouraged me to keep trying when he already knew the answer, just so I could feel the victory.

"Take off his head!"

Men rushed to the front of the green to achieve spitting distance. Everyone was shaking their fists. Everyone screaming. The young boy next to me on the balcony yelled, "Kill the ratbag!"

I thought about how Rulloff always knew just what everyone needed to hear, what was deep in their heart: Hornberger, the slavecatcher, Maggie, Mrs. Jacobs, Thornbush—me. I remembered that awful night at the jailhouse, when men had come shouting for his death, Rulloff had asked what kind of pies I liked.

Who had ever stopped to listen to his heart? To understand the depth of his pain? To realize his monomaniacal ambition was an attempt at self-respect?

Certainly not me.

The hangman took his position on the scaffold. A group of priests jockeyed for position near the noose. A parade of officials pushed through the crowd in a narrow path held open by a group of soldiers. Rulloff was out of my sight for a moment, but the thunderous roar grew again. I didn't see his face until he climbed the steps to the scaffold, a head above the men who surrounded him. Someone had scored a direct hit with their shit pile.

He stood stiffly, in shirtsleeves. No coat. Ropes pinned his arms behind his back. Certainly he'd asked to die in his suit, like a gentleman, but it was not a dignity they'd granted him. Someone spit far enough that it landed on the knee of his trousers.

If I'd let Pa hang him years ago in Ithaca, at least it would have been over quick. A few hundred spectators maybe. Maggie would be alive. Merrick would be alive. Scores of merchants would still be in business.

Sometimes a difficult thing needs doing.

Rulloff scanned the crowd, and I realized this was the last view he would ever see—ten thousand people full of abject hatred. He skipped the front rows and the VIP platforms, looking into the distance at the men climbing lampposts for a view, at the writhing crowd bearing the stifling heat for this event. His head turned in a slow arc. I wanted to look away, but found I couldn't manage it. I deserved to feel his abhorrence for this unfathomable humiliation I'd forced him to endure.

Finally, from two hundred feet away, in a crowd of thousands, his eyes found mine—piercing my soul from all the way across the green. I stopped breathing, melting into guilt. Then he nodded at me. Just a tiny tip of the head, but it was enough of a sign from a man I knew so intimately.

I forgive you, it said.

I bowed to him, low and deep, risking exposure to Phinneas, but it was a necessary sign that went beyond gratitude. He deserved to be punished for his terrible crimes. But if so, he also deserved to be honored for his gifts. The crowd saw a monster, a one-sided caricature of a person.

It was easier, was it not?

By not looking deeper, they could avoid seeing themselves—or themselves as they could have been. They could see the fact that his methods were dreadful, but avoid knowing that his intention was pure, genuine in its desire to be of service to the world.

When I stood, I held my hands up to both sides of my face so no one would see me weep.

The pastor approached Rulloff with his Bible. The sheriff glanced up at the town clock, which still read seventeen minutes to noon. He spoke something to Rulloff who nodded, then the sheriff stepped forward and raised his arm in the air. If the intent was to silence the crowd, it had the opposite effect. The deafening roar nearly split my eardrums. I thought about how he'd arrived in Binghamton years ago, on the other side of those bars, having worked a miracle to set me free.

They untied his arms for the final step, but left his ankles bound. I watched him carefully place his hands in his pockets, declaring himself unafraid, making a statement with the gesture that even those in the back of the crowd could see. The sheriff placed the hood over his face, then the hangman slipped on the noose and tightened it around Rulloff's massive head.

I thought about how he'd looked that night on the bank of the Chenango, his slumped silhouette backlit by the descending torches, holding the limp piece of rope in his hand as he registered the depth of my betrayal.

I gripped the railing with both hands and took a breath that I didn't think I'd ever let go. Everyone pushed and shoved to get a better view.

The sheriff dropped his arm.

The hangman pulled the handle.

Rulloff dropped like a boulder through the trapdoor. He hung at the end of the rope, feet still shackled, body twisting, left arm thrown loose of the pocket.

As sure as the hangman had pulled the lever, I'd put it in his hand.

People began to point. The boy on the man's shoulders behind me shouted.

"Why's he doing that?"

Then I heard the crowd gasp, and looked up to see Rulloff's body still flailing at the end of the noose. As he'd anticipated, the fall hadn't broken his neck. Instead, he was slowly suffocating to death. I watched in horror as he struggled to put his left hand back in his pocket.

Did the crowd understand the gesture as I did?

Despite all the jeers and the hatred, he was still trying to prove himself. To die with honor.

Seconds turned to minutes. The writhing continued, but I couldn't take my eyes from his hand, Rulloff's last vestige of humanity and honor. The crowd did notice and grew quieter. Five minutes elapsed on the courthouse clock.

On he struggled, thrashing about, trying to put his hand in his pocket, even as he was being asphyxiated. The torture looked endless and cruel. Even the remaining jeers stopped as ten minutes elapsed.

Still, he battled, the misery ceaseless. A disturbed hush spread over the crowd.

Fifteen minutes.

He moved more slowly, but was still trying to gain control of his hand. Many people had quietly ceased watching. They'd come for a quick and triumphant death. They hadn't wanted to pity the man.

Eighteen minutes.

"Good God," a woman said.

"Do we need to shoot him?" A man asked no one in particular.

Twenty.

With a gruesome jerk, Rulloff managed to secure his hand firmly in his pocket.

Despite themselves, the crowd cheered.

At twenty-two minutes, Rulloff ceased writhing and fell still.

The crowd breathed a hesitant sigh of relief. A physician climbed down the steps and held a wooden tube to Rulloff's heart. No one breathed. Finally, he waved his hands. It was over.

The triumphant announcement was greeted with silence.

No one seemed to know what to do. How could they cheer his death after cheering his victory? They stayed so quiet I could hear the pulley squeak as five soldiers hoisted his body and removed the noose and sack. So quiet I could hear the thunk of the blade as they lopped off his head for study by phrenologists. Everyone avoided each other's eyes. Who could explain their feelings of pity for a man they were supposed to hate? Each seemed to feel the shame of their revenge gone awry.

Then the sheriff shouted, and his voice carried for blocks over the silence.

"Here is your murderer!"

The crowd found clarity and redemption in that single, profound word: Murderer. The ovation went beyond anything I'd ever experienced. Screams to break windows. Hats thrown in the air. Arms raised like offerings to the heavens as many fell to their knees.

Thanks be to God. Order is restored.

When the sheriff kicked Rulloff's headless body off the stage into the crowd, they set on him like wolves, ripping off his clothing for souvenirs.

46

AS I CAME OVER THE HILL, I SPOTTED CARTS TRAVELING up and down Clinton Street. I passed the cemetery and the Ithaca brewery, then walked across the bridge, practically expecting to hear Josiah holler at me. Instead, I heard his echo in the rush of the river.

Cayuga Street was quiet as I walked up to the courthouse. The pear tree had grown, while the steps that had once seemed so large had shrunk considerably. The jail was empty though, the annex piled with dirty clothes, a plate streaked red with beet juice, the rungs of the ladder to my old bed coated in dust. I remembered the drunken stupors and boot shinings, but also the lessons: how to clean a rifle, skin a badger, grind the coffee extra fine, make new candles out of scraps of tallow, trap a squirrel.

I staggered back into the blinding sunshine and followed the well-worn path to State Street. A bank stood on what had once been an empty lot, and a hardware store had replaced the saddler. An army recruitment office advertised cavalry positions for qualified officers. A discarded newspaper proclaimed RULLOFF'S BRAIN MEASURED, THIRD LARGEST EVER RECORDED!

I expected to see a face I recognized, but people walked past me left and right, all unfamiliar. I tried to remember what had been on the corner before the new sash-and-blind factory.

Then I saw Grant's and felt my heart swell. The bar looked as wondrously ratty as ever, with its raw plank siding and faded red curtains blowing in the late summer breeze. If anyone knew where to find Pa, it would be the barkeep at Grant's.

I took off my hat, cradled it in one hand, and smoothed my hair back with the other. Then I stood for a moment to gain control of my trembling hands before walking through the sloped doorway into the dim saloon.

Confident, articulate, and poised.

Just enough light filtered through dust-caked windows for me to see the gaps between the planks in the floor. I walked past the same unvarnished tables and chairs with missing spindles that I remembered from my childhood. I was surprised at the depth of my nostalgia for such a broken-down place.

At the end of the bar, turning a whiskey glass in a half-circle, sat the unmistakable shape of my father. Slumped and slack, with uncombed gray hair, he was staring through a generous pour of whiskey, moving the glass forward and back as if to increase the optical effect on the wood grain, moving his eye closer and then farther away, like a scientist with a magnifying glass.

I could barely breathe and stared dumbly at the back of his head, unable to either step forward or turn around and walk out of the bar.

"Jesus and Mary."

It was Thomas's voice. I hadn't seen him standing under the elk rack. He had a slight paunch around his belly, but the same matter-of-fact look on his face.

"Jarvis." Thomas knocked Pa on the shoulder. "Your boy's back."

Pa didn't turn—he just swatted at Thomas. He was only half-drunk—lucid enough to give me a beating, drunk enough to make the outcome of our reunion unpredictable. He took a sip of his whiskey.

"Pa," I said. It took everything I had to make it a statement, not a question, to remind myself that I was a man, not a quivering child.

He put the glass down at the sound of my voice, but it took a full minute before he turned his head around.

Could he not even stand to look at me?

Finally, he twisted his head on his shoulder until I could see his grizzled beard. He looked at me with flat, emotionless eyes and said nothing.

"I've come back to face up to what I've done."

I gave him plenty of time to say something. Anything. Even Thomas's cheek twitched like he wanted to speak, but Pa only ran his eyes over me, from my battered hat to my mud-soaked trouser cuffs.

My heart beat so furiously that I was afraid my voice would waver. I held myself as straight and tall as I could.

"I owe you a profound apology for what I did. I'm truly sorry that I didn't listen to you."

Still Pa said nothing and the awkwardness of the quiet grew ever more painful. This was it then. Stone silence.

"I understand," I said. I rested my thumbs on my belt. "I didn't expect forgiveness, but I had to say my peace. I owe Eph Schutt an apology too. If one of you can tell me where to find him, I know he'll have words for me."

Pa continued to stare. Finally, I turned to the door. I'd tried. It was all I could do, but the disappointment of his silence burned through me until I felt as inconsequential as ash.

"California."

Pa's voice.

I spun around.

"Don't know if he's alive. No one's had a letter."

There was no more than fifteen feet of lumber between my shoes and his, but I felt like I was on a stage a hundred feet high.

"Thank you."

I wanted to kick myself for using such dumb words.

"Sheriff Andrews?"

"Dead. Three years."

"Is Babe—" I couldn't finish the question, too afraid of being directed to the cemetery.

"Still ornery as a goat? What do you think?"

I laughed. Couldn't help it. Just a chuckle. But I saw a squint come to Pa's eye. I stood as straight as I could, wishing I was clean, polished, respectable in some way.

"You got tall." Pa cracked his neck, then turned back toward the bar. "Buy your old man a drink, then?"

I fished a coin out of my pocket, walked forward, and palmed it onto the bar.

"It's my last quarter." Honesty loosened my shoulders. "No matter, I suppose. Won't be needing it where I'm going. You still feed slop to the prisoners?"

" 'S'all different," he said, eschewing both progress and decay in the same sentence. "But they still get Jarvis's famous raccoon stew, that's sure."

I smiled, remembering the stew, made invariably with potatoes, beets, and the occasional squirrel—never a plump raccoon.

"No prisoners now?"

"I get work, time to time," he said. "Man don't need much."

I scratched at a few weeks' growth of beard.

"He's dead now, Pa. Rulloff's dead."

Pa's eyes flashed anger suddenly.

"You think we ain't got papers here, fancy boy? You think me 'n Thomas didn't ride clear to Binghamton to watch that man swing? You think I'm surprised to see you show up here, now he's gone?"

My jaw dropped. My brain felt muddled, and I stumbled, as if the earth had shifted and I was the only one who'd felt it. I hadn't imagined it would be so obvious. I'd never even thought to look for Pa in the crowds at Binghamton, but of course, he'd be there. It seemed so logical now.

He took my silence as acknowledgement.

"You think your old man's so dumb," he said. When he swallowed the whiskey, I could see the back of his throat through the glass.

"What if I told you about Third Avenue?" he said.

"You read about us in the papers?"

"Papers?" he sneered. "The papers say it was the second house from the corner? Papers say the old lady kept a yellow bird in a cage?"

I had to grab the bar to keep my knees from buckling.

"You *found* me? When? Why didn't—"

"You'd made your choice," Pa said. "What was I going to do, drag you back?" I looked into his bloodshot eyes, the spidery red lines around his nose. "Seemed you had the life you wanted there. Books and papers."

I grew light-headed. I pulled out a low chair from a nearby table and sat.

Pa turned away from me, looking back toward the bottom of his glass as if he could read the future in it.

"I thought he could give you more."

I thought of how Rulloff had been sure we were being followed and I'd been sure he was paranoid. I thought about how much self-control and humility it must have taken for Pa to turn around and let the man who'd ruined his life become a father to his son. He thought I'd chosen Rulloff over him, that my dreams had come true. Ideas turned in my head like a wagon wheel slipping on ice. I thought all these things, but I couldn't make words come out.

"I wasn't so kind to your ma always," Pa said, grinding the toe of his boot into the bar's support post, a low voice echoing from his glass. "Only asked me one thing before she died, that woman. Made me swear you'd grow up right." I watched the ripple along his jaw as his teeth clenched.

"I didn't do so well at that either."

I wanted to ask what else she'd said.

"How'd you find me?" I asked instead.

"We watched the library," Thomas said. "Jake said you'd make for the library."

What else had they worked out?

"Did you—" The robberies stuck in my throat.

"Learn how you got all that money?" Thomas said. "We did not. I'm the sworn sheriff now, so careful what you tell me."

I smiled, finally. Shook my head.

"I should have known. I suppose that means I'm turning myself into you, Thomas. I guess I'm pleased it's you."

Thomas stood tall. Wary, with a steely gaze.

"Well, then I owe you a wallop for that nasty laudanum hangover, and Eph Schutt would want to see you burned alive, but he ain't here. What's there to interest the law? The man's dead. Fact that you're standing here, I've a mind you had a hand in bringing that about, but I don't want to know nothing 'bout that either."

"All I want to know is how you made them tracks in the snow disappear," Pa said. "You give him wings?"

"Aunt Babe never told you?"

"The hell did she know about it?"

"Nothing. She wasn't part of that," I thought of the people she was probably still hiding with that tunnel, and worried I'd spoken too plainly. "It's just she'd made a few modifications to the house—for guests," I said cautiously.

Pa's hands fell to his lap, as he figured out what I didn't say.

"Son of a bitch," he said. "All these years?" I saw his belly quiver in a half-chuckle, his cheeks tensed trying to hold back a look in his eyes that might have been pride. He scratched behind his ear, then rested his chin on his palm. Finally, he looked at Thomas. The grin was winning out.

"You ever figure Babe had it in her?"

I saw a tenderness in the way Thomas looked at Pa, just for a second. The way they shared a secret glance. I remembered how close they'd been, how often Pa had traveled to Dryden when Thomas lived there. It was a look of love. Maybe the friend kind, maybe the other. But either way, I saw Pa in a different light. A drunk bastard, but still smarter than I'd thought, kinder—at least in his own way. In that look I saw that Thomas would take care of Pa, that he had been taking care of Pa all these years.

"I'm sure I don't know what you mean, Jarvis." Since Thomas was sheriff, slave catchers could fine him thousands for turning a blind eye, but he was never one to let a few words on paper redirect his moral compass.

The room grew silent, an awkwardness creeping back after all the confessions. If I wasn't going to jail, I wasn't sure what I was doing here, or what to do next. Maybe I'd have to keep walking. Maybe I didn't deserve to belong anywhere.

"Your aunt might appreciate a hand," Pa said, turning back toward the bar. "Harvest coming up. Grain to cut and thresh."

I nodded. Reunion over. I pressed myself toward the door, head spinning as if the fever had returned. If she let me, I would clear her fields, set her up for the winter.

"Come back sometime. Buy your old man another drink."

I stumbled out, feeling almost drunk myself, suddenly seeing my own past differently in the warmth of the sun, the chirping of the cicadas. I walked until I stood on the grassy banks of Cayuga Lake. The water shimmered in the golden sunlight like a forty-mile diamond. Boats plied the surface, rowboats sprouting fishing poles, sailboats with canvases luffing. A breeze picked up the first of the autumn leaves and scattered them gently across the surface. Somewhere below, a lady and her baby stared at each other with wide eyes, never blinking.

THE PATH WAS SHORTER than I'd remembered, or my legs had grown longer. Soon I crested the hill overlooking Aunt Babe's house. The cornstalks had grown tall, and the wheat hung heavy with seed. On the flagpole, a Lincoln-Hamlin pennant flapped in the breeze. Aunt Babe was outside, wrapped in her shawl. She looked hunched, and smaller than I remembered, dragging her obstinate donkey back to the barn. As the sun cast its luscious orange glow over the fields, goosebumps rippled over my body.

It took all my effort to put one foot in front of the other. It had been easier to face the prospect of jail. The afternoon light faded fast, with charcoal clouds pressing in from the horizon. When I peeked through the barn doors, she stood mostly in shadow, stroking Bailey's white whiskers.

"Aunt Babe?"

She paused, hand still on Bailey's nose, until he shook it off. Still, she said nothing, her chest rising and falling in that same old blue-checked dress. Wisps of gray hair had pulled out of her bun and curled around her neck. She snatched the bridle off the ground, hung it on the peg, and dumped an armful of barley straw in the trough. She wiped her hands on her apron, picked up the handle of a wooden bucket, and swept past me, pressing the rope into my palm.

"Take this," she said. "And don't forget to wipe your feet."

I followed her to the porch, carpeted with the first yellow leaves of September. The remnants of summer heat wrestled with the chill of autumn. Dappled light stretched into long shadows. I breathed in the familiar scent of damp earth.

Aunt Babe climbed the steps with military precision, strode to the door, and then stopped. Her shawl slid from her shoulders, and I could see a quiver run across her back. I wasn't sure what to do, whether she was furious or ill. Then she spun around and threw her arms around me.

"I'm so sorry," she said before I could breathe a word.

I dropped the pail to hold her in return, surprised at how small and fragile she felt in my arms.

"It's my fault, Aunt Babe," I said. "You never did anything but good."

"That's not the truth at all," she said, wiping her eyes and pressing her hair back up into its bun. She stood up straighter. Sniffed. Laughed. "But never you mind. I've a pie in the oven. Have a seat in that rocker. I'll bring out some supper." The last light of the day reflected a cautious joy in her face as she patted my hand. "What matters is you're here now."

A boat sat motionless on the glassy lake in the yellow-orange afternoon, barely a ripple to disturb the surface. From deep in the woods I heard the triple chirp of a cricket, followed by the hoarse squawk of a blue heron across the lake, topping up his belly with frogs before heading south ahead of the coming winter. The seasons had come and gone, one by one in my absence. Always in transition, always the same.

"You're home in time to vote," she called from the kitchen. "Lot of ways to change the world, you know."

She was right, as always. Soon I would have greater cause for that gunpowder poultice than I could have ever fathomed.

But in that moment, I set my hands in my pockets and filled my lungs with the optimistic scent of the air before a storm, thick with dank mud, rotting leaves, and the tinge of sulfur that promised both release and danger when the clouds broke.

I was no hero. I was no coward. What I was, was home.

Afterword

Truth is stranger than fiction,
but it is because fiction is obliged to stick to possibilities;
Truth isn't.

——MARK TWAIN

As impossible as it may seem, this novel is based on a true story.

The man born John Edward Howard Rulofson, best remembered to history as Edward Rulloff, "The Educated Murderer," came to my attention one life-altering night, when I discovered him lurking in my family tree. From that moment on, the same woman who gets nightmares from your average Halloween special found herself unable to resist obsessively researching one of the most notorious serial killers of the nineteenth century.

As I probed, I discovered the shocking truth underpinning this novel. Rulloff's unimaginable talents, relationship with the jailkeeper's son, silk thefts, and at least five known victims, are well documented in the historical record. I also found a dozen other astonishing facts I elected to omit because, frankly, they would have seemed too unbelievable.

If you find yourself curious about Rulloff's scandalous affair, his most atrocious con, or his secret relationship to the head of the National Photographic Association, download the free e-book *Edward Rulloff: The True-Crime Story* at CheyenneRichards.com/Rulloff.

Acknowledgments

Perhaps because novels get published under a single name, we tend to believe that isolated writers birth genius from cabins in the woods. The reality is usually more like a feature film—a novel's credits should play for at least five minutes past the point you've made a beeline for the bathroom.

Sure, there's a lot of solo time. But underneath the author, there's also a massive, invisible (to the reader) support structure that encouraged a love of literature, bolstered her confidence, made her laugh at her follies, and brought cups of tea when they were most needed. *I'm looking at you, family.* Thank you to Suzanne and Brian Bayley; Mose Richards; Colin and Aidan Ross; Katie and Jake Louderback; Chris, Sunny, Lindsay and Spencer Richards; Kevin and Rob Bayley; Bonny James; and Christine Mix. Not only would this book never have existed without you, nor would its author, in any recognizable form whatsoever.

Additionally, between the pages of anything you've ever enjoyed reading, hides an army of writer's groups, beta readers, and editors of all sizes that helped shape a pile of poop into a piece of art. Thank you with all my heart to the editing dream team of Alan Rinzler and Leslie Tilley, as well as these particularly wise and generous literary geniuses that have my endless gratitude: Tamim Ansary, Courtney Becks, Eileen Bordy, Mark Chu, Stacy Davids, Dana DeGreff, John Foley, Harriet Garfinkle, Ann Gelder, Mollie Glick, Laurence Howard, Elise Hunter, Gordon Jack, Shelly King, Julie Knight, Peter Manos, Avantika Mehta, Rudy Ravindra, Rich Register, Matt Rosin, Beth Sears, Val Shay, Laurie Steed, Ellen Sussman, Mary Taugher, and Lolly Winston.

And many, many thanks to Laura Duffy, for her amazing cover artwork, Karen Minster for the extraordinary interior design, and Debra Nichols for her incredible proofing prowess.

I'd also like to extend my undying appreciation to the most important contributor of all: You, thoughtful reader. Before you picked it up, this book was merely a collection of words. Your imagination provided the alchemy that breathed life into inanimate symbols, making the world and characters manifest. Thank you for lending this work your beautiful mind.

If you enjoyed the experience, please consider leaving a review on Amazon or Goodreads.

About the Author

Cheyenne Richards is an author, sailor, and writing coach who loves everything on the planet except Swiss cheese.

A tomboy who loves polka dots, a Palo Alto native drawn to the past as much as the future, Cheyenne is an outdoors-loving bookworm who's most at home under a cozy blanket with a good book.

She's lived in California, Australia, Singapore, and most recently Mexico, with her boyfriend, aboard a small sailboat named Pristine.

Cheyenne is also the great-great-grandniece of Edward Rulloff.

You can learn more at CheyenneRichards.com or follow her on Facebook, Instagram, or Twitter @CheyWriter.

CPSIA information can be obtained
at www.ICGtesting.com
Printed in the USA
LVHW091405150921
697884LV00015B/342/J